WAR

Book 3 in the Twin Worlds Series

Richard Arthur

Published by: R A Walton

Email: publisher@rawalton.co.uk

Apart from one metaphorical allusion, made in protest against aggression here on Earth, the characters portrayed in this book, and all the events are fictitious.

Other than the above-mentioned allusion, any similarity to real persons, living or dead, is coincidental and not intended by the author.

Published by R A Walton

Email: publisher@rawalton.co.uk

Cover design and illustration: Philip Bannister

ISBN: 978-1-9196529-2-4

Dedication

To the women in my life,

Audrey, Jackie, Helen, Mary, Jackie

and now—Lucy

Table of Contents

Foreword..

Maps..

Part 1: The Beginning of the End..

1 Escape...1

2 Oakbridge Abbey..3

3 Elmhouse..10

4 Artificial Rivers..15

5 The Slave Market in Knot-on-Lesser..18

6 The Northern Wild Lands...27

7 Northern Culture and Religion...38

8 Rivermouth 1..48

9 Shay's Progress...55

10 Thar and Shar—a domestic interlude..58

11 Cray's Visitation...65

12 Phalanx-Ball..73

13 Consolidation...80

Part 2: War..87

14 Council of the North..87

15 Pootini...99

16 Cray takes a hand..118

17 Control of the Borders...131

18 A Bad Mother...136

19 Edwin's Vision....148
20 Zoni....156
21 An Illicit Correspondence....161
22 Politics & Progress....166
23 Council of the North in Knot....170
24 Omens & Portents....179
25 An unexpected Ally....185
26 Rivermouth 2....189
27 Thay Wakes....195
28 Outside Midborough....202
29 The Battle of Midborough 1....212
30 The Battle of Midborough 2....227
31 The Battle of Midborough 3....239
32 The Battle of Midborough 4....248
33 Return from the Dead....263
34 Well Met....273
35 Mother and Child Reunion....279
36 A Brave New World....288
Appendix 1....296
Appendix 2....301
Appendix 3....307
Appendix 4....312
Acknowledgements....318
About The Author....319

Foreword

Once the Geosians had visited their neighbouring planet, Duplos, it was clear that they had the capability to travel between the main continent and the neighbouring island of Isla, thereby ending the latter's isolation. This capability was realised at the end of the second book in the Twin Worlds series. At that juncture, it had been nine years since the hero of the first book, Arté, had been marooned on the continent. In that time a lot had happened on Isla, much of it consequent on his experience.

I felt this to be part of the story that needed to be told, and this book does just that. While (I hope) the background from the first two books would be helpful to the reader, it should not be essential and this story should be accessible to the reader new to my world of Duplos.

One of the disadvantages of this form of publication is that to keep the printing costs under control, maps do not come out as well as I would like. Page size is necessarily less than ideal and many maps also benefit considerably from the use of colour. For this reason I include a free download on my website of an A4, colour PDF of all the maps.

Please visit www.richardarthur.uk

There is also a free download of the appendices available on the site.

Richard Arthur

Worcestershire UK, April 2024

Maps

Map 1 Duplos: Isla

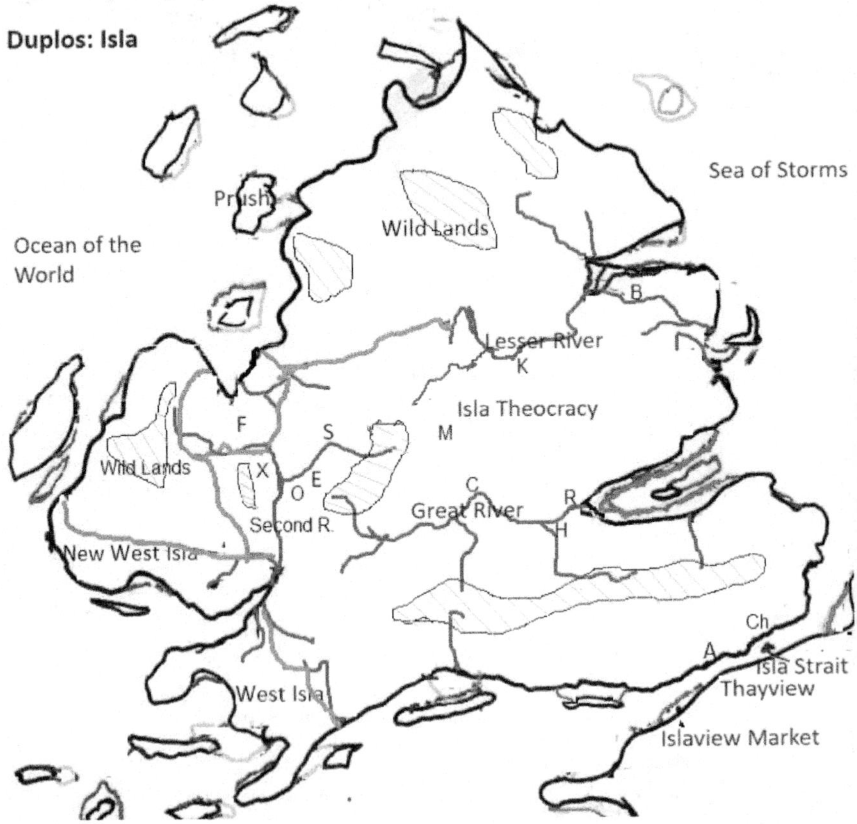

Approximate Scales

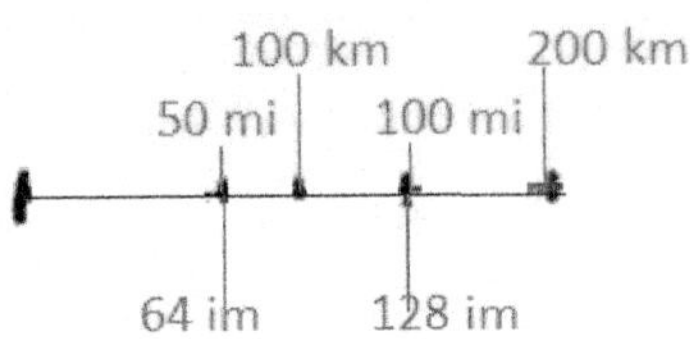

Key

A Thay's Estate **B** Barton **C** Cattlebridge
Ch Chalcliff **E** Elmhouse **F** Fort
H Honeyfield **K** Knot **M** Midborough
O Oakbridge **R** Rivermouth **S** Street
X Springhills

Map 2: Shay's Proposed Navigations

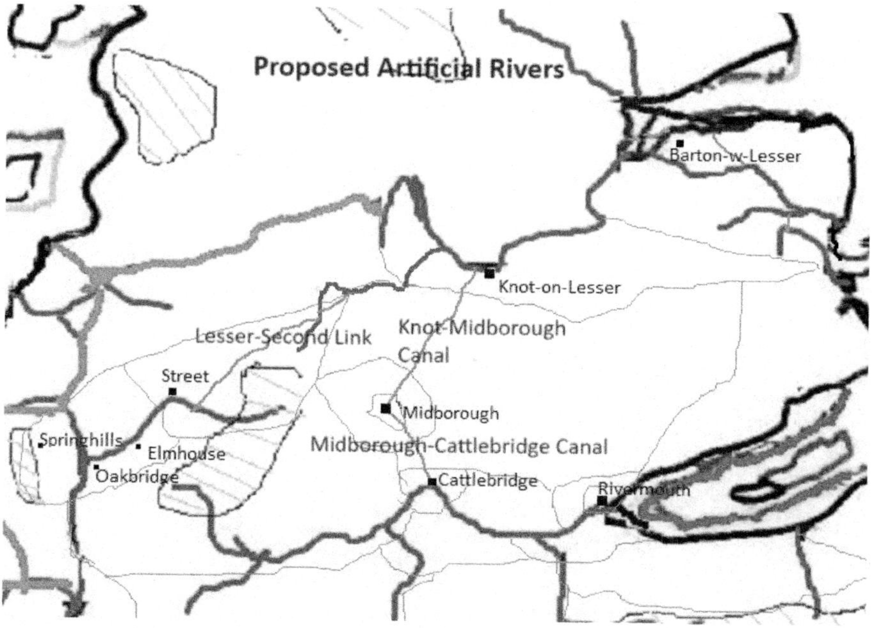

Map 3: The Northern Wild Lands (Northlands)

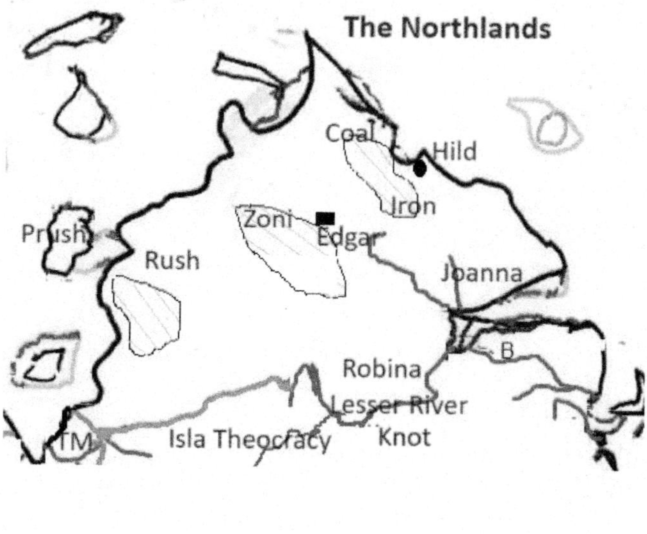

Part 1: The Beginning of the End

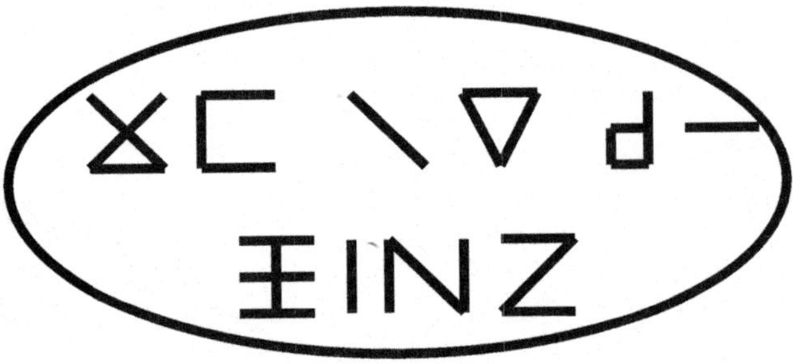

Twin Worlds III

1
Escape

As I heard the splash, I cried out "No!" The cry seemed to give me renewed strength, and I broke free from my captors and smashed my elbows into their respective chests.

I heard them both, surgeon and priestess, scream in pain as they clutched at their tits and gasped for breath under their broken ribs. I am a big woman and physically very strong. Turning towards the surgeon, I swung a mighty kick between her legs. I was wearing boots with pointed steel-tipped toes. The sound of a very satisfying crunch told me certainly that I had broken some bones and the growing crimson patch on her tunic made me smile.

"That for your treachery," I called, "may you never enjoy a man again." I turned on my heels and ran as fast as my long legs could carry me.

I was naked under the cloak that now streamed behind me, my speed over the two imiles to my transport, unencumbered by gown, was fast. I believed I would have outrun any woman in all the history of the Theocracy.

The transport awaiting me was a team and carriage, and separately, two fast horses. I took one of the horses and told my waiting companion to take the carriage with the spare horse to Elmhouse, my estate near the second river.

"No man then?" She queried.

"No", I replied. "We were caught making our escape and the man ended up in the strait. I have taken some revenge on the woman who betrayed us. She will need a lot of attention from her surgeon colleagues if she is ever to walk again, and with luck she will be incapable of sex for the rest of her miserable life. I am going to Oakbridge where I have some business to attend. I want you to start the survey work we discussed and I'll catch up with you at Elmhouse in about a period. I shall travel fast, changing horses when this one tires, and plan to reach Oakbridge without a break."

"Shay, that's a long journey, must be over 256 + 128 imiles, you'll need more than one change."

"Yes, I will, I have made all necessary arrangements in case of this contingency. If all goes to plan, I'll be in Oakbridge in ten ihors".

Brinda shook her head. She was glad she didn't have to attempt such a journey, but she knew that I was exceptionally strong and if anyone could do it, I could. "Well, good luck to you", was all she could think of saying.

2
Oakbridge Abbey

Most women would be shattered after such an arduous ride; but I am not most women. On admittance to the ancient abbey, I demanded to see the head priestess immediately. I was a woman in a hurry.

Most high priestesses would be offended at receiving a peremptory summons, even from a woman as important as me. However, Wilda is not most high priestesses. She appeared to be intrigued that the foremost chief of the north eastern region of the Theocracy was seeking her out in this way. She knew that I had unexpectedly inherited the Elmhouse estate from my late mother, but also realised this was not a normal social call from an aristocratic neighbour. Wilda herself is very much an outsider among the governing classes of the Theocracy and not one to stand on ceremony. The clue is in her name, which is not one of those traditionally adopted by new priestesses. Nor indeed by anyone else as far as I could recall.

"I'm pleased to meet you Wilda," I said, "Thank-you for agreeing to see me at no notice. I hope I can further impose on your hospitality by having a bed for the night. I have come directly from my sister's estate near Chalcliff without taking a break, and need to talk with you at some length before continuing to Elmhouse."

"A bed for the night is no problem, but what is it that brings a leading chief to my abbey? Let me hang up your cloak and please take a seat and I'll order us some refreshment."

"Better leave the cloak, I'm naked underneath."

"You intrigue me, I can't wait to hear your tale." Wilda rang a bell, and asked the answering servant to have a room prepared for me and to bring suitable refreshments for us both.

"Thank-you, Wilda, you may recall that twelve years ago my mother, Chay, bought a young man from this abbey. He was given to my sister as a coming of age present and was thenceforth known as Arthay. I want to learn as much as I can about him. I also regret that I am the bearer of bad news to his mother and to any who might have known him."

Wilda went a bit pale but soon recovered herself to respond. "Yes, I remember Arthay well. He was Arval when here. His mother Valray is a farmer near Street. Arval was also my half-brother and I was very fond of him. We never had the chance to say goodbye. At the time I was locked up in solitary as a punishment for the heresy of suggesting he should be passed off as a woman. When I think on it, I can still feel the accompanying whipping. Since I have risen to my present position I have abolished such punishments, though not without opposition from some of the older and more conservative priestesses. You'd better tell me the worst."

"That makes it even harder for me. I'm sorry to have to report that Arval is no longer with us. It's a long story and you deserve to know the worst, including my own partial responsibility. I shall call him Arval as I prefer not to use my sister's name. She had sentenced him to sacrifice to Nepa for an offence not of his making, but of mine. I set out to rescue him and we had almost succeeded in making our escape when we were caught and he was dragged to the cliff edge. He shook off his captors but was cornered between them and the sea. I might yet have succeeded in rescuing him; but before I could do so, he jumped into the sea.

The only silver lining is that he escaped the mutilation required by the sacrificial rite."

"That is indeed a comfort, but what a waste of his life. He really was special, you know."

"Yes, I do know now, and it will be to my lasting regret that my war with my sister led to his loss. I will at least ensure that he did not die in vain, but I must make my confession."

I then told Wilda the whole story leading to the current state of affairs[1]. "So you and I also have in common our determination to end the sort of beating that we have both suffered. I have decreed laws against the most brutal forms of corporal punishment within my domains. I haven't outlawed it completely, but it is illegal to beat a child under the age of seven with any form of stick or whip or other instrument, to give more than three strokes to a child under twelve or more than six to anyone else, teenager or adult, male or female."

"I applaud your action, despite the hurt of Arval, I'm sure we will deal well together. Arval would not have wanted me to hold a grudge against either you or your sister."

"Which brings me to your mother, I feel I ought to be the one to inform her and give her the opportunity to heap some coals on my head for my part in the loss of her son. If you could give me her direction I shall visit her before returning to Elmhouse."

"I will certainly give you Valray's direction, but she is not my mother. Arval and I shared a father, not a mother."

---

1 See the first book in the series, Twin Worlds: First Contact where this history is recounted in detail.

"It is my turn to be intrigued, it is most unusual to know about paternity at all, let alone shared paternity. You must have a strange history."

"Yes I do, including my name! Let me tell you about it, but first we'd better get some more booze in, I can see we're likely to have a long evening." She rang again and ordered another bottle of wine.

When she'd replenished both our glasses, Wilda continued. "Valray was part of an expedition into the northern wild lands to capture some slaves. My mother was heavily pregnant with me at the time and was easily captured. According to her, my father was unusually big and strong and eventually managed to escape during the journey south. Before his escape, Valray had grown lustful and made good use of him to keep her itches scratched, which had actually helped him in achieving his escape. She later found she was pregnant with Arval."

"So your mother was a slave, but as you would have been born here you would be free. Is your mother still alive?"

"Yes, you can meet Wilja later. When I was born I was indeed technically free; but never had a choice other than to remain with the order. I considered the name I was given at birth to be a slave name, and even when it was changed when I became a priestess, I still considered it wrong. That is why, when I became head priestess, I changed to my present name of Wilda, in honour of my heritage. I also freed my mother and all the female slaves in the order. One or two, from the west, even returned to the wild, but most, like my mother, have remained with the order here. I would have liked to end slavery altogether, even for men, but that seems too much to ask. Anyway, back to Arval. When it turned out he was unusually intelligent, Valray came to consult the order here and he was sold to us. A few years later, when he was about eleven, my mother recognised him as the image of his father at the same age. She made enquires, and when she was told who his mother was she realised the truth. She then told me, because she was concerned to warn me not to have sex with him, as she was sure I might otherwise have done in due course. Obviously, I didn't attempt any form of sexual liaison with him, even though he made me itch like there was no morrow-phase; but I did befriend him and did what I could to help him. Some of my contemporaries even went so far as to suspect me of closet homosexuality because of my refusal to join in their sessions with Arval. I can tell you that there was much anguish among the younger priestesses when your mother took him away."

"Thank-you for sharing all this with me, I can see that we are going to become much closer in the future. As you may have realised, I am ambitious. I already control the politics in the north-east of the Theocracy and have made several secret treaties with tribes in the northern wild lands. I have a monopoly of trade on the Lesser River and now I have inherited Elmhouse, I intend to extend my influence to the Second River. I have a water engineer working for me, surveying the Street River, with the intention of opening navigation between here and Elmhouse and eventually all the way to Street. She has extensive experience of cutting canals on the Lesser delta and my further ambitions extend to connecting the Lesser and Second rivers. I already have some important allies in the region here. Girls I was at school with, now in influential positions. I hope to extend my hegemony throughout the northern half of the Theocracy, and beyond into the Marches and the Wild Lands. Part of my means and my goal is to do with slavery. We could become valuable allies."

"How do you mean. I'm not sure of some of the implications of what you are suggesting."

"I have already given the north-eastern wild tribes guarantees that I will not allow them to be raided for slaves. Once I gain full control of the border lands, I will outlaw slave raiding completely. At that time I will also use my influence to free any non-criminal female slaves. Beyond that I hereby make this vow: in honour of Arval I will do all I can to end the practise of female ownership of men and give men rights to their own bodies, to refuse sexual exploitation. I will do this despite the irony that my rape of Arthay shall become the trigger for me to end all rape of men in the Theocracy. That must be my atonement."

"Fine sentiments, I applaud them and will be your ally in this endeavour. Ideally, and ironically, we should seal this in bed, but I cannot bring myself to have sex now under the shadow of my late brother."

I responded, "I too cannot indulge in sex for the same reason. That is why I asked to rest here. I could have gone to a dear friend in the town but she would have insisted we shared her favourite together. However, there is an even better way to seal our alliance."

"What do you have in mind?"

"I have already told you that my desire was to bear Arval's daughter. Even though it is too early to know, I am certain that I have been successful. This daughter, whom I will call Shar will also be your niece. It is fitting that you should stand Goddess to her."

Twin Worlds III

"That is indeed fitting. It is an honour for me far greater than the mere sharing of a man, and I agree with you. That can be the seal of our friendship and alliance."

3
Elmhouse

I decided to call in at Elmhouse before going on to see Valray. This would be my first visit to the estate as owner. I knew it well from my childhood, as I had spent exeat weekends there while at school in the village of Springhills twenty imiles away. Oakbridge is actually nearer, only twelve imiles. I left after breakfast and arrived in good time for lunch. I was met by a groom who rushed out to take care of my horse, while I went inside.

"We weren't expecting you so soon." The housekeeper was somewhat flustered. "We'd had a message from Brinda that she would be arriving in about four ihors time, saying she expected to meet you here later. I'm sorry if everything is a bit of a mess, I'm still finishing up the preparations for your arrival."

"Don't worry, I'm sure you're doing a great job, and I realise that my arrival is unexpected, and you haven't been given a proper amount of notice. Daubey, isn't it? I remember you from when I was a schoolgirl. You worked in the kitchen as I recall."

"Yes m'lady, My mother was housekeeper then, Lady Chay allowed me to take her place when she died. I have been keeping things going for you since her ladyship passed on."

"I am most grateful to you and I'm sure we will get on splendidly. Right now, this is a fleeting visit. I'm just going to have a bit of lunch, if that's not too difficult. When my horse is properly rested I need to press on to Ludray Farm near Street. I don't know how long I'll be gone, but I will return to see Brinda. Please look after her until I get back."

11

Twin Worlds III

"As you wish, m'lady. I'll tell cook to prepare something for you and get the boy to light a fire in the library. I've finished cleaning there and you should find it comfortable. Shall I tell cook to bring the food there for you."

"No, I'll come to the kitchen and eat there. Tell cook I don't need anything hot or elaborate. Some bread and ham, or sausage roll will be plenty. Oh, and a jug of ale. And, before I forget, there's no need for the m'lady stuff. Unless we are entertaining top brass, call me Shay."

"I'll try to remember m' er Shay. If you'll excuse me, I'd better go and instruct the chef and the boy. I did get an iferk[2] of beer in but it won't be ready for drinking for another few ihors yet. When he's lit the fire, I'll get the boy to fetch some from the pub. Will a couple of ipints be sufficient for you?"

I replied in the affirmative and then went into the library. Daubey scurried off to the kitchen to give her orders.

I was amused by Daubey's formality. The staff in Barton became used to me some years ago and remained informal when I took charge of the estate. I had forgotten how things tended to be between mistress and servant in the grand country houses, and compared to Barton, Elmhouse counts as grand. I found the estate book in a desk drawer and began to study it. I knew I had a lot to learn now I had come into the property. I noted that I employed two adult women, three girls, four men and a boy. Daubey was housekeeper in charge of the indoor staff. These amounted to the three maids, the male cook and the boy. The other adult woman was described as 'outdoor estate manager'

---

2 An iferk is the Isla equivalent of a ferkin, i.e. a quarter ibarrel = 8 igals = 64 ipints.

and was in charge of the groom and two gardeners, all male. I supposed that nominally all the males belonged to me.

I didn't want any unnecessary delay, so timed my departure an ihor before Brinda was expected. The ride to Valray's was uneventful and took me just a couple of ihors to cover the seventeen imiles to Ludray Farm, which is situated on the north bank of the Street River just three imiles west of Street.

Clearly Valray knew me by reputation, but we had never met. She appeared somewhat flustered by my appearance on her doorstep. "Your honour, this is quite unexpected, my modest abode is not really fit to receive such as you. Oh dear, that didn't come out quite right. I don't know what to say."

"Valray, you don't have to apologise to me, rather the other way round. I assure you I've been in far more modest dwellings than your fine farmhouse. Just let me put my horse somewhere and let us go in. I really need to talk to you seriously."

"Yes, your honour, one of my men can stable your horse for you." She shouts across the yard, "Orval come and take this lady's horse to the stable, be quick about it." A man, presumably Orval, ran out of a barn, took hold of the bridle and led my horse away. Valray ushered me into the house. "I hope I've done nothing to offend your honour, I always try to do as I should and I'm not into politics, leaving all that sort of thing to my betters, like yourself."

"Valray, you have nothing to fear from me. Honestly the boot is very much on the other foot. Let's sit down and have a comfortable talk. And please, none of the 'your honour' stuff. I'm just Shay and, despite what I'm about to confess, I hope we can become friends."

13

Twin Worlds III

After I had related Arthay's history and confessed to my part in it, Valray responded. "I never expected to hear anything of my son again. After all, we don't usually concern ourselves with them. However, his father was special. His name was Edgar and he was the handsomest man I have ever seen, and I've never had sex to rival the begetting of Arval. If Arval was half as good, I can't blame any woman for wanting him. I am sorry he has died but glad you saved him from the sacrificial mutilation. I've made my peace with Wilja, Edgar's woman. I will never again go on a raid into the wild lands.

I don't see the need for you to require my forgiveness, and I would be proud to become your friend. You know that Wilja's daughter, Wilda is Arthay's half-sister and has become great herself as Abbess of Oakbridge. With her and you as my friends, I feel very honoured."

"You are generous. I promise I shall do all in my power to deserve your friendship. You said that you won't go raiding again. One of the things I want to do is to outlaw the taking of slaves from the wild lands. I have already made agreements with several communities on the north-east coast. I have given them my personal guarantee that they will be safe from slavery, and have established valuable trading links which have proved of mutual benefit. Could you see your way to supporting me in my endeavours?"

"Well, I don't know what I can do, but you certainly have my whole-hearted support. I do have a couple of slaves myself. I did have three; but one has now passed on. However, I have been increasingly uncomfortable with the practise. After all, men are people, not animals, and it seems wrong that we should own them."

"My thoughts exactly. I agree there is little you can do except treat your men well. On the other hand I do have a position in the Theocracy, and with my recent inheritance of Elmhouse, I will enjoy a position of considerable influence here in the north. In the years to come I ought to be able to enforce a ban on slave-raiding in the northern lands and begin at least to chip away at the whole institution of slavery."

"I certainly wish you luck. I'm too old to bear arms myself, but I'll do what I can to support. I fear that your plans could lead to war. Not everyone of your class, or indeed mine, will be happy to give up their slaves."

"I fear you are right. My plans will take that very much into account. On the other hand, I fear that war with my sister may well be inevitable anyway. We might as well have a just cause."

"Things are really that bad between you and Thay?"

"They were always that bad; but the Arthay business and our mother leaving Elmhouse to me has made things between us impossible. While Chay was alive, neither of us would move against the other, but now! My Goddess, Cray, will do her best to keep the peace, and I am truly sorry for her, but she won't prevail on either of us. It's just a matter of time and I intend to be ready when the time comes."

"When do you think that will be?"

"Oh, some years, yet. I have much to do, and the first task is to consolidate my position here in the north-west."

4
Artificial Rivers

"Extending the navigation to Street is not too difficult from a purely engineering standpoint. The obstacles will be political."

"You can safely leave any politics to me. Your part must be to carry out the necessary works. What does your survey tells us needs to be done?"

Brinda laid out a map of the Street River on my library table. "Currently the navigation is open from the confluence with the Second River upstream as far as the quay three imiles west of Elmhouse. The paths from the quay to Elmhouse are poor and the terrain is not ideal. If we build a lock and weir just beyond the quay we will be able to add a further six or seven imiles to the navigation. I then propose a short canal from about half-way along that stretch into Elmhouse. That will be better for your access than to build a road from the quay. To navigate all the way to Street we need three more locks and a bit of dredging. You also asked about the river upstream of Street. It's not too difficult to extend by ten imiles or so but I can't see the point of it. There are no significant settlements close to the upper river and I can't see it being commercially viable."

"How long will it take?"

"That depends on the politics. You control the land needed for the extension to Elmhouse, but you will need to negotiate the rights with other landowners for the other locks. Then there is the question of the labour force. We'll need a lot of labour. While we can import some experienced navigators from the Lesser delta, they will be relatively expensive and will need to be accommodated, and also supplemented by others. The workforce requirement is a major stumbling block."

"OK, we can start with the Elmhouse section. If you select some experienced crew from the delta. I can get additional labour from the northlands on a promise of exemption from slave-raiding as well as payment. I also note that one of your locks is on Valray's land and I'm sure I will get her permission. I'll work on the others through the local wapentakes. I am going to resign my Lesser Coast seat on the Superior Wapentake and instead represent Oakbridge and District. The representative for Upper Street is an old schoolfriend of mine. I'm sure that between us we can deliver the support of both wapentakes and ensure the necessary permissions."

"In that case, with enough labour, we could be open to Street within a year. I still don't see the case for going beyond."

"That, my dear Brinda, is because I haven't shared the bigger picture with you." I unfurled a sketch map showing my larger vision. (See Map 2).

"Phew! That is what I call ambitious. It will take several years even if you were to control the whole Theocracy."

"The question is: do you think we could do this in a decade?"

"Well, certainly it will take at least that. The technical challenge of the canal linking the Street to the Lesser is immense! I must say, though, that I'd love to give it a go, and to see your sister's face if you link to the Great River itself and challenge her monopoly there."

"It's not 'if', Brinda; it's 'when'. Incidently, would you like my Lesser Coast seat on the Wapentake. It's yours if you want."

Twin Worlds III

"No, Shay, I really can't be bothered with the shenanigans involved in politics. Anyway, I'll have quite enough to do with all those artificial rivers. Do you mind?"

"That's OK, I expected your answer, but I wanted to offer you the first refusal. I'll go ahead with plan B and get another of my former school friends to take the seat."

5
The Slave Market in Knot-on-Lesser

I'm Shay's daughter, Shar. I recall celebrating my third birthphase while staying at Ludray farm with my grandmother Valray. My Goddess, Auntie Wilda, was also with us for the celebration. The conspicuous absentee was Mummy. I didn't like it but was nevertheless used to her frequent absences on business. "Poor Mummy, she's always having to work," I used to think. I was just as much at home at Ludray as at Elmhouse. For one thing, Grandma Valray always had time to spend with me and never seemed to be too busy. Even when she was at home, Mummy was always busy, and even Daubey, who is very kind to me, had lots of jobs to do around the house. Ludray Farmhouse is much smaller and didn't appear to need anything like as much housework. Valray often took me to the river to feed the ducks and let me play on the bank and talk to the boaters going through the new lock.

Of course I could also play by the river and new canal at Elmhouse, but Daubey always fretted that I might get hurt and so I had to be careful about just how much I let on about my adventures. Valray always seemed more relaxed and didn't mind if I splashed about in the water and got a bit wet. Grown-ups are so strange.

19

Twin Worlds III

The reason for my absence on this occasion was that Brinda and I were visiting the northern wild lands in a bid to recruit more labour for the canal. A great deal had been accomplished in the three and a half years since I first laid out my plan for linking the major rivers in the Theocracy. As anticipated by Brinda, the navigation was opened to Street within the first year. Since then the Upper Street Wapentake had approved the canal linking the Street river to the still un-named tributary of the Lesser. The first short cuts had been completed to provide the junctions to the two rivers. As originally planned, the junction with the Street was about ten imiles beyond the village, which was expected to grow into a town on the strength of the river trade.

At the far end, work on the Lesser had extended the navigation to the confluence with the tributary, which had itself been made navigable for about seventy-five imiles to where a nine imile canal, needing only one lock, had been dug to cut across a long loop of river, rejoining the river just downstream of the proposed junction with the planned link canal.

Brinda had just completed the detailed survey of the route and was ready to start the construction which would include a couple of short tunnels and a major lock flight of a dozen locks to reach the summit level before the river junction.

Brinda explained the challenges that this would bring. "Shay, I've done the best I can with route selection but there's no getting away from it. We have to raise the canal through a hundred and twenty-eight plus sixteen feet over an imile, as well as needing two tunnels of over a quarter of an imile each. Both these feats are much greater than anything that has ever been attempted before. I'm confident in my calculations but even so there's a lot of risk involved and I'll need a much bigger workforce both for the tunnels and the locks." Brinda pointed to her sheets of notes and calculations, which I pondered with an air of puzzlement and surprise.

I shook my head. "Brinda, I'll get to the labour issue later, but first I think we need to talk about your calculation methods.

You must be aware that there is an elite religious order that controls advanced calculation. I'm a member and am supposed to report on developments that might threaten their supremacy. Your work is definitely in that category, and I don't anticipate a happy ending for either of us if it comes out.

For entirely snobbish reasons, I doubt that you would be admitted to the order, and instead would almost certainly be denounced as a witch. Well, I've made some advances myself which I have chosen not to reveal and I'm not going to say anything about your methods either. But please bear in mind that you have come upon dangerous knowledge and must be careful how you use it. I think for the sake of public consumption you had better say nothing about calculations and instead fall back on divine inspiration. The temples are much readier to believe in visions of the Goddess than in clever arithmetic."

Twin Worlds III

"Wow, thanks for the warning, I'd rather not be burnt at the stake. You'd better advise me on what I should say to the Wapentake when presenting the route details."

"Now, I want to make sure I understand your calculation methods properly. You seem to have based your system on sixteen unique symbols using one symbol to represent nothing and to represent numbers by strings of these symbols with each successive symbol in a string implying multiplication by sixteen. Is that right?"

Brinda nodded.

"OK, I understand that, although I doubt if anyone else on Isla would. I've done something similar but using only eight symbols. The best methods known otherwise haven't come up with the idea that nothing can also count as a number or that using the order of symbols to represent larger numbers can be so powerful. Anything else?"

"Yes, using this sort of representation, I've found good algorithms for multiplication and division by any number, not just repeated halving. I've also designed a mechanical aid to do multiplications and divisions. I can then calculate in the field, so to speak, as a quick check, leaving a more accurate calculation to be done later if needed."

"How interesting, tell me more."

"I'll show you." Brinda took out a ruler from her bag. "See this ruler. Its middle section can slide from side to side. Both the middle section and the outside are marked with the numbers from one to sixteen, but not evenly. Suppose I want to multiply two numbers together, say two times three. I slide the middle so as to align its one with one of the multiplicands on the outside. In this case with two. I then look for the other multiplicand on the middle section and find where it is aligned on the outside. In this case with six, the required answer. The big secret is in the way the markings are spaced. This is done so that the length between doublings is constant. Thus the distance between the markings for one and two is the same as that from two to four, from four to eight and from eight to sixteen. The other markings are all placed using the same principle. Finally, I've only needed to mark the bottom half of the ruler in this way. In my earliest prototype I marked the top half uniformly so I could use it for addition by the same method. But in this ruler, I decided it was more useful to mark the upper half with the squares of the lower half, giving me a simple way to look up the result of multiplying a number by itself. With practice, I find that I can do quite complicated sequences of multiplication and division very quickly and with adequate accuracy for most of my purposes."[3]

I was impressed. "That is amazing. You are a genius. I'm afraid the temples would definitely condemn you as a witch!"

"Oh dear, and there I was hoping to make money out of my invention." Brinda said this with a wistful smile on her face. It was clear that In actuality she has no such thought.

However, I had to take it quite seriously. "And you deserve to make a fortune, but we'll have to wait a while. Please be very careful. If even a hint of this gets out we will both be in the most tremendous trouble and I'm not joking about the inevitable charge and conviction for witchcraft. Furthermore, in their supreme arrogance, the elite authorities will refuse to believe you to be capable of such arithmetical advances and will accuse me of divulging secrets; and conducting private occult research that

3 See Appendix 3 for more details of Brinda's sliderule.

should have been declared to, and regulated by, the authorities in advance. It just makes my ultimate political goal that much more urgent. We must break the power of the temples. The whole religious stuff is just nonsense and it's holding the whole of society back."

"Right, I understand you. I will indeed be most careful to conduct all calculations privately in a secure room. I shall also keep all my devices locked away. However, what would Wilda have to say about your temple agenda, would she still be your ally if she knew your ultimate goal?"

"I think she would. She's no fool, but is pragmatic. We've talked a lot about such things and I'm pretty sure she doesn't believe in the Goddesses either, and certainly not in the surrounding mumbo-jumbo. To get on in temple politics it helps not to be too devout a believer.

But back to our original problem. You and I need to travel into the North and see what we can negotiate in the way of labour. We'll need to get on with it because once Thay wakes up to the reality of the Lesser-Second link, she'll start to agitate and we may find that Isla politics begin to get heavy. But that's for later. For now, we must concentrate on the labour force. Morrow-phase we must go to Knot and then cross the river into the wild. I am well-known to, and on friendly terms with, most of the tribes East of Knot. Outside of Knot itself my no-slave-raiding policy is accepted by both the Lesser and Lesser Coast Wapentakes and it is now rare for raiding parties to venture into the East. I have all but blocked off all river crossings East of Knot to raiding parties and I have hopes of extending that to the whole river. I think we can expect a good reception.

We should get some rest here before setting out, and when in Knot, I'm a member of a very comfortable club where we can get some pampered treatment and maybe share the attentions of a scrumptious man."

"I'm up for it, but isn't it a bit hypocritical what with our anti-slavery stance?"

"No, not at all. A man doesn't have to be a slave to allow as to have a good fuck. As long as they're willing we can enjoy ourselves. And, believe me, mostly they are very willing as long as you also respect their needs and comfort."

"Well, here's to morrow-phase then. You realise you'll be missing Shar's birthphase."

"Yes, but it can't be helped. Shar must learn that the world doesn't revolve around her and that her mother has other obligations. As it is, Daubey and Valray indulge her excessively, with Valray being a particularly doting grandmother."

My club lived up to my promise and Brinda rose from her bed with a feeling of profound satisfaction. The gorgeous young waiter paid her the major share of his attention, while I was content with a more passive supporting role. The same waiter came in to wake her with a lovely hot drink and then gave her a good massage and allowed her a quickie before she eventually dressed and came to join me for breakfast.

On the way to the town landing stage, we were passing the slave market when I stopped suddenly. "That place is an abomination and one phase I will get it closed down. I tried a selenth ago but my move was premature. I've been banned from entering the place, but they don't know you. Go in and see if you can find anyone suitable for the canal work. There may even be some women among the slaves for sale, as they will have all been taken from the wild lands."

Brinda was taken by surprise. "But we are opposed to slavery, and in any case, as you say, I am unknown here. They won't accept my credit for more than a couple of men."

"We are also realists. Slavery is a fact of life here in the Theocracy. We can contribute to the welfare of the slaves by treating them well and eventually giving them their freedom. You must make the purchase on behalf of the Street River Navigation Company, which will have sufficient credit. You must also explain the nature of the work to any prospective employees and give them a free choice to accept or reject your offer. You should also promise them their freedom on completion of the canal."

Not without some misgivings, Brinda did as I asked. She outlined her requirements to the slave mistress. The latter then went to the local temple to enquire about the bona fides of the SRNC while Brinda was allowed to address an audience of slaves, and then interview any she liked the look of. In the end Brinda purchased two women and a dozen men, all of whom had been captured from lands close to the north bank of the river to the west of Knot.

In the meantime I went to the temple to ensure that adequate funds were available for the prospective purchase and then returned to the landing stage to arrange suitable river transport. When Brinda showed up with the slaves we all boarded one of my craft and headed down-stream towards the Lesser Estuary. After a couple of ihors on the river, we left the slaves in the charge of the Captain to transport to my Barton estate where Brinda would later give them some initial training on canal technology. We then left the boat and set off on horseback through the wild lands.

6
The Northern Wild Lands

"I keep having that feeling that we are being watched, shadowed even." Brinda was nervous. This was the first time she has crossed the Lesser into the wild lands.

"Of course we are being shadowed," I answered matter-of-factly. "I would expect nothing less. Eventually we can expect to be met by one of the local tribal leaders. Right now they will be assessing whether or not we pose a threat. Once they've decided that we don't, someone will be along for a parley."

"How can you be so relaxed? We could easily be ambushed and killed. I've heard they can be terribly savage."

"Nonsense, tales to frighten children so they don't go wandering into these lands and get lost. The people here might not live under the sort of discipline we are used to, but they are not stupid. They know we would be missed if anything happened to us and that a major punitive raid would be the likely outcome. They live in small communities that can't defend themselves from even a modest force with our superior weapons."

We were now riding through a large deciduous forest. Some of the trees being of great size and antiquity. After about half an ihor we rode into a clearing with a particularly massive oak in the centre. Under this tree stood a tall woman wrapped in a long green cloak. On either side of her stood two others wearing deer-hide tunics and carrying wooden staves of length equal to their heights. "What brings two fine ladies from the Goddess-botherers into our lands? You can't be looking for slaves, otherwise there would be more of you. Anyway I hear that your grand lady Shay has forbidden such ventures. Am I not right?"

We halted and I slid off my horse to approach the welcoming party on foot. I smiled and held out my hand. "You are indeed right, and I should know, since I am that Shay. My companion is my friend Brinda. Whom have I the honour of addressing?"

"I hice Robina and lead our small community in this part of the forest. Shay, you are indeed welcome among us. Although we have not met, I know of you from my mother's sister's daughter, Joanna who dwells further East by the river from the North, and has had dealing with you." She then chuckled, "and my cousin has not exaggerated. You are the only woman I have met who is taller than me and I am reckoned taller than most."

"As indeed am I. But you do breed some tall people here in the north. My dear friend Wilda, whose mother was taken as a slave, is perhaps a smidge or two shorter than me and her half-brother Arval was the only man I have ever seen to exceed two strides."

"We must have more speech inside. At this time of year we live in the trees hereabouts. This clearing is the centre of our village. You may leave your horses safely here to graze. My servants will fetch them water. Please come to our meeting house with me." She then led us into the forest for about fifty strides and up a ladder into a large tree house, consisting of one large room with a small ante-room where they could hang their outer garments and exchange their footwear for soft slippers. I also hung up my sword and bow and arrows, instructing Brinda to do likewise.

Taking my cue from our hostess, I confined my conversation over dinner to small talk. After we had eaten we retired to a sitting area where the floor was strewn with cushions. A male servant filled our mugs with mead and then departed leaving us with just Robina and one other younger woman.

"Now we are comfortable let me hear what has really brought you across the river into our lands. I take it you are not here just for the fresh air." Robina took a swig of her mead and lay back against her cushions.

"You are right. I do indeed have an ulterior motive in coming here. I have ambitious plans; but to fulfil them I need more labour than I can find within the Theocracy. I believe that what I am doing is just as much in the interests of you in the northern lands as in my own. I don't want slaves. I want partners. I want to challenge and change the status quo and enable a new beginning in relations between us all."

I then outlined my immediate plans for an artificial river system to link the island's major rivers and to further productive trade throughout the Theocracy that extended into the northern lands.

"Look," I said, "this will make me personally richer; but that is not the point. The benefits that will flow to you will also be considerable. As my power grows I will be able to enforce my ban on slave-raiding, and ultimately hope to rid at least the northern half of the Theocracy of the stain of this vile practise. It will also open up opportunities for both men and women in your northern lands to travel safely in the Theocracy and to engage fully in trade with us. As you may have heard from your cousin, I have turned a blind eye to the export of some metal goods and I promise that when the time is right I will openly oppose the current ban and will engage in unencumbered trade between us, both in goods and knowledge. I truly believe there is much that we can learn from you as well as being able to help you develop your own economy. I look to bring real peace between us. Free trade is the enemy of war and distrust. The sort of good communications to be had from my canal network will provide the foundation of that free trade."

"OK, I get that but what exactly do you have in mind? Do you really think you can achieve what you say without fighting, without any bloodshed? There will be sceptics here, people that will never trust a southerner. Surely on your side of the border there will also be those who are far from ready to bury the hatchet."

Brinda and Robina's companion both kept quiet during this exchange but it was clear from their body language that both thought there was a lot of truth in Robina's words.

"I'll be honest with you. I would love to refute what you suggest but it wouldn't wash. There will be real opposition both within the northern wapentakes and even more so in the more distant parts of the Theocracy. I think I will eventually bring the north round without open fighting but I do expect real trouble from my own sister and the Rivermouth establishment. It seems to me that it is inevitable that this will lead to war. I don't only need labourers. When things get tough I will also need an army. However, here too I have plans. By the time it becomes necessary I will have a stockpile of superior weapons and will have new and superior tactics. My army will be better trained and superior in all respects. I will train men alongside women and open the ranks of my army to volunteers from your lands who will receive equal training, weaponry and pay to everyone else." I kept a determined look on my face. Brinda looked shocked.

Robina shook her head in some disbelief. "Do you mean what you are saying? Isn't it treasonable in the Theocracy to train men in war, and even more so to arm and train people from the northlands? Don't you fear the splits?"

"Treason doth never prosper. I will prosper, so it won't be treason and no-one will dare to split me in twain. My ankles will not be nailed to the posts on Rivermouth bridge. As far as I'm concerned all people are equal. Men as much as women, denizens of the northern lands as much as citizens of the Theocracy. So, Robina, do you think you can help me? Are there women and men who will cross the river to dig my artificial rivers. To link the Lesser to the Second then the Lesser to the Great; and even to enlist in my future army? All who do will be free people, will be paid for their work and be able to return to the north afterwards. Each and every one of them will be given my token to guarantee their freedom from slavery in the Theocracy, to be enforced by everything in my power. This I swear."

Robina thought carefully before responding to this impassioned speech. Then she spoke slowly and with deliberation. "You interest me, our men are not our slaves in the way that they are in your territory. No individual woman can claim ownership of any individual man; but nor are men considered our equals. They are definitely subordinate in almost all of our communities and generally play a subservient role in our culture just as in yours. I can't order any woman or man to work for you but I can advertise the opportunities you offer and I expect some may answer your call. However, our population in this forest is small and I doubt you will get the numbers you require. We must travel further from the border to find greater numbers. I suggest we start by visiting my cousin and then go on an extended walkabout. Shay, I trust you and believe you are sincere, but you do not yet exert the power you will need to back your promises. Many will be sceptical both of your promises and your ability to deliver them."

I responded in measured tones. "And they will be right to be sceptical. I can ask no more of you than you have offered and I thank you profusely. Tophase my writ runs throughout the wapentakes of Lesser Coast, Oakbridge and Street, and in much of Lesser and my guarantees will hold throughout those districts. I assure you that once the Lesser and Second rivers are joined that I will have the power to bend the town of Knot-on-Lesser to my will and all of the Lesser Wapentake with it. Borders will then come into line swiftly and much of the northern Theocracy will be mine. To extend throughout the Theocracy will take a war, but I will win. The only question in my mind is whether I complete the join to the Great River before or after the war."

"And your sister, do you intend to split her?"

"Don't tempt me; but, no, much as I would gain personal satisfaction. Deep down, I know it to be wrong. I just might give her a scare though! Just as I will end the sacrifices of men to Nepa I will also end all such barbaric punishments. A death sentence is sufficient in itself. There is no place for adding torture. If someone, man or woman, must be executed, it must be quick and as painless as reasonably possible. Anything else degrades the executioner as much as the victim. On my fifth birthphase I was beaten savagely. That beating has coloured my whole life for both good and ill. On the good side it has brought me to reflect on the morality of punishment. Although it has taken me many years to reach my present position, I am now passionate in my quest for just dealings both between individuals and between people and the institutions of society."

Robina shook her head, "I would never want to be on the wrong side of you. I think we have said enough for now. You have given us much to ponder and we should turn in to rest. Would you like some male company, or perhaps, Shay you would like to join me with one of my favourites. My companion here will be pleased to share with Brinda if she would like that."

I thought of refusing. I was quite tired. But I didn't want to seem impolite and anyway surely a bit of sex is always welcome. "What a kind offer. I will be delighted to join you. I'm sure Brinda will be pleased to have her fun without me in the way. Although I have set her a tiring pace tophase and she might just crash out. Up to you Brinda, I'll wish you pleasant dreams and go off with Robina here, who's bound to have a first rate taste in men."

Whether Brinda indulged herself or not, she didn't say and I was not going to ask. Robina's favourite was both good-looking and well-endowed and I have no complaints but as I am so often finding, sex is never as satisfactory as in the times before Arthay. Well, I suppose, if that is my punishment from the mythical goddesses it is no more than I deserve.

Robina was true to her word and spread the news of our offer through the forest and when we set out a phase later we were accompanied by some dozen recruits from both sexes. Our whole cavalcade set off on foot eastwards through the forest. The plan was to reach Robina's cousin who resided on the banks of the northern river where we hoped to swell the numbers of recruits further. Brinda would then take them down to the estuary and cross over to Barton where she would establish a training centre. I planned to remain in the north and make a longer tour to promulgate our labour requirements further, to learn more of the geography and communities of the lands and to pursue additional trading objectives.

The journey through the extensively forested countryside was interesting but uneventful. We encountered a few scattered communities and gained a handful more recruits on the way.

When we arrived at Joanna's village I recognised her immediately as someone with whom I had dealt while trading for coal and ore, copper and iron. She welcomed us warmly and provided a sumptuous feast for our entertainment. The next phase we were joined by Audreeda from further down river with whom I have enjoyed a long and prosperous trading partnership. Indeed it was Audreeda who had first introduced me to Joanna.

Audreeda is short for a woman, just seven feet and two thumbs but has one of the sharpest intellects I have ever encountered. She immediately took the lead in our discussions and was quick to grasp the import of my plans and the opportunities for us all.

"Look," she said to Robina and Joanna. "What Shay is offering is a once in a generation opportunity for us. OK, it could go pear-shaped, but I don't think it will. I don't like the idea of war any more than you do, but it will be inevitable if we are ever going to get away from the current divisions on our common island. Surely it's worth some risk to go for the big prize. I think Shay can win and that we can make a material difference to help that along. And in winning with Shay, we will break the power of the temples and not have to pay the price of conforming to their religious fundamentalism. Free trade and no slavery, either to people or

Goddesses. That is the bright vision ahead of us and we should grasp it for our children."

Joanna butted in, "Yes Audreeda, but you have always had a bee in your bonnet about religion. You and your weird sister. Trade I can understand, and an end to the threat of slave-raids. I want peace with the Theocracy but don't necessarily want to embrace their lifestyle. For example, we've managed without metal goods forever, and I don't see they are that important except for weapons which we won't need if we are at peace. Anyway, despite what they think down south, we actually know enough about metallurgy, if we so choose, to make our own pots and pans. I just want to live and let live."

Robina nodded, "our lifestyle in the forest is simple but easy. We don't want to lose that by absorption into the Theocracy."

I countered. "I am not proposing absorption into the Theocracy. It is important that you should be free to live as you want. I'm totally with Joanna in terms of live and let live. But Audreeda is right, there is a unique opportunity here to end some barbaric practises and to engage in peaceful trade in a way that respects all of our rights to live as we please as long as we respect others' right to also live as they please. With your help we can do this."

In terms of our recruitment drive the next couple of phases were very successful and Brinda led quite a force downstream along the river to the estuary where she was able to arrange to ferry them all to Barton. She then set up a camp outside the town and started a training programme on canal building and maintenance. After about three periods of training she decamped, taking river transport to the head of navigation on the

Lesser and its tributary ready to embark on the major canal works to join to the Street river and thence connect all the way from the Lesser to the Second estuaries.

Meanwhile I set out on horseback with Audreeda and Joanna and a couple of menservants into the North-East of the country. This was further than I had ever before penetrated into the Northern wild lands and eventually the forest gave way to moorland as we climbed into more mountainous country.

Joanna explained that these mountains were the source of the iron and copper ore deposits that she had been supplying and that we would need to negotiate with the local tribes if I were to increase the rate and volume of supply.

When last in Barton I had met with the blacksmith who had been experimenting with more efficient steel production using coal for the heat source. She had invented a much hotter form of furnace and was able to reduce the costs of production substantially while also obtaining a much more consistent quality of steel. She had told me that the main bottleneck preventing her from stepping up production was the supply of ore and coal. Apart from the need for labour for the canals, my other goal for this northern tour was to see what could be achieved.

Although Joanna knows that the purpose of the ore is for metal extraction, those who actually did the quarrying did not know why their rocks were in demand. I decided to enlighten them and after several phases of negotiation I was able to strike a deal that was satisfactory to all of us. The only downside is that I am now committed to wholesale breaking the Theocracy's ban on trade in metal goods. Among other things I have undertaken to supply copper ware and metal jewellery in return for the ore.

37

Twin Worlds III

Apparently the coal comes from even further north and in addition to quantity of supply there are transport issues to solve. However, I am optimistic and morrow-phase we will continue our expedition to treat with the coal-producers.

7
Northern Culture and Religion

Our stereotype of the northern lands as 'wild' and the people as 'barbarians' is just so wrong on many levels. This trip with Audreeda and Joanna gave me the opportunity to get to know them really well as people and also to learn much more about the societies in these lands.

Unlike in the Theocracy there is a wide variety of society and culture. Communities are small and largely independent of each other. While, for the most part, they are matriarchal as elsewhere, there are a few exceptions. In particular I learnt that the community raided all those years ago by Valray treated its men as more-or-less equal with women and even sometimes had a man as leader. Indeed, until about a year previously Arval's father, Edgar, was the leader of his village, and was held in great respect by neighbouring villages. According to those I spoke to from the moorland community, after he escaped from Valray, Edgar took up with Wilja's younger sister Wena who gave birth to a son who was establishing a formidable reputation as a warrior and huntsman.

Relationships between communities are not always peaceful and over the years Edgar had established hegemony over quite an area in the central highlands some sixty-four imiles due north of the Lesser river. Although Edgar had retired from his leadership position, his legacy was still very much in evidence and it was made clear to me that, as a southerner, I would not be welcome in that part of the country. For that reason we kept very much to the Eastern side of the Northlands. Perhaps in the years to come I shall be able to repair our reputation sufficiently to attempt a reconciliation with Edgar and his people, whose attitude to us from the Theocracy is totally understandable.

Apart from the obvious distrust of the Theocracy caused by our slave raiding, there remained concerns about our ruthless enforcement of religious uniformity. As I hope has become clear, I do not have strong religious beliefs, and not only doubt some of the theological myths, but am absolutely certain that the temples are not the authority on whatever truth there may be about the Goddesses. Thus, for my part, I had no issue with the variety of beliefs held in these parts.

Audreeda is especially erudite and knowledgeable in theology and she and I would discuss such matters long into the evenings. Joanna tended to leave us to it during such times, as she is neither devout nor very interested in the deeper theological questions.

According to Audreeda most of the northern communities retain the basic pantheon as in the Theocracy but exhibit a range of different rituals and degrees of emphasis. However, in most cases, they are tolerant of differing views and do not try to impose on others. Many, like Joanna, have little interest and do no more than show some outward conformity to the majority practises within their community, while not letting religion interfere very much with their ordinary lives.

In the more primitive communities the regular pantheon is often supplemented by local 'goddesses' who look after specific localities or natural features: for example these may include goddesses belonging to rivers or streams, or particular hills, caves and waterfalls. In some cases even ancient trees are cited as hosting a goddess. Both Audreeda and Joanna were dismissive of such beliefs.

Audreeda herself was sceptical about the established pantheon and its myths which she feels are largely rubbish and promulgated by a self-serving priestess class to their own profit. On the other hand, she acknowledged that there are deep questions about life and the natural world that cannot be answered by our own knowledge and experience; and that surely there are spiritual truths out there that we do not understand and need to be addressed through faith and contemplation. She described herself as a sceptical agnostic engaged in a constant internal struggle to gain a glimpse of the true nature of life and the universe.

I asked her about her sister who Joanna had earlier described as a religious weirdo.

Audreeda's response was interesting. "Ah yes, my younger sister Elguy is a member of a rather austere community living a secluded moorland existence in an abbey high on a cliff above the East coast. However, it is not an abbey as would be familiar to you. They do not believe in the Goddesses at all. Their main belief is that there is exactly one Goddess/God. They argue, reasonably in my view, that there is no theological need for a whole community of Goddesses but that a unique creatrix of the world is all that is required. Furthermore, they argue, that since this creatrix is unique she has no need to be associated with one gender but will incorporate both female and male within the one godhead - both Creatrix and Creator. In some vague sense they claim that people were created in her own image, but that we were created female and male to enable us to procreate children without having the creative power that must uniquely belong to her."

"Wow, that is quite a theological leap, but I can see how it attracts, tell me more. I would very much like to meet your sister and learn from her. How come you haven't joined her?"

"There are indeed attractions to the basic monotheistic idea. On the other hand there is also a lot of associated mumbo jumbo, as they ascribe properties to their Goddess for which there can be no real justification. For example they have very restrictive views about sex and have even gone so far as to develop phobias regarding the human body. I could never go along with such things."

"Please explain more. Surely at least with their Goddess being both female and male, they do not subjugate men in the way that is common throughout our cultures."

"You might think so, but you'd be wrong. They still regard women as superior, as I suppose we are to some extent, and they are no different from our mainstream religion in limiting priesthood to women. Indeed, they do not acknowledge any spiritual dimension to men but claim their sole purpose is to serve women, literally for procreation, and also to free women for prayer and spiritual contemplation by meeting our physical needs by doing all the work. I think that's wrong. Men are the weaker sex. That seems clear, but surely it becomes our duty to nurture them, even to indulge them a little. To give them some compensation for their weakness. Anyway, that's how I approach the men in my life."

"You interest me. We must have further discussion on the treatment of men some other time, but explain about these monotheists' views on sex."

"Well it's like this. They consider that the sole true purpose of sex is for procreation and that there is something dirty about its misuse for enjoyment. They do acknowledge that people are weak and will only rarely live up to ideals. However, for them the ideal is to only engage in sex when you are trying to get pregnant, and therefore also to limit yourself to those times when your rhythms indicate that as a likely outcome."

"Ouch! You mean just once a selenth, four times a year. Surely they'd all go mad."

"I do mean that is their ideal of the perfect woman. Our inability to live by such a restriction is merely a sign of our inherent weakness and sinfulness. But apparently the Goddess understands us and makes allowances, if we but strive to approach the ideal as best we can. In practice the devout women of the abbey try to go without for as long as they can stand it. When they finally succumb they hang a token at the door of their cell. Each night there are men on duty to patrol the corridors and when one comes upon a token he enters and provides for the woman. However they are not supposed to enjoy themselves properly. All the devotees wear a long grey hooded gown, tied at the waist with a girdle, which they never remove except to change it once a period for washing. When having sex they merely raise the gown to the waist to give the man access while both man and woman wear a blindfold so they do not see the other's genitals. The only speech is for the woman to say whether she wants one, two or three servings. Officially she only asks for more than one if she is indeed trying to get pregnant."

43

Twin Worlds III

"That's bizarre. I can see why you haven't joined your sister's order. I can't understand how anyone would. Do they really never takes their gown off, what about when bathing?"

"Well, I did say it was a small order. And Joanna did call them weird. But no, they never undress. When bathing they only remove the girdle and enter the water in the gown, washing themselves beneath it. Even when changing, Elguy says she puts the clean gown on top of the old one which she then removes from underneath. It is regarded as sinful to gaze on a naked body, even one's own. Even when nursing an infant, they wear a gown that opens at the breast and minimises exposure. And they never feed an infant if there is a man in the room."

"How come others tolerate them. Surely most people would be afraid that these ghastly ways might spread."

"Well in their defence, they do not try unduly to convert outsiders; limiting their preaching to presenting their beliefs and hoping to gain the occasional adherent, as they do. They also engage in good works which are of value to their neighbouring communities. For example they establish schools for girls and give comfort and care to the sick. They do all this without imposing their religious opinions or seeking other than voluntary charitable donations to help further their work."

"Well, if we have time after conducting our business I would like to meet them to learn more; but I assure you that even if they convince me about the unique Goddess I will not join their way of life."

It took us several phases over inhospitable mountainous terrain to reach the coal fields in the extreme north-east of our island. I'm sure that in doing so I have travelled further north than anyone else from the Theocracy. The language spoken here is quite unintelligible to me but Joanna and one of the menservants were able to interpret.

I had no difficulty with the locals agreeing to supply more coal but they explained the very difficult transportation challenges. To deliver the quantities I am looking for requires significant improvements to the paths and tracks linking the coalfields to a point on the north river where barges can be loaded for the journey to the Lesser estuary and Barton.

I was given a tour round one of the larger coal quarries and noticed how they made use of carts pulled along on wooden rails to ease the effort needed. This gave me an idea that perhaps we could lay steel rails over some of the trickier terrain and so improve transportation. Of course there is a bit of chicken and egg here, we would need more coal and ore to make the rails as well as significant amounts of skilled labour, and then we need the improved transportation links to obtain the necessary coal and ore. Still I thought it worth considering just where the optimal balance lies and I'm sure that with some of my experts back in the Lesser delta region I could come up with a plan.

Interestingly, the local communities said they would welcome the work and thought there would be no difficulty in supplying the labour force. The people here are very attached to their locality and resistant to moving. Thus while there were few, if any, willing to join my workforce on the canals in the Theocracy, there were many who would work on improving the local roads.

45

Twin Worlds III

All in all I judged the trip to have been successful and I looked forward to a restful sojourn with Audreeda's sister in her abbey. We rode south by easy stages on the cliffs overlooking the East coast. Eventually we came to the abbey which is situated in a commanding position with views over the sea of storms to the East and the moors to the north, west and south. It is rather exposed to the weather and, when we arrived, there was a biting East wind blowing from the sea. Elguy welcomed us on behalf of the abbess and I explained my desire to debate with them and learn about their beliefs and way of life.

We stayed at the abbey for a full period and I enjoyed many discussions with Elguy and her abbess, Hild. I learnt a lot. While Audreeda's description of their practises is correct as far as it goes, the full truth is much more nuanced. Hild was able to explain that their austere way of life was never intended to be for everyone to follow but was for just a few who felt called to deeper meditation of the relationship between Woman and Goddess. For most women (and by implication, all men) it is sufficient to believe in the one creatrix and her gift of life through the creation of both female and male.

Hild explained to me that the Goddess's attitude to our sexual behaviour is not as harsh as described earlier. She has given us the gift of sex primarily to enable us to have children but understands that we would take pleasure from the act itself and delights in us doing so. However, Hild warned that there is danger in us abusing the gift through over-emphasis of the physical, distracting us in our relationships with each other and thus with the Goddess herself.

All this has given me much food for thought and I must say I am attracted to a lot of the ideas. While I am certainly not called to such an abstemious lifestyle as offered by Hild's abbey, I find monotheism much closer to the truth than the mish-mash of the pantheon. There does remain the question as to whether any Goddess is required to explain the purpose and existence of the world and the life in it. Such a question seems to be unanswerable, but it seems clear to me that at most one Goddess is sufficient!

It is generally held in the Theocracy that the wild tribes in both the north and west are illiterate. Thus I was astonished to be shown a beautifully illustrated prayer book produced in Hild's abbey. The writing was similar to ours with just a few different characters in use. The main difference is that all lines are written from left to right in contrast to our practice of continuing lines in a boustrophedon pattern. I asked Audreeda about it.

"Well," she said, "you are right that literacy is rare, and there is no historic tradition for reading or writing. However, we are not totally isolated from what you do down south. Although rare, a few of your slaves do escape and find their way home. It is thought that some of those had learnt to read and write and brought the ideas here. Personally, I come from the north bank of the Lesser Estuary and have spent time in Barton where I learnt to read. And, before you ask, I went by the name of Maudree when living in the Theocracy. The innovation to write all lines from left to right is very recent, and pioneered in the few abbeys that have produced devotional books. The oldest such book I have heard of was written a bit over sixty-four years ago. Older books only contain pictures, generally illustrating deeds of the Goddesses."

This was quite an important revelation because there remains a prohibition from the Arch Convocation on the export of literacy to the wild lands. As far as I'm concerned this was always dubious, but now I had the evidence that should enable me to confront the temples and have the prohibition lifted.

I parted from the others when we reached the Estuary where I was able to take passage on one of my barges to return to my property outside Barton.

8
Rivermouth 1

Despite my orders that I was to be undisturbed, my slave was brushed aside and Cray came storming in. "Thay, it's long past time that you pulled yourself together. You've neglected your duties for four years now and it's not fair on the people of Chalcliff and Strait that you fail to attend the Superior Wapentake on their behalf, let alone that you neglect your business interests and the duty you owe to the family."

"I gave orders that you weren't to be admitted. I'm in deep mourning still, and such energy as I have must be devoted to my daughter. Thar is over three now and quite a handful. Craya is managing my business for me and I'm sure she's doing her best."

"This state of affairs cannot continue. I've indulged you as far as possible, and far more than is reasonable. You locking yourself away and moping is not going to bring Arthay back from the sea. And Thar is no excuse. Your mother managed you and Shay; I managed Craya and Crayza, while maintaining our positions in society and Government. You can do the same while Thar is growing up. Although we don't see much of her in Rivermouth, I gather that Shay is leading a very active public life in the North despite having Shar who is the same age as your Thar. As for my daughter Craya, she is indeed doing her best for you, but she doesn't have your abilities and finds it a struggle. It doesn't help that you've landed her with that cripple[4] who keeps dripping poison into her ear. So snap out of it. I'm not leaving until you accompany me back to Rivermouth and remember your place in the world."

The trouble is that I know she's right. I do have to go back to my life. It's just that my life feels meaningless without Arthay. It's only Thar that keeps me sane. She is all I have left of him and I know I owe it to her to give her a normal upbringing, but it just seems too soon. Until she reaches school age, surely we can exist in our own bubble.

"I don't care if Craya does less well with the business than I might do. I'm sorry about the surgeon. I just can't stand the thought of ever having to deal with her myself; while I know it is my duty to ensure she is looked after. She betrayed me first, and then changed sides and betrayed Shay. She got what she deserved but she was my employee and I couldn't abandon her completely. I haven't been completely idle. I have managed my estate here and kept in touch with the goings on in the Wapentake through Craya. Now that she represents Honeyfield, she has been able to keep me informed."

"Well, we must talk further. Right now, I've had a long journey and am famished. You can order up some lunch and I can meet Thar. Then we can discuss further on a full stomach."

---

4 I ought to put a trigger warning here, and I apologise if this usage offends anyone. When I was growing up the word was in common parlance. However nowadays its use is much rarer as it is seen as (and is) disrespectful. However in the context of the primitive and brutal society on Isla, it is appropriate within the norms of the culture. There are 4 uses of this word in the book.

I knew I was beaten and only put up a show of resistance. The next phase we all set off for Rivermouth. Not much had changed since I was last there over four years previously and I soon settled down to my routine of business and Wapentake affairs. I caught up with Craya and realised what her mother had been getting at. The surgeon, I won't say her name, had indeed turned her vehemently against Shay. Obviously that doesn't bother me. Having Craya as a staunch ally against my sister is only good news for me. On the other hand I want no more direct dealings with the treacherous surgeon and quickly came to an agreement with Craya on the subject.

Otherwise Craya has stepped into the role as my lieutenant and we have become quite inseparable. My sex life has never recovered properly from the loss of Arthay but Craya does invite me to join her occasionally which, though rather unsatisfactory, does meet my basic physical requirements.

Thar is my delight and consolation. I suppose I do indulge her somewhat. I talk to her a lot about her father, which is most unusual in our culture. On the other hand I don't say much about my sister. I really just want to ignore her existence. Fortunately she comes to Rivermouth very rarely and Craya and I do what we can to avoid her, which I think suits us all. I have never seen my niece, Shar, because Shay never brings her to Rivermouth. That is also how I like it.

However tophase is going to one of those rare exceptions. Shay is in Rivermouth and is due to attend the Superior Wapentake. There is no way that I can avoid encountering her. A crisis is brewing concerning the authority of the Superior Wapentake and Arch Convocation over the individual Wapentake and Hundred courts.

Twin Worlds III

The immediate cause of concern is a ban on slave-raiding into the Northern Wild Lands imposed by five of the northern Wapentakes, namely: Lesser Coast, Lesser, Central, Upper Street and Oakbridge and District[5]. While this doesn't cut off the trade completely, it makes it extremely difficult and increases both the costs and the risks involved. The only official routes open are now across the Second river via the territory of West Bank and thence through the Isla Marches either directly into the North-West or into the Borders territory, where the Wapentake is itself under pressure to introduce the ban.

All this has been driven by Shay acting personally, and is indicative of the immense influence she now exerts in the north. Indeed her power grew considerably during the years of my isolation following the loss of Arthay. I had been so overwhelmed by my own grief and guilt that I had failed to notice Shay's activities, although Craya did try to warn me.

Actually, even though I can't possibly support Shay, I do agree that men should be well-treated and our power over them should not be abused. However, going so much against the natural order as to free them from female ownership seems to be risking the total breakdown of society and civilisation as we know it. It is also good to refresh the population through importing men from outside the Theocracy. Perhaps we should look at better ways of doing so than the current practice of raiding.

Anyway, Shay did not please everyone in her locality. In particular her actions have destroyed the majority of the business

5 See Appendix 2 for the political geography of the Theocracy with accompanying map.

of the slave market in Knot-on-Lesser which used to be a major contributor to the economy of the town and of the whole Lesser region. Indeed the Lesser Wapentake resisted Shay for some time, and I still don't understand how she persuaded them eventually to support and enforce the ban.

Shay is less successful with the religious establishment. Isla-of-the-Knotted-Bends College, which had a significant financial interest in the slave market, has presented the ban as a threat to the religious foundations of our Theocracy and challenged it through the Arch Convocation. The result is the present position. Arch Convocation supported the College by eighteen votes to four with two abstentions. It is hard to see how this will end well. It isn't just about slaves. The political balance between Wapentake and Temple is delicate and an open split could be extremely dangerous; possibly even provoking civil war. Bloody Shay, if she isn't put in her place she could end up destroying us all.

What a fucking shambles! Cray's attempts at a compromise, followed by trying to talk me into rescinding our ban were pathetic. I suppose I didn't really expect to win but I had thought that maybe enough members would be sufficiently concerned about interference from the temples and regional rights to sway the vote my way. I predict the final compromise won't last.

As I later explained to Wilda, the whole thing is an unworkable fudge, but I suppose it has prevented an immediate civil war. The motion coming out of Arch Convocation was split in two with each part voted on separately. This was Cray's doing in an attempt to head off a constitutional crisis over the rights of regional Hundreds and Wapentakes. I don't blame her but perhaps I might have won otherwise.

The first vote was on the assertion that female ownership of males was as ordained by the Goddesses and a constitutional right blah blah blah. We lost by thirteen votes to eight with four abstentions. Actually that's not too bad. I was surprised that Upper Great River and West Country Rural voted with us, and pleased that Cray herself recorded an abstention from Rivermouth Central. My only disappointment, apart from losing, is that I failed to persuade Borders into my camp, but at least they abstained.

The second vote was on whether regional Hundreds and Wapentakes had the right to legislate on matters of slavery. We won that vote convincingly, with Cray coming off the fence. The vote was eight votes to fifteen with two abstentions. I'm sure it would have been even more convincing but for Thay's pressure on her neighbouring regions.

So it's a dog's breakfast. Male slavery is a religious requirement, but individual Hundreds and Wapentakes have the power to legislate on the matter.

I really don't have the inclination to waste my time politicking in Rivermouth. There is so much to do back in the North. The link between the Lesser and Second rivers is now open to traffic and Brinda is starting work on the canal to link Knot-on-Lesser to Midborough. The Midborough Hundred opposes me on pretty well anything so I haven't revealed my complete plans and will leave it to the last before undertaking any work within the

Hundred boundaries. On the other hand I have full co-operation from Central and negotiations with Midborough Rural are going well.

The Lesser-Second link is already bringing major economic benefits to both Knot and Street. Street's population is increasing to the extent that is will soon be declared a town. It was by using the economic leverage that the link gives me that I was able to overcome the opposition to my slave-raid ban in the Knot council and Lesser Wapentake. When it came to a choice between the benefits of my river transport or the slave market, the opposition soon buckled. Hence, I suppose, the move by the College to stir up trouble in the Arch Convocation. One phase we are going to have to face up to the power of the temples and get rid of the Theocratic strangle-hold on the whole island.

Twin Worlds III

9
Shay's Progress

I really don't have the energy for the Rivermouth scene. Now that Thay's come out of her self-imposed purdah we're only going to clash if ever I attend the SW[6]. It's also clear that for the time being I'm not going to achieve anything there. Consequently I have decided to send a proxy to attend future meetings on my behalf. I have advised Cray accordingly and, although she made a token remonstrance, I think she is secretly pleased. She doesn't like conflict and especially not when it's between me and Thay. She tries her best to keep the peace between us and also to act as a sort of surrogate mother to us both. Actually I do both love and respect her, somewhat more than I did with my real mother, but I'm not going to let her thwart my ambitions for the future of the Theocracy.

Right now that means keeping up the momentum on my canal projects and concentrating my political activities here in the North.

Regarding the former, we have just opened the first sixteen imile stretch of canal south from Knot. This brings us over the border into Central and is likely to bring an economic boom to the village where it currently terminates. There have been some issues with locals concerned about the antics of the workforce, but thus far we have had no serious incidents.

It helps that the workforce is mixed and actually has a surplus of men. This has helped contain the wilder women since at least

6 Superior Wapentake

they are getting sufficient sex within the encampments. I don't always approve of the way they treat some of their male colleagues and Brinda has sometimes had to intervene when a man has been promoted to a leadership role over some of the women. However, most of the problems of this nature were ironed out during the digging of the Lesser-Street link.

At least we've had no more murders. Oh! I forgot, I haven't described that incident. I suppose, having now mentioned it, I ought to go into the details. Anyway about a year ago a man was promoted to lead the gang working on a pair of locks and a few phases later he was found floating face down in the canal. Although at first sight it looked like an accident, Brinda was suspicious and called me in to investigate.

Careful examination of the body and other facts made me pretty certain that foul play was involved and that the man had been killed before being chucked in the water. Finding who did it took a while but eventually I tracked down the culprit, a woman from my estate at Barton-within-Lesser who was resentful that she hadn't been promoted. She also held unreconstructed views on the role of men in society.

Of course she had denied it, and then explained that she had been drunk and couldn't recall her actions. This last might have been true. She did have a problem with alcohol and subsequent violence. One reason she had been passed over for promotion to a position of responsibility.

I was having none of her excuses. It is important to maintain strong discipline in the work camps and I felt that an example had to be made.

Twin Worlds III

I'm afraid her execution was not pleasant and I would have preferred a more humane ending, but there was no place for showing any form of leniency that the tough women might misinterpret as weakness. I had her feet nailed to a high branch and left her hanging upside down for two whole periods, then I allowed her body to be cut down for wild animals to finish off.

As I said, there have been no repeats.

Also, the canal was finished on schedule and the current work is progressing well.

Politics are more challenging. Thus far I have dealt bilaterally with the various Councils, Hundreds and Wapentakes. And as for the Temples, they can be a nightmare, even with the strong support I receive from Wilda and Oakbridge Abbey.

I have decided that the time has come to establish an appropriate multi-regional forum which I am calling the Council of the North. To this end I've invited the Superior Wapentake members for all the northern regions, together with the Arch Convocation members for Temples within those regions. Two of the first things I plan to do is to open the council up to observers from the Isla Marches and the Northern wild lands, and then to try to extend the slave-raiding ban to all the regions bordering the wild lands.

10
Thar and Shar—a domestic interlude

While their mothers were engaged in the high and low politics of the Theocracy, the near twin sister-cousins were growing up in very different styles. Not only was Shay physically absent for much of the time while she pursued her political and business objectives, but even when her body was at home in Elmhouse her mind was often elsewhere, leaving Shar very much to her own devices. Shar desperately loved her Mummy and wished she would spend more time with her, but she was both bright and a realist and thus had become very independent and quite grown up for a young child.

She didn't actually lack for adult attention. Daubey saw to her phase to phase needs and acted very much as a surrogate mother. Also Valray often came to stay or had Shar visit the farm and was ever the indulgent grandmother. Even Wilda and Brinda made time for Shar whenever their busy schedules allowed. These two also took the trouble to berate Shay for her neglect and did what they could to persuade her to take maternal breaks from her concerns.

In this they were at least partially successful. Shay promised to try to do better. Indeed, she adored Shar as much as any mother of an only daughter. It was just that she was driven by her ambition and couldn't let go, or even let up.

Shar enjoyed stability of home. Shay never took her to Rivermouth or Knot and only very rarely to Barton, so Shar knew Elmhouse and Ludray as her homes, wandering through the local countryside, playing by the river and new canal or around the farm, all the while developing a strong imagination and a taste for exploration that would never leave her. She learnt to read early and was fluent not long after her third birthphase. As well as delighting in such children's books as she was given, she also made good, if, at first, secretive, use of the Elmhouse library; thereby acquiring knowledge and sophistication well beyond her years. What she really lacked was the society of other children. This didn't worry Shay but Wilda, in particular, was very concerned.

"Look Shay", she would say. "Children really need each others' company. Not just to play, but to learn how to become social beings. How to share, how it is not to be the centre of the universe, lots of things vital to their personal development to ready them for life beyond childhood. I know it's early but you must consider sending Shar to school. She's big and old for her age and will easily cope with being a year ahead of her age group. Let her come to me at Oakbridge."

"I'll think about it", was Shay's customary response. "Shar's too young to board and Oakbridge is too far for her as a home-based girl. Anyway I thought your minimum age for boarders was eight. And, much as I respect you and your school, I am looking to send Shar somewhere more academic. Probably my old school in Springhills."

"You say you'll think about it but you don't." She wouldn't have to board in the regular way. After all, I'm her Goddess and we get on fine together. She can stay in my apartment with me during the three school-phases, and it isn't too far for her to return home for period-end rest-phase. I agree she can be expected to outgrow what we offer at Oakbridge but we can prepare her for Springhills so she is ready to transfer at a sensible age of ten or eleven. If she had suitable child company here it would be different, her cousin for example, but she doesn't. It's bad for her to be limited to adult company all the time. Even though you don't value it now, I assure you that you benefited considerably from your early life with Thay, before the dreadful experience that thrust you apart and, in all honesty, I have to say has marked you both for life."

Eventually, Shay gave in. At the tender age of four and a half Shar went to live with Wilda for the three school phases out of four each period in term time.[7] Her first school-phase was at the beginning of the Autumn term which always falls on the first phase of the twenty-third period of the year, or thirteenth phase of Autumn as it is more commonly known on Isla. Although at this time Isla, or indeed the rest of Duplos, didn't number their years; this was in the year that would later become know as 2611 GDY, or eventually as 3 BC[8].

Throughout this period of her life Shar was ignorant of the existence of her sister-cousin, Thar. Shay never spoke of her and told her very little of her own twin other than she existed and they were sworn enemies. She was more forthcoming about Shar's father, praising him as exceptional among men, while being economical with the truth about his demise. Shar was only told that he had fallen into the sea and drowned following a dispute between the twin sisters. Shar soon learnt that she might speak freely about Arval, who was, after all, not only her father, but her

---

7 On Isla the school year is divided into three terms of six periods each. The remaining twelve periods in the year are vacation breaks. Three periods over new year, two periods between the other two terms and a long Summer vacation of seven periods.

8 GDY = Geosian Decimal Year; BC = Before Contact; The All-Duplos Harmonisation Convention of 10 AC wll agree a common dating from contact year 2614 GDY as year zero (or Contact Year - CY)

Grandmother Valray's son and Auntie Wilda's brother. On the other hand any questions or discussions concerning Thay were sharply discouraged as off-limits. The other adults in Shar's life took their cue from Shay and also never spoke to her of either Thay or Thar. Shar also learnt that her infrequent visits to Rivermouth always put her mother in a bad mood.

At Thay's house on the South coast, Thar's early years were quite a contrast. Thar was just five phases younger than Shar but, although physically they appeared as the sororal twins that their genes dictated, if you had met her aged five you would have taken Thar as much younger.

As pointed out earlier, Thay went into a self-inflicted purdah following Arthay's leap into the strait. When, to her delight, Thar was born she doted on the child, wrapping herself in her baby and hiding from the world. Certainly Thar didn't lack for love and affection or luxury, but the isolation and almost smothering attention of her mother, keeping her close at all times, meant she didn't enjoy the freedom to roam and explore that dominated the life of her sister-cousin. She was also not told of the existence of Shar while being fed the line of Shay's wickedness and culpability in the death of her wonderful father.

Eventually, as we have seen, Thay's mother's cousin, Cray, forced her way into their lives and dragged Thay, with Thar in tow, back to Rivermouth to resume a more normal life.

Thereafter Thar's world was split between the grand palace in Rivermouth that Thay had inherited from her mother, Chay, and the South coast estate. As one might expect, Thar was a bright child and quickly advanced in her understanding. There was some dispute regarding her schooling. Thay remained reluctant to let go of the baby, while Cray urged her to start Thar in the Spring term which started just one phase before her fifth birthphase.

In what seemed an ironic reversal of that time when Shay was made to wait another selenth before starting her school career, Thay was keen to delay Thar until the Autumn, which she was entitled to do because Thar was still technically only four on the first phase of the Spring term.

Cray won. Not by any force of argument but the news reached Thay that Shar had started her schooling the previous Autumn and Thay was not going to allow Thar to be a whole year behind. The bitter rivalry between the twins was by no means forgotten. So it was that on the first phase of the tenth period (twenty-first of Spring) in what would become 2 BC, Thar started at the Rivermouth Academy for Future Ladies, the most prestigious preparatory school in all the Theocracy.

Unlike Shar, she didn't have to board. The academy was located in the same fashionable district as Thay's palace and a young man was engaged to drive Thar in a carriage to school every school-phase and then collect her at the break times. During term time both Thay and Thar lived in the palace and then returned to the South coast for the vacations.

While in Rivermouth Thay attended the Superior Wapentake when it sat, which was not all that often, and never in school vacation time, and divided her time between her political and business duties. Cray's daughter, Craya remained Thay's trusted lieutenant and under Thay's closer guidance the various business interests prospered. Craya as SW member for the Rivermouth South and Honeyfield Hundred was also Thay's most loyal political supporter and could be relied on to further Thay's interests at all times, even on those occasions when it put her at odds with her own mother.

In her turn Cray had become the senior member of the SW. As always, she was a conciliator, trying to work in harmony with the various political factions in the lay house.

Although she had accepted that she was not going to reconcile Thay and Shay, she was still going to do all she could to prevent their feud from damaging the fabric of the Theocracy. It pained her that her only remaining daughter was so strongly allied to Thay in opposition to Shay, just as they had been as children. Now for political as well as personal reasons, she mourned the tragic loss of her dear Crayza. How different things might have been if she had lived. Cray's glasses were never so rose-tinted as when she thought of her younger daughter.

With Thar living much of the time in Rivermouth, Cray got to see quite a lot of her. Indeed acting as a sort of surrogate Grandmother to her and often having the child to stay on the rare occasions that Thay had to be away. This arrangement suited all parties. Craya had no children, leaving Cray with no grandchildren of her own, so building this important relationship with her late cousin's granddaughter filled a gap in her life. While for Thay and Thar the benefits also went beyond the mere convenience of the practical arrangements. Thay missed Chay and still felt guilt at having denied her a granddaughter while she still lived. Cray made an excellent substitute, apart from the regrettable circumstance of her being Shay's Goddess and thus retaining both duty and affection for her.

In her turn, Cray was also aware of her nagging feeling that she needed to do more for Shay. She knew from bitter experience that any attempt to reconcile the twin sisters was doomed to failure, but Shay remained her Goddess-daughter and she loved her and felt keenly that she should make an effort to maintain the relationship and to also get to know the child, Shar, that she had never seen.

11
Cray's Visitation

It was the 14th phase of Summer in the year that would eventually be known as 2 BC. Shay was in her library with Wilda, discussing Shar's progress over her first year at school. The morrow would be midsummer phase when the long Summer vacation would begin and Wilda had brought Shar home following the last school-phase of term.

Shar had made excellent progress, being extremely bright, like both her parents. "We're going to have to bump her up a year to keep her from getting bored even though she is already a year younger than most of her present class," opined Wilda. "It's a good thing she's big for her age."

There was a knock on the door and Daubey put her head round to announce: "Excuse me for disturbing you Shay, but Brinda has just ridden in and says she needs to speak with you. It seems quite urgent."

"Show her in, I'm sure Wilda won't mind interrupting our chat for a bit."

Brinda was shown in still wearing her riding clothes, obviously having been in a considerable hurry.

"Not another mishap on the Midborough canal, I hope."

"No, nothing like that," puffed Brinda, "but I thought you would want as much notice as possible. I happened to be in Midborough to pick up some supplies when I noticed a bit of a commotion. It turned out that your Goddess, Cray, has been resting in town while on her way, apparently to visit you. She is making somewhat stately progress in a fancy carriage drawn by six horses and with a baggage carriage following behind. She stayed with the Mayor for her sleep-over and was then setting off on her next stage. I made further enquiries and learnt that she is intending to to spend her next sleep-over in Street before coming on here. I thought you might want to be prepared."

"Indeed, you thought correctly, I'll get Daubey to make the appropriate arrangements to enable us to cope with this honour. I wonder what has caused Cray to stir herself. She rarely leaves Rivermouth, but I suppose she was bound to come sometime. I've been neglectful of her because of Thay and she has never met Shar."

Wilda butted in. "She's never met me either. I must say I'm curious to meet her. By now she must be the senior lay representative on the SW and could well be in line for President of the Isla Council when the current temple presidency ends next year. Perhaps she's come to enlist your support."

"Maybe, but I expect it's going to be more personal than that. Even so it is inevitable that there will be some political discussion and I'll need us to exercise some caution. I don't want to show my hand yet. So, in particular I don't want her to become too aware of our military preparations. Brinda, can you ensure that any training during her visit is not too obviously warlike? Oh, and by the way, how much is Cray likely to have learnt about the current canal construction?"

"I would rather not have the troops idle, but we could avoid weapons training, especially with pikes, and perhaps limit ourselves to phalanx-ball and tug-of-war? As for the canal, the construction is still well short of Midborough and Cray won't have passed anywhere near the actual workings. Neither will she have learnt anything in Midborough itself, as we are still keeping a very low profile there. Of course, when she stays in Street she will see the river traffic and hear about the economic benefits of the Lesser-Second link. I expect she'll also be lobbied to declare Street a town."

"Right," decided Shay, "it is imperative that Cray does not learn about pikes or about the new steels. Hide anything to do with them. Tug-of-war is fine. That is a well-recognised sport. I'm reasonably relaxed about phalanx-ball as well, provided the teams are kept reasonably small. Let's say no more than seven in the front rows. However, definitely no Pike-Push. We can explain the encampment as navvies on a rest break. The sport will help, and if you can arrange for a bit of maintenance work on the Elmhouse canal arm and local locks, that could help the cover story. We could give her a lock demo and perhaps a presentation on the canal arm and Street navigation. She's aware of the Lesser-Second link following all the fuss in the Arch Convocation and Superior Wapentake last year. She just won't have a full realisation of the economic implications. Whatever she learns in Street won't matter too much and I have no problem with their advocacy for town status."

"OK, I'll get to it," answered Brinda. "I'll leave you two to your own business and to sort out domestic arrangements with Daubey. When things are quieter I'll give you the latest brief on the Midborough canal. There are a few minor issues but nothing for you to worry about right now, and also some good news from the Central and Midborough Rural Wapentakes."

Thus it was that when Cray's carriage made its stately progress up the long drive to Elmhouse Manor late on midsummer phase, Shay was ready for her and waiting outside the front entrance.

"Welcome to Elmhouse, Goddess. Do come in, we are prepared for you, and Daubey will arrange matters with your staff. There is some lunch ready in the dining room."

Cray alighted from her carriage and preceded Shay into the house. "Hmm, I see my surprise visit is not a surprise after all. You have made some changes to the decor since I was last here, but I think I remember my way."

"When was that? I don't recall you visiting at all, you hardly ever venture out of Rivermouth."

"Oh, I was last here with your mother about ten years ago while you were holed up in Barton. It's true I don't get out much nowaphase. I'm a town girl and don't maintain a country estate. Anyway Wapentake business keeps me very much in the capital. This is good chicken though, maybe there's something to be said for rural ways."

Conversation over lunch was largely trivial. After they had eaten Shay led her Aunt into the library where they could discuss more serious matters.

"So, what is the purpose of this visit? I suppose you have come to remind me of my responsibilities to the Superior Wapentake, or is is really only a social call?" was Shay's opening gambit once they had settled into comfortable chairs and Daubey had served them drinks.

Cray's response took Shay a little by surprise. "Actually, I fully understand your reluctance to come to Rivermouth. This really is a social call. I have been feeling guilty about neglecting you, while seeing a lot of both Thay and Thar. I refuse to take sides in your sisterly feud, but you are my Goddess daughter and I remain attached to you and your interests both by reason of personal affection and a sense of duty. Besides, I have not yet met Shar which I consider very remiss of me."

Shay grew thoughtful. She too had been feeling a bit guilty about neglecting Cray, which she had rationalised by convincing herself that Cray had indeed taken Thay's part. "Well we can soon remedy that, Shar is home from school for the summer vac. You should also meet Wilda, the abbess at Oakbridge, who has become a very close friend; and my right hand woman, Brinda, who is the Engineer in charge of all my navigation works. Incidentally, it was Brinda who tipped me off about your visit, having seen you in Midborough. While you are here you must let Brinda show you our river works, which are bringing great prosperity to the region."

Cray remained at Elmhouse for a full period. She found herself more interested in the canal work than she had expected. She had never visited Barton and the Lesser delta and had not considered the possibilities of artificial rivers. Shay and Brinda did not reveal the full extent of their plans but concentrated on those parts that were already complete, namely the connection between the Lesser and Second rivers. Cray was well aware of the economic benefits of river transport. After all Chay's and now Thay's monopoly of the Great River traffic from the estuary to Rivermouth and Cattlebridge had brought them great wealth. She also knew that Chay had been very impressed by Shay's development of the Lesser, a consideration which probably influenced her late decision to leave the Elmhouse estate to Shay. What none of them could have anticipated was Shay's vision to connect the two rivers, something that anyone else would have dismissed as impossible.

Cray was also somewhat taken aback that the task of explaining locks and their maintenance was given to a man. It turned out that this man was actually in charge of the crew looking after the locks on the Street river, including that on the canal arm leading up to the wharf at Elmhouse. This was despite there being several women employed in his crew.

She was even more astonished to learn that all the men working for Shay were considered to be unowned and were paid a wage at the same rate as a woman doing the same work.

She took Shay aside: "I know you are trying to abolish slave-raiding, but how is it that these men are allowed to be without an owner? Doesn't that destroy the whole fabric of our society?"

Shay's response was firm and to the point. "I am not only opposed to slave-raiding, I am opposed to all aspects of slavery. I'm not stupid, and know I can't insist on abolition, but I can set a personal example. On my initiative the Wapentakes of Lesser Coast, Upper Street and Oakbridge have all legislated to allow for unowned men and to abolish female slavery altogether other than for fixed-term judicial punishment. The Lesser Wapentake has not gone so far yet but has made it legal for unowned men who are normally resident elsewhere to visit or transit the region without being subject to ownership laws. All men working for any of my enterprises are free and carry my passport to guarantee their freedom. These passports are legally binding in all the above four constituencies and in practice are also honoured in Central, Midborough Rural and most of North Cape and Borders. My guarantees of immunity from slavery to those men and women from the Northern Wild Lands to whom I have extended my protection are also honoured in the same parts of the Theocracy. Furthermore, among my employees I insist on equality of treatment between men and women and assign responsibilities entirely on merit."

Cray shook her head. "I'm sure you know your own business but I find it hard to comprehend this notion of equality. I suppose I'm just set in my ways and too old to change. I've not heard of any such movement in the South of the Theocracy and can't imagine how normal society could flourish in such conditions. I'm not particularly religious but surely the temples don't allow you to get away with such heretical practices."

"Well, of course there is a lot of resistance here too but the temples are less powerful than in the South. Furthermore, Wilda is entirely on side and Oakbridge wields a lot of influence throughout the North, and Fenwold is loyal to me as lady of the Barton manor and the major benefactor of the temple. Not that I've had it all my own way. As you know Isla-of-the-Knotted-Bends College made a considerable fuss in the Arch Convocation and I had a lot of trouble getting the Knot-on-Lesser council to fall in line. It took some rather unscrupulous economic pressure before they caved in."

All this gave Cray much to think about and some concern, but at least, she thought, there is the silver lining that Shay was likely to be sympathetic to her goal of reducing the power of the temples in general, and in particular of diminishing the power of the Arch Convocation within the Council of the Theocracy. Anyway, she told herself, this is all secondary to her aim of rebuilding her family relationship with Shay and getting to know her great-niece.

She found Shar to be a delightful child, very intelligent and more mature and independent for her years than her sister-cousin. When she happened to mention this she learnt that Shar was ignorant of the existence of Thar and knew very little about her Aunt Thay. After some diffidence on Shar's part, she became quite inquisitive about her unknown family and pressed Cray for as much information as she was prepared to impart. Cray was extremely diplomatic but Shar indicated that she was well aware of the need for discretion on such matters in front of her mother and that she could and would keep her own counsels where both Thay and Thar were concerned. Thus Shar learned something of her mother's feud with Thay and how between them they had caused her father to be drowned when each of them had decided to honour their own mother's desire for a granddaughter fathered by Arthay.

In her turn Cray was astonished to learn that Arthay was known to Shar by his birth-name, Arval, and that she was in regular contact with her paternal grandmother, Valray. Furthermore Wilda was not only Abbess of Oakbridge and Shay's friend and ally but also Shar's Goddess and Arval's half-sister through a shared father. The fact that such paternal relationships were recalled and celebrated was quite extraordinary and, to Cray at least, somewhat disturbing.

12
Phalanx-Ball

Cray was enjoying a pleasant walk with Shar when their peace was shattered by a raucous noise coming from just over a low rise ahead of them. It sounded to Cray like a minor battle in progress, or possibly a football game. "What in the world is that racket?" She exclaimed.

"Oh I expect it's just a game of phalanx-ball. I think the work force are due for some recreation time. There's a tug-of-war competition being planned but I think the phalanx-ball is due first, or maybe the other way round. I'm not really sure. But either way it'll be exciting. Shall we go and watch?" was Shar's reply.

"I've no idea what you're talking about, I know about tug-of-war but what is phalanx-ball? I've never heard of it."

Shar paused before answering. It suddenly occurred to her that her mother would not want Cray to know about the military purpose behind the game. She had already been warned about not mentioning pikes and had been disappointed that a planned tournament of the very bloodthirsty Pike-Push had been postponed. She liked violent sports! "Oh, its a sort of football but much more disciplined. There's a properly marked out playing field and the two teams start in the middle and push against each other each with the aim of pushing the opposing team back to the end of the field. They have a ball placed between them by a Lieutenant and the aim is to keep possession of the ball within their own phalanx and then fall upon it when they get over the goal line. It's quite violent and exciting to watch. There are other complications but the push is the main thing and I can explain most of the rest to you as we watch."

"Sounds appalling, but healthy young women need to let off steam and these games do provide a relatively safe outlet for them. Show me the way and I'll come and see for myself."

Shar looked worried. "Er you should know that its not just women, men join in too, although the higher officers are usually women. Things can hot up a bit and sometimes a woman has been know to deliberately pull a man's pants down, sort of accidentally on purpose. That always makes me laugh."

"You shock me. And your mother encourages you to enjoy such a spectacle?" Cray looked as shocked as she was.

"Oh Auntie Cray, don't mind me, I'm not all that bad really. Mummy doesn't so much encourage me as just being unaware of what I get up to. I'm on my own quite a lot, what with everyone being so busy, and I'm used to being left to my own devices. That's why Auntie Wilda persuaded Mummy to send me to school at Oakbridge so early."

"I was wondering about that. Surely you're too young to board and it's quite a long way to Oakbridge from here."

"Well, I don't board in the regular way, but stay in Auntie Wilda's apartment with her. I then come home each period for the rest phase. Sometimes Auntie Wilda brings me, and sometimes they send a carriage to collect me. I like school. The work is a bit boring, but I like to play with the other girls. Look over there!" she pointed ahead of them. "You can see them playing. The red shirts have pushed the whites right back to their sixty-four. And they're playing with big phalanxes, I think there are seven in the front row. That means sixteen plus six in the central phalanx and I think there are six corporals on each side as well as the three officers, making one less than thirty-two on each side. And the white lieutenant is a man. Hurry up we could be about to see a score." Shar pulled on Cray's arm in an attempt to speed up their progress.

Just then the white phalanx collapsed in a heap with the reds falling on top of them. A woman in a blue shirt blew a shrill whistle, raised one hand in the air and, with the other, pointed towards the white end. The players picked themselves up and trudged towards the white line while the red lieutenant grabbed the ball and followed them. The phalanxes locked together again and the blue-shirted women said something to them after which they got back to pushing against each other while the red lieutenant put the ball back into the middle of the competing phalanxes.

Cray asked Shar to explain what was going on. "And who is the woman with the whistle and the other two also in blue who seem to hanging about doing nothing?"

Shar explained. "The one with the whistle is the General. She's in charge of both teams and they have to do what she tells them. She makes sure that they keep to the rules. The other two are the Colonels, and they assist the General. You're not supposed to let the phalanx collapse and in this case the General must have decided that the white shirts were at fault and she ordered a red restart thirty-two feet closer to the white line, but still directly ahead of where they were before. See the two posts sticking up towards the centre of the line. If the reds ground the ball between those posts they get two points, whereas if they ground it on either side of the posts they get just one point."

The pair continued to watch the game. After about half an ihor[9] there was a break, following which the teams swapped ends and the game restarted from the middle. After about a further half ihor or so with the score at 4-0 to the red shirts an incident occurred of the sort that Shar had presaged. The white shirts had let the ball out of the back of the phalanx and their Lieutenant was a bit slow and fumbling as he tried to pick it up. Two of the Red Corporals jumped on him. One made a grab for the ball while the other went for his shorts, ripping them off. She then ran off round the field waving her trophy while the lieutenant chased after her. Shar pointed and giggled, look at his bits wobbling as he runs she exclaimed. Meanwhile the teams broke up and started to push each other around. The General blew her whistle several times, while the Colonels ran in to help her restore order.

Eventually things calmed down, the General took the two Majors aside for a good talking-to, the white Lieutenant had his shorts restored and the offending red Corporal was sent off the field for the duration of the game, leaving her team one short. The ball was then handed to the white Captain who kicked it far down the field where it bounced over the side boundary quite close to the red goal line.

The phalanx was then reset thirty-two feet in from the side line and sixteen feet short of the goal line. The white Lieutenant then had the job of feeding it into the middle of the phalanx.

After remembering to reprimand Shar for her unladylike behaviour, Cray asked for an explanation of what was going on.

Shar grinned. "Well it was funny. Debagging the Lieutenant is against the rules so the General penalised the red team. The

---

9 An ihor equates to 1.125 hours. There are 64 imins in an ihor.

Corporal has been sent off and will probably also get fined. The white team was awarded a penalty kick, which enabled them to get lots of extra territory. If the ball had gone over the goal line the reset would have been on the sixty-four feet line. If it had stayed within the field of play the reds could have tried to regain territory by kicking it back or running with it. This could go on as a sort of ping-pong until someone gets sacked while holding the ball. By sending the ball out of play the phalanx gets reset level with where it goes out, but at least sixteen feet from the goal line."

"I think I see", said Cray. "This makes it much easier for the whites to push the phalanx over the line.

"That's right, and see, it's worked." The General had again blown her whistle as the white shirts pushed the reds over the line to score a point. The phalanx was then reset in the centre of the field with the red Lieutenant having the put in. After several more imins the General blew her whistle three times in succession and the game was declared over. There having been no more scores, the red shirts had won by 4 points to 1.

"That's the end of the game. They play for thirty-two plus eight imins for each half. There'll now be a break of about twenty imins before the tug-of-war competition begins. We could stay and watch that. It will be exciting."

Cray shook her head. "You've had quite enough excitement for one phase, young lady. It's time I took you home for your tea and bed-time."

Shar pouted and looked glum for a few isecs but then perked up and bounced happily along beside Cray as they made their way back. "I've had a lovely time with you, Auntie Cray, Mummy and Daubey are always too busy to take me to watch sports and it's only when Grandma Valray is here or sometimes when Auntie Brinda wants to watch that I get a chance to see any of the games. It's Auntie Brinda who knows all the rules and teaches me. She and Mummy invented Phalanx-ball and some of the other games they play, but Mummy isn't very good at explaining things to me. She just says that the workers need to exercise and let off steam and she prefers they do so in a disciplined way that encourages team work. She won't let them play football."

"Well, I can understand that, at least. Football is totally without discipline and can get very rough with fights breaking out and very often some people getting killed. If what we have just witnessed had been in Football the Lieutenant wouldn't have stood a chance. Several of the women would have forced themselves on to him including some from his own side and he would very likely have bled to death. Of course if it had been Football, men wouldn't be playing, and every sensible woman would have kept their men well away from the event."

Shar decided it was her turn to issue a reprimand. "We don't allow women to own men here. It's a disgusting practice, and men are entitled to go about their lives unmolested. There was one man who Auntie Brinda had promoted to lead the team building a lock further up the river. He was murdered by a woman who thought she should have been given the job. Mummy was furious and discovered the guilty woman and had her publicly executed. It caused quite a stir but since then there has been only a little trouble from women thinking they are automatically superior. I wish my Mummy was less busy all the time, but I'm proud that she does so much to make things fairer."

Twin Worlds III

All this gave Cray much cause for thought. She recalled that she had never been that keen on football. Both she and Chay had observed this form of inter-village warfare from the sidelines during their youth, but neither had really taken part. Chay had said that it was a pastime for the lower orders and not at all proper for women of their class. And where Chay led, Cray invariably followed. More recently she had come to hate it. She recalled that it was football that had triggered the events leading to her loss of her darling Crayza.

At the time, Chay had exiled Shay to Barton, and Crayza missed her cousin and started to go off the rails. Now she thought about it, Cray realised that Shay's own excesses had always been carefully calculated; indeed, disciplined was a good term for her. Shay had been a good mentor to Crayza, and until her exile, had exerted a positive influence on her young cousin. Anyway, Crayza, aged seventeen, had slipped out to partake in a particularly rowdy football event in an unsavoury part of Rivermouth. She got extremely drunk and indulged in various acts of wanton violence and vandalism before being arrested by the watch. Cray had had to go to bail her out. She then gated her for a couple of periods, and put in place various other restrictions on her activities. Crayza's inevitable rebellion was to seduce her sister's man Orcray, which in the end led to her taking a boat out to sea and eventual destruction. Cray had never forgiven herself. If only she had gone to Chay and begged her to let Crayza join Shay in Barton. Crayza would still have seen that as a punishment, but one she could accept, and now would still be with us — probably working alongside Shay, she mused.

13
Consolidation

Cray's visit has given me much to think about. She has always been good to me and I do appreciate her efforts even though I cannot see any real prospect for conciliation with my sister. Reconciliation is not the appropriate word since we have been at odds ever since early childhood. There is no 're' about it. Many threads have come together and it is time for me to get a stronger grip on things.

The first phase of my navigation is complete and my monopoly on traffic along both the Lesser and Second rivers is proving extremely profitable and has bound most of the northern and western regional councils to me. Of the northern border constituencies only Borders remains outside my political control, and even there I have a considerable following. As a result the slave trade has been eliminated in the East, and although there are theoretical trading routes through Borders or The Isla Marches, the opposition to the trade in Oakbridge and Upper Street means that only a small trickle makes it as far as the slave markets in Midborough and Cattlebridge. It's true that I have been unable to persuade the West Bank Wapentake to co-operate but they are most concerned with the trade from the Western Wild Lands which I have not been able to influence. This was always a much lower volume trade than from the north and even here I have denied the use of transport on the Second river, thereby forcing the use of overland routes through Upper Great River or Second Estuary.

Of course this success has come at some cost. The Southern Hundreds are experiencing a considerable economic downturn and it is highly likely that this will lead to conflict. Closer to home, Midborough has become the centre of opposition to my policies and work on my new canal going South from Knot has been halted at the border between the Midborough Hundred and Midborough Rural Wapentake, with the Hundred council refusing permission for the canal to enter their territory. As I'm not ready to take them on just yet, I have told Brinda to cease operations there, but meanwhile to start on the stretch to the south pressing on towards Cattlebridge. The Central Wapentake has taken note of the prosperity being enjoyed in Upper Street following the opening of the Lesser-Second link and is keen to facilitate my plan to link to the Great River, if necessary by bypassing the territories of Midborough and Cattlebridge Hundreds.

As Brinda keeps reminding me there are substantial challenges to be overcome in any such routes, but I'm keeping the options open, at least in political discussions. In reality the commercial and technical advantages of linking through both the towns of Midborough and Catllebridge are such that I'm sure that is what we will do, but I suspect we might have to win some real military battles first.

That's where my other activities play their part. The industrial work in Lesser Coast centred on the village of Steele is coming on apace. Raw materials have been arriving steadily from the North-East and the steel production has reached quite unimaginable proportions. From the new steels we have large scale production of munitions: swords, shields, steel-tipped pikes, and Brinda's new development of a crossbow. This is quite a fierce-some weapon that can fire steel-tipped bolts with considerable force over a long distance, rendering it particularly effective against charioteers and heavy horses. The downside being, it is unwieldy, requiring two operators and having a low firing rate. Furthermore we have devised protective armour for both soldiers and horses, the latter because I am considering the potential of fighting from horseback.

Then there is the military training. Phalanx-ball is not just a sport. Brinda and I have conceived it as part of our training programme to prepare completely new military tactics. For a long time the military strength enjoyed by the Theocracy has been the effectiveness of fighting in phalanx against the undisciplined rabble that is the main feature of the forces put together by the various tribes in the wild lands. This is all well and good, but will not answer against forces equipped like ourselves. We have come up with the pike, a long pole, with a deadly tip as the weapon of choice against the traditional phalanx of women armed with swords and shields. My game of Pike-Push is even more directly aimed at military training. The lethal pike-heads are replaced by cushioned ends — I don't want to kill off my work force — but otherwise the exercises are a close simulation of actual battle.

As I've just said, I'm also considering the potential for greater use of horses in battle. Maybe we can develop a few elite solders to fight from horseback as a more versatile force against both infantry and charioteers. Beyond that, Brinda is looking at what might be done to reduce the defensive strengths of town walls and fortified buildings, and thereby avoid the difficulties of a protracted siege of such strongholds. I fully anticipate that in another year or two I'll be able to field an army capable of defeating any opposing force within the Theocracy.

This is all so well and good, but my grip on regional politics has stalled. The couple of meetings I have chaired of my Council of the North have not resulted in any real progress. It's true that on the back of the prosperity I have brought I have managed to get several of the northern wapentakes to back my anti-slavery agenda, at least in name, but I haven't yet persuaded them to come together as a more united political unit, or to embrace the closer inclusion of the Isla Marches, let alone some of the communities in the wild lands. We shall see what the forthcoming meeting planned for next period brings.

To which end, I'm expecting Wilda to arrive any moment now to discuss the issues and help prepare. Actually, I think I can hear Daubey letting her in right now, so time for me to stop my musing and get down to real business, once we've got over the pleasantries, settled down with drinks and biscuits and so on.

"OK, Wilda, as I see it the background to next period's Council is more hopeful than previously. Remarkably, this hasn't come about through my pushing, but the meeting has been set up in a bit of a hurry as an urgent request from Borders and Lesser. Furthermore, Borders actually want the attendance of representatives from the Marches. Even more remarkably, the only opposition has come from Midborough, although they will attend, if only to try to prevent us achieving anything."

"I hadn't known that", responded Wilda, I had just assumed it was you in a rush as usual. But I have heard rumours of unrest along the borders and even some refugees from the Marches seeking shelter from troubles there. In fact I've even heard of people crossing into Borders and Lesser from the Northlands, encouraged, I guess, by our slavery ban."

"That's interesting, the two Wapentakes were rather vague about their motivation. I expect they are really concerned about the economic impact of immigration from the north and want to re-impose slavery or something like that. Indeed Borders hasn't actually adopted the ban either on slavery itself or on the trade, but merely operates a half-hearted moratorium, intended to keep me off their backs."

"Maybe, but from what I've heard there's more to it than economic fears or even the usual xenophobic stuff. There are indications that people are genuinely fearful. In fact now I come to consider it, I've noticed more movement into Oakbridge than usual." Wilda frowned as she said this, suddenly struck by the way her thoughts were running.

"Well, no doubt, we'll hear all the details in due course. Brinda's crews have lots of northern people. I must ask her to dig about a bit. I'm sure she'll come up with something to help us manage the situation. In the meantime what I wanted us to do tophase was to compare notes on the current political position, who we can rely on, who are opposed and what we need to achieve. You know, the usual baggage.

As I see it we have the complete support of Oakbridge, Upper Street, and Lesser Coast, our heartlands. Lesser is more-or-less onside but there remain factions there that are still sore about the closure of the Knot slave market, as well as being resentful of the wealth I have gained from the river trade. Other allies are Central and Midborough Rural. The latter is largely because of their animosity to Midborough, while the support of Central has been a surprise to me. That gives us at worst a six-five majority."

"It's not that bad", interjected Wilda, "Neither North Cape, nor Upper Great River are actually opposed to you. They may need convincing over some of our agenda. After all, they both border the Southern Hundreds and have some concerns about the potential for a North-South rift, but they have been reasonable. After all, they didn't have to accept your invitation to join the council. Of the others, Midborough is implacably opposed to you, largely because they think they should be the leading centre here, as well as their strong lobby in favour of the female ownership of males, for which they do have some legitimate arguments. Similarly, West Bank's real problem is with their border with the Western Wild lands. Cattle raiding is still very much a problem for them and it is unsurprising that they are opposed to abolition, or that they have any real interest in your northern policy. That leaves Borders, who are very much split. Think about it from their point of view. They have a long border with the north which is difficult to police without the benefit of the barrier formed by the Lesser. While less important than for Lesser, slave raiding and trading formed an important niche in their economy and they haven't benefited much from your river trade. On the other hand they do welcome your initiative for closer co-operation between the Northern Wapentakes, and hence for the council."

In the end we concluded that the forthcoming Council provided us with a good opportunity to make progress on our wider agenda. Although it turned out that we would be blind-sided by the enormity of the crisis; it also served our long-term ends, notwithstanding that all of us would have preferred a less drastic scenario.

Wilda and I agreed on three major objectives, and planned to use our response to whatever was behind the Borders and Lesser Wapentakes' concerns to shape the outcomes our way.

1. To consolidate the role of the Council of the North as the strategic voice of the Northern Wapentakes, and the primary forum to oversee formal relations with the Northland communities.

2. To obtain the formal adoption of the slave trade ban across the whole northern border (i.e. to get Borders to formally adopt the policy and to enforce it actively). This would leave the only remaining route for such trade into the southern part of the Theocracy to be the economically unviable and problematic one via Isla Marches, West Bank and Second Estuary.

3. The full inclusion of representatives of the Isla Marches in the Council and the invitation to representatives of some Northland communities to join as observers.

We did debate whether we might go further with the general recognition of free (i.e. un-owned) men throughout the North with some associated male rights but we decided that was unrealistic at this juncture.

I also undertook to get a brief from Brinda and our various contacts in or from the Northlands to discover more about the situation that was causing the refugee crisis. (I am now using 'Northlands' rather than 'Northern Wild Lands' because in my view the latter term is insulting and gives a false idea of the communities living there).

Part 2: War

14
Council of the North

I banged my gavel on the table to call the meeting to order.

"Welcome to you all to this meeting of the Council of the North. The reason we are all here tophase is at the instigation of the Wapentakes of Borders and Lesser. But before I invite the Borders' leader to address us I would like us to approve..."

I got no further, being rudely interrupted.

"I must protest. Who appointed you as President of this Council? Midborough is the largest and most important town in the Theocracy outside the capital. As the Mayor of Midborough and lay representative of the Midborough Hundred, I demand priority and that you stand down as a usurper of authority."

The meeting around us broke into general chaos, while Wilda, sitting on my right, whispered in my ear. I banged the gavel again, several times.

"Order please, ladies. The representative from Midborough does have a point, although I would reject any notion that the nature of her office bestows any right of preference among us. Are we not all the undisputed leaders of our independent Wapentakes, Hundreds or Temples? However, I will stand down for the time being and pass the gavel to The Abbess of Oakbridge, as the senior cleric here present and thus outside the direct politics of our lay authorities. Wilda, over to you."

Wilda then addressed the meeting. "Do sit down Lady Mayor, you're making the place look untidy. I assure you my tenancy of this role will be brief." The Mayor of Midborough sat down still grumbling. Wilda continued. "The business of this council is primarily secular in nature. Thus it is appropriate that it should be led by one of you lay leaders. The lay representative for Midborough Hundred has just nominated herself for the position. I would also nominate the lay representative for Oakbridge and District Wapentake. Do any of you lay representatives wish to nominate yourselves, or indeed any other of your colleagues."

There was no response other than some murmuring, as several representatives shook their heads.

"Right, I'll take that as a no then. I propose we settle the matter by a show of hands from the eleven lay representatives here. The Mayor of Midborough has stated her claim on the grounds of the importance of her town. I would remind you that the Oakbridge claim is based on her personal vision for the northern half of the Theocracy and consequent foundation of this Council. As we all know both ladies and their qualities, I propose we waste no time on debate and proceed directly to a vote. Please show hands in support of the Midborough candidate."

Two hands were raised, Midborough herself and West Bank. "And for Oakbridge". All the remaining nine voted for Shay.

"I declare the lay representative for Oakbridge and District, Shay, is the preferred President of the Council, by nine votes to two with no abstentions. I shall now return the gavel to her and without more ado let's get on with the business at hand, which I am led to believe is urgent."

Twin Worlds III

I took back the gavel, and stood up. "Thank-you Abbess, and thank you too, all of you, for your vote of confidence. I will do my best not to let you down. As I was saying before this important interruption, before inviting Borders to speak, and since I understand the nature of the crisis concerns our northern neighbours I propose that we ask representatives of the Isla Marches to join the meeting and also for a representative of one of the Northland communities to come in as an observer. I invite both lay and temple representatives to vote on this."

The vote was carried with all but the Midborough lay and temple representatives in favour. Wilda went to the door and ushered in three women who had been waiting in an anteroom.

"At least they're all female", muttered the Mayor of Midborough. "I wouldn't have put it past Shay to bring in a man."

"Right, thank-you all. May I introduce the Earl of the Isla Marches who incidentally is also Mayor of Fort, and the Chief Priestess of the Temple of Isla in Marsh, who are respectively the secular and spiritual leaders in the Marches. And Audreeda who is from a community on the north bank of the Lesser estuary."

The visitors sat down, amid various murmurs of greeting from the assembled company.

"Now that we are all assembled, let us please hear from the lay representative from Borders."

A middle-aged lady stood up. She was probably about fifty years old but looked older. A veteran of many cross-border raids and skirmishes, she sported a number of visible scars including a long one down the right hand side of her face topped by a black eye patch covering battle wounds from the same blow that had scarred her face. She addressed her peers in a low, sombre voice.

"I've never known it so bad. There's always been a certain amount of unrest over the border as outsiders migrate from further north, putting pressure on the communities already in occupation. However it has been rare for anyone to actually seek refuge among us as they have a general distrust of the Theocracy and also fear that they might be enslaved. The spill-over into our territory has generally been in terms of raids on our cattle and occasional attempts to annex some of of our farms along the border. Usually we beat them back, take a few prisoners for slaves and make it clear that their anarchic behaviour will not be tolerated. Then, after a bit, things settle down and we rub along more-or-less contentedly with a small amount of cross-border trade and mutual tolerance.

However in recent periods it has been very different. There has been considerably more upheaval north of the border, but rather than this spilling over as encroachment on our farms, we have experienced a number of people, both men and women, crossing the border and actually asking for refuge and the opportunity to resettle within the Theocracy. While some of this may have been influenced by the changes brought about by Shay's policies on slavery and the greater tolerance of religious plurality within our northern temples, as led by Oakbridge, this only explains the greater trust on the part of the refugees. The major issue is that so many northern people feel the need to escape the turmoil they are experiencing from the force of numbers fleeing southwards. We only hear garbled rumours about the pressures driving them, but it appears that a new regime has emerged in the far north-west that seeks to impose itself on the surrounding areas in an extremely violent way. We don't really understand what's going on because we hear so many contradictory tales, but it is clear that whatever is the truth behind it all, the situation is out of control and we are bearing the brunt of the fall-out. We have sought assistance from our allies in the Marches but they have reported a similar situation with many refugees entering their lands bearing tales of north-western expansion and imposition of a harsh and intolerant regime."

"Worrying indeed," I opined. "But what do you want us to do as a council? I'm sure there will be a lot of sympathy for your plight, but I am not clear as to what practical measures we might be able to take to help you."

"That's a major part of the problem. I don't have any useful proposals to make. Perhaps some sort of commitment to accept some of the refugees, giving them guarantees of fair treatment on a par with our own citizens would help relieve some of the immediate pressures on our local economy. Another option might be some kind of punitive raid into the far North. But any such adventure would have to involve a pretty large and well-disciplined force, as well as operating with the approval of the wild communities close to our borders. We would need to go to the root of the trouble, which I believe is somewhere in the far North-West of the wild lands, and even then I'm not sure how far we should go."

I responded. "We will have to debate this more fully. As to the first suggestion I am sure that many of us will be able to help a bit. Certainly, I will commit both Oakbridge and Lesser Coast to take some refugees, but our own social and economic constraints will limit what we, and indeed any other of our Northern regions, might do. Consequently, I suspect we will at best provide some temporary relief and not actually solve the problem. We do have to face up to the issue at source, whether by military or diplomatic means. I believe we can assemble an appropriate force but I do not think a traditional 'raiding party' will answer, irrespective of the size of force. As a very minimum we must learn more about the nature of the threat and then plan any military response with great care — I recognise the representative from Midborough, I see you are eager to say something."

"I most certainly am. This is a load of tosh. We all know how to deal with such emergencies, and the only reason we are in this situation is Shay's namby-pamby views on slavery and her encouragement of peaceful dealings with the wild tribes as if they were our equals instead of the blasphemous illiterate savages that they are. You should show the strength and courage of your ancestresses. All incursions should be met with force. The savages should be driven back, or killed or taken into servitude. Reopen your slave markets and fill them with these so called refugees if you don't have the stomach to send them home. Two strides of ground for a grave is all the territory they should be given."

Most of the chamber fell silent, with just a hear-hear from the High Priestess of the Midborough Temple and some mumbled assent from the West Bank representative. Wilda then got to her feet.

"Well I for one am glad that we have risen above such barbarity. And you call the Northerners 'savages'. Are they not women and sisters, are their men not also people? Do they not bleed when cut, or feel when hurt, do the men not give pleasure and children? I am ashamed for the Mayor of Midborough and wonder at the callousness of the High Priestess. Your so-called savages are also beloved children of the Goddess. For those of us in service to Isla through the Abbeys and Temples, it is our bounden duty to succour any of her children who come to us in need. We must give whatever aid we can to the refugees and to the Borders Wapentake. However, I also agree with Shay that this will not be sufficient. While I sincerely hope and pray for a peaceful resolution through dialogue with the North-Western oppressors, I fear that some violent action will prove necessary in what will most certainly be a just cause."

The Abbess of Fenwold rose to her feet. "In other words, your reverence, you are saying that any military expedition will be engaged in a just war in accordance with the Goddess's ordinance. I also agree with you. But to comply with the strict conditions of such an enterprise we must be sure that we target the true cause and, even then, exhaust all possibilities for peaceful coexistence."

The Earl of the Isla Marches was signalling to me. I called the meeting to order and invited her to speak.

"Lady Shay, and distinguished lay and spiritual leaders of the Theocracy, thank-you for allowing me this opportunity to address you. I hear what you all say with great interest but with some trepidation. I am able to add to the information vouchsafed by the honourable lay representative for Borders. The source of the trouble lies directly to the North of our borders. Until recent years the communities in the North-West were small, disorganised and relatively peaceful. They squabbled among themselves from time to time but none was ever sufficiently large or powerful to give us any trouble. Occasionally a refugee from one of their squabbles would seek shelter in the Marches but even that was rare. East of the mountain ridge, Edgar's people maintain a loose hegemony over the North-central communities and resist any Eastward incursions. But, while maintaining control over their borders, they have shown no inclination to cross into the remote regions of the North-West.

This peaceful situation changed in recent years. There is a fairly large inhabited island off the west coast, which its inhabitants call Prush, about the seventh double of imiles north of our northern border[10]. This island is about four more than the fifth double imiles long and twenty-three imiles wide and supports quite a large population by wild land standards. It can be reached from the mainland at low tide. Some fifty years ago (fifth plus fourth double or so) a populist by the name of Hilta deposed and murdered the ruling princess. She then crossed to the mainland and forced the community there to cede territory to allow her to relieve population pressure on Prush by colonisation.

Once her colony was established she sought ever more expansion together with the extermination of the original mainland inhabitants. She called it cleansing the land. Her thuggish soldiers under the command of her sister, Stala, would round up everyone they could catch and herd them into small crowded camps from where they were taken every phase to work from sunrise to sunset with the bare minimum of food. Anyone too weak to work would be killed on the spot and buried in a mass grave outside the camp. After about five years of this the remaining neighbouring communities put aside their differences to fight the invader. Indeed a few of our own people from the Marches joined the war. Victory took a further five years. Hilta was caught and executed and the Prush territory on the mainland was cut back to just a small foothold extending just eight imiles

10 That is 128 imiles or about 100 miles/160 km. The island dimensions translate as 28 x 18 miles or 45 x 29 km.

(6.25 miles, 10 km) inland from the coast opposite the Prush low-tide beach (sixteen imiles long). After this, most of the allied communities went back to their previous mode of existence. The one exception was to the East of the mountain ridge. Edgar's predecessor, Churchee had played a central role in the allied victory and she returned to lead a small number of communities in a federation retaining a strong commitment to mutual defence. Edgar himself had served with distinction during the war and as you are aware eventually came to lead and expand his communities despite the obvious disadvantage of being male.

Going back to the aftermath of the war. Unknown to the victors at the time, a year or two before the war ended, Hilta had given birth to a daughter who was smuggled back to Prush. She was raised by some of Hilta's acolytes who escaped the attention of the victorious parties. When she reached her fifth double Hilta's daughter, Pootini, emerged from the shadows and soon rose to power on the island.

In her speeches Pootini repudiated her mother's actions and at first appeared to be a moderate, if somewhat autocratic ruler. However, as her grip on power tightened her mask began to slip and after five years in power she was proclaimed leader for life, while her henchwomen gradually started to undermine the neighbouring communities, murdering her opponents — at first anonymously, but most recently openly. Then two years ago Pootini issued a decree claiming hegemony over all the former territories ruled by her mother and aunt. By this time she had built a formidable army which she sent to invade her neighbours and force them into her empire. Edgar is now too old to fight but his son Edwin has built quite a reputation and his people alone have resisted Pootini's expansion. Elsewhere, armed resistance has been futile and people have fled in great numbers. Hence the refugee crisis in Borders and also in the Marches.

In the past few periods the crisis for us has deepened. The flow of refuges across our northern border slowed and has now halted. Units of Pootini's army have been observed just a few imiles from our borders and look to be preparing for an invasion. We have sent envoys to treat with her and have been assured that the army is merely on exercise and that their only activity is to protect us by preventing the exodus of refugees. Finally, and without appearing to see the irony, Pootini claims that her actions have been necessary to forestall the rise of Hilta's politics within the communities she has now over-run.

Needless to say we are very concerned and fearful for our future. Shay, I am here not only to support Borders but also to beg your assistance in the face of Pootini's threats."

Wow, that does appear to change things. I'm going to have to do some quick thinking here. "Er, our thanks to the Earl for this full historical account which gives us a great deal to think about and reinforces our need for decisive action. I, for one, was not aware of the extent of the war against Hilta. It is no more than a minor footnote in the history that I was taught at school. I recall learning that one of the main drivers for the treaty of alliance with the Isla Marches was the outbreak of unrest between some of the wild tribes leading to worries that they might threaten to invade the Marches and then our own lands. All we learnt of the war was that with some intervention from the Marches the tribes settled their differences and returned to the status quo ante. It seems it was much more serious, but that luckily for the Theocracy, we were not dragged into the war. This time it looks that, at least here in the north, we will not be so lucky."

Twin Worlds III

The ensuing debate was somewhat rambling and didn't add much light to the situation, but did mean that most of the Wapentake leaders had their say and were able to feel included. There was general support for Borders and the Marches. Only Midborough remained opposed to offering any help. The West Bank leader, while remaining resolutely opposed to any concessions over slavery, was visibly shocked by the threat to the Marches and pledged her willingness to support them in the event of invasion.

I was also successful in persuading Borders to join in the ban on slave raiding, close their remaining slave market and legalise the existence of free men. Further qualified support for this agenda was also given by North Cape. Central and Midborough Rural were already on side which only left Midborough and West Bank implacably opposed with Upper Great River ambivalent.

Then, just as we were about to break up the meeting, we heard a commotion outside the doors which then burst open to admit a breathless woman who rushed over to the Earl. After no more than about three imins the Earl banged her shoe on the table to quieten the hubbub and stood up.

"Lady Shay, I offer my profuse apologies for this unseemly interruption. Matters have become even more serious. This messenger has newly arrived from Fort bearing the most shocking news. Despite all previous assurances, Pootini's army has crossed our border and is marching through the land, destroying settlements as they go. We are attempting to organise a defensive line along the South bank of the March river which as you may know separates the small transmarch communities from the majority of our lands.

As you know we have a small population and according to our best estimate women of military age, excluding those who are pregnant or have a baby under one year, number about the ninth plus the eighth double. Of these, our active militia is just the eighth double in strength, and only about half of those are deployed to the northern border. We estimate that the invading force is at least the ninth double. Your assistance is now urgent."[11]

11 Populations on Isla are small, consequently so are armies. A force of 512 is extremely large by Isla standards. The number of women of military age in the Marches is around 800. Men only rarely have a fighting role.

15
Pootini

That certainly forced us into rapid action. I was able to supply the eighth double[12] in well trained troops from the army I was building, together with a company of sixteen charioteers. Of course my army is mixed gender which shocked some of the others, though not the Marches, which had rushed a defensive force of 128 men to defend the only bridge over the March river. These men were rein-forced by the retreating remains of the northern border force (70 women with 56 male supporters, the remaining 58 women and 20 or so men having been killed or captured by the invaders). These retreating forces were joined by such of the transmarchers as managed to escape - some 300 out of the estimated population of 512.

Some of the refugees were able to give us intelligence about the invading force and even of its goals. Apparently the initial stated goal for Pootini was to take the whole transmarch region[13] which she claims is historically part of territories taken into her mother's empire. Indeed this region had only been settled and then incorporated into the Marches some years previously (128 according to oral history). This land would be part of Pootini's territory of Rush. Beyond that she wanted to replace the 'illegal' ruling regime in Fort with a puppet regime of her own. She

12 Enough of this! Richard Arthur will edit numbers in most of what follows to make it easier for the reader from Earth.

13 Shown as TM in Map 3.

claimed that Isla Marches were massacring or enslaving the Western tribes and that she intended to liberate the whole of the Western Wild lands from exploitation by the evil regimes in the Marches and Theocracy.

Well that was more than enough to enrage the West Bank Hundred, which immediately doubled its contribution to the assisting force. Each of the constituencies in the council of the north, apart from Midborough, had agreed to send assistance. In the case of Borders, they would station almost their entire militia on the Border to deter Pootini from using their territory as a supply route but for obvious reasons would be unable to spare troops otherwise. Each of the remaining constituencies agreed to supply 64 fighting women with 32 male supporters, all to be placed under my command. Actually West Bank had insisted on a separate command but that suited me fine. The now 128 strong West Bank contingent (with the customary 64-strong male support team) were deployed to strengthen the defence of Fort, whereas my forces headed towards the front line.

I was too late. The estimated size of Pootini's army was grossly understated. Although they were poorly equipped compared to the Marches militia, having no metal for armour or weapons, and with the majority being ill-trained and, at best, reluctant soldiers; they were able to overwhelm the defenders by sheer weight of numbers together with a suicidal disregard for casualties. They also had one innovative weapon whose like had not been seen before, either in the Marches or the Theocracy. This weapon was a huge catapult with a strong wooden frame mounted on ski-like slides with an alternative wheeled option. Later at the battle for Fort I saw that they had five of these monstrosities. Their operation required a lot of personnel, and could fire no more that four times an ihor, but nevertheless they hurled massive rocks and boulders, destroying walls and buildings or causing major casualties when aimed at a phalanx of soldiers in the tight formations that are customary to defend against infantry or chariot attacks.

In consequence, by the time we got close to the River March we encountered refugees from the Marches militia and the few lucky transmarchers that had escaped the slaughter. From the small numbers we encountered I feared that some seven eighths or the population and militia had been massacred. Fortunately this was too pessimistic a view, as many had been able to cross the border into the Theocracy where they were assisted by the Borders' authorities. The invaders respected the border and didn't pursue the escapers. Clearly, they were not yet ready to take on the Theocracy.

I learnt that the bulk of the invading army, together with all their heavy weapons were marching south, headed for Fort and the border to the Western Wild Lands. They had left just a few troops to occupy the transmarch region, harass the few remaining locals and await further reinforcements from the north.

I decided to split my force. I took my own 256 strong phalanx together with sixteen chariots and the levees for Oakbridge and Upper Street to follow the enemy to Fort. This left the other levees with a total of 384 regular troops plus half that number of men in supporting roles and a few charioteers who had attached themselves to the levees. It is normal practise in the Theocracy militias for some wealthier citizens to append themselves to a fighting force, slightly independently from the main command. Such women supply their own war chariots, horses and equipment. Many of these women operate their chariot single-handed, while others bring a man to actually drive the chariot, leaving the woman freer to use her weapons. The usual disposition of a fighting force is for the majority to be part of a phalanx, a tight formation of 64, 128 or 256 women for a major battle. A phalanx generally fights in a wedge shape which is almost impenetrable by less co-ordinated infantry. Rapid re-formation into a square provides an effective defence against the more mobile attacks by enemy chariots. A few soldiers are generally deployed outside the phalanx as skirmishers to harass the enemy, and together with the charioteers, to drive them into direct confrontation with the phalanx(es). These forces are also very effective when mopping up a fleeing enemy.

It is unusual for a Theocracy army to meet a similarly organised enemy, as the wild tribes have not yet been observed using similarly disciplined formations. Indeed much of the innovative training that I have undertaken with my own force is to develop and practice strategies and tactics to be used when confronting a traditional Theocratic army, as I might expect in my anticipated struggle with Thay. Central to my plans is the use of pikes as designed by Brinda. However, I was not prepared to compromise my future war by unveiling this weapon prematurely and I had deliberately left the pikes behind when setting out on the current expedition. The members of the phalanx are armed with swords, daggers and spears, while wearing breastplates, arm and thigh guards and helmets. They carry long shields. The skirmishers are more lightly armoured, often just wearing a thick leather tunic and helmet for protection and carrying a smaller, lighter shield. They are also armed with sword and dagger and usually carry a few spears or javelins and a staff in a holdall on their back and sometimes have a small bow and quiverful of arrows.

Charioteers normally wear breastplates but otherwise are armed very much like the skirmishers. The wheels of most war chariots are festooned with knives and some have spear-like stakes protruding at various points to provide extra protection against close fighting. Many of the horses also carry some form of light armour. War chariots are generally drawn by just one or two parallel horses. The general and maybe some other senior officers usually ride on horseback.

As you will realise, with the above weaponry, almost all fighting is at close quarters. Until we saw them, the catapults used by Pootini were unknown to us, although Brinda is working on weaponry along similar lines. Some of our soldiers may carry a hand-held catapult capable of shooting a small stone or dart, but armour is an effective defence, so such weapons don't really feature much in war-fighting. And our bows are neither very powerful nor accurate. They are between two and three feet long and have only a short range. Among the other innovations Brinda has been pioneering is a crossbow which is much more powerful, firing a heavy bolt capable of piercing most armour and covering a much greater range. I have four of them with me — more are in production. Each requires two soldiers for efficient operation, but even so can only fire at a maximum rate of sixteen bolts per ihor. Bolts are also in short supply. I took these crossbows with their all-male crews on the march south to Fort.

Our part was a breeze, a walk in the park. By the time we caught up with them, Pootini's army was engaged in heavy fighting at the gates of Fort. Their catapults had destroyed many buildings and defence barricades in the north end of the town and the route was open to them to enter. The defenders were heavily outnumbered but fighting back resolutely, inflicting huge losses on the invaders. It appeared that Pootini herself was there 'encouraging' her soldiers. Her tactics were crude in the extreme with wave upon wave of soldiers, both men and women, hurling themselves into the defenders in an attempt to triumph through sheer weight of numbers. Any who tried to turn back were killed by their own comrades. I'd never seen anything like it.

As we approached, some of the enemy turned to wave at us, as if in welcome, before resuming their action against Fort. It became clear later that they had no intelligence as to who we were, but had thought us to be reinforcements that they were expecting.

I soon disabused them. I deployed my main force into two phalanxes, keeping my chariots to the rear with just a few skirmishers to prevent the enemy coming round our flanks to attack from behind. When the van of my army came within easy crossbow range, I ordered a salvo of bolts with which we took out the officer in apparent command of the catapults and three of the catapult operators. The bowmen then retreated into the centres of the phalanxes, which then moved in to attack.

The enemy rearguard panicked. Their soldiers ran about like headless chickens, yelling and screaming, while their officers were unable to gain any sort of control. It was a massacre. The troops assaulting the town turned to join the mêlée while the defenders, led by the West Bank contingent moved forward from the barricades to harry them further. In actuality, I think the enemy were responsible for more killing through sororicide as they turned on each other, whether in confusion or in an attempt to force the soldiers back into battle.

Twin Worlds III

The only organised resistance we encountered came from a group of thirty-two horsewomen who rode at one of our phalanxes in an attempt to scatter us. It didn't work. The Phalanx concerned happened to be commanded by my most innovative young officer and she quickly hit upon the defence of re-forming into a defensive square with a shield wall with swords thrust out at an angle of about 40 idegs[14]. The two crossbows that were at the Phalanx centre aimed at the leading horses while other soldiers also fired regular arrows into the oncoming charge. This tactic worked. The enemy lost about half its force, either horse or rider, and the remainder withdrew and fled. Three of these were intercepted by our charioteers but the rest got away and, I believe, eventually returned to their home territory. These included their commanding general, but among the dead was a very small, richly dressed woman, who was identified by some of the few survivors as Pootini herself.

This was great cause for celebration. The corpse was decapitated and the head set on a long spear to be carried with us in triumph.

As it turned out, our celebration was premature. Much later we discovered that Pootini employed a number of 'body doubles' to masquerade as her, as she herself would never venture into a risky situation. Our victim was just one of those doubles.

However, just after the battle of Fort we were in very high spirits. We had completely destroyed a much larger force, while our own casualties were negligible, and the Earl of the Isla Marches, as Mayor of Fort, and the townsfolk welcomed us with open arms as liberating heroines. A banquet was held in our honour, and many of the men in the town were made available to

14 56.25 degrees on Earth, (64 idegs = 1 rightangle)

my female solders. All in all, my whole army enjoyed a wild time. Indeed we were enjoined to stay longer to revel in the local hospitality.

However, I was keen both to maintain discipline and also to return to the fight. Even though I believed we had killed Pootini herself, I didn't want to leave her 'empire' intact. Relieving Fort was just the first stage. The security of the Theocracy depended on chasing all of the invaders out of the Isla Marches and then carrying the fight into the Northlands and right to the heart of Rush.

I explained all this to the Earl, who was very much in agreement. And, after a rest for a phase to enable my troops to sober up, we marched out back North.

I didn't want to be encumbered with the captured catapults on my march north, but also I didn't really want to leave them behind. I wanted to study their construction and capabilities as I had seen their efficacy against town defences. I negotiated with the Earl who was not in a good position to deny me. I agreed to leave the two damaged machines with her in Fort where she could have them repaired for her own arsenal. The other three she agreed to transport to the Second river for loading on to barges and onward transportation through my network to my workshops in Steele where my engineers could study and improve them.

Apart from the catapults, one other part of the enemy's tactics was new to me. In our armies the only actual military use of horses is with the war chariots, which don't really play a significant part in the main battle. As I think I mentioned in an earlier chapter, I have been contemplating the potential of mounted troops but as yet haven't developed the concept further. The idea of actually charging infantry while on horseback was new to me. Apart from the aforementioned chariots we use horses for transport, or occasionally for running messages on the battlefield. Despite the ease with which we dispatched their mounted force, I can see the value in such a capability and have decided to pursue my ideas further and introduce the concept into our own operations.

When my army arrived back in the transmarches, I found that the force I had left behind had completed their mopping-up task and were now awaiting me at the border with the Northlands. A few of the transmarchers had crossed the border surreptitiously to gather intelligence and had returned with valuable information. The true residents of the borderlands had been forced to succumb to Pootini's rule and were ready to welcome us as liberators. Further north, Pootini's grip was tighter, but even so, there were some who resisted, and the country was very much living under a military occupation.

I gave the order to cross the border and as we marched north we gathered new recruits from the liberated lands while Pootini's forces offered only scant resistance as they retreated.

One phase into our northwards march, Audreeda rode into our camp. She had been travelling through various Northland communities to exchange news on the developing crisis. To the Eastern communities, Pootini was a distant figure of little relevance, but in the central regions people were more concerned, while those villages closer to her activities were becoming alarmed at the growing incursions from the west; especially as most lacked the means to defend themselves against territorial expansion.

According to Audreeda, Edgar's domains were an exception. Over the years since the raid in which Valray had captured and then lost Edgar, a number of villages had banded together in a defensive alliance that had been successful in resisting further raids from the Theocracy and also in maintaining supremacy in local squabbles. Wilja's sister, Wena, and Edgar had been at the forefront of the evolution of this alliance and in recent years Edgar had been recognised as its military leader, although now at 65 years of age he had long retired from actual fighting.

When we camped for a rest-break, Brinda and I sat down privately with Audreeda to dine and hear her news. "I was a bit shocked to see how frail Edgar has become and fear he will not live much longer. Although he retains the title as war-leader, in practice the position has now been taken by Edwin, his son with Wena. Edwin was not present during my visit, so I didn't get to meet him. The lands considered within Edgar's defensive remit extend westwards into the foothills of a mountainous region that is virtually unpopulated. These mountains constitute a kind of buffer between Edgar and Pootini's empire. For the past year Edwin has been leading a guerrilla campaign aimed at discouraging further expansion by Pootini's forces. Wena didn't elaborate on how Edwin's tiny force was able to manage this, but nonetheless claimed that so far they had been successful. Pootini's troops are now reluctant to venture far into the mountains where many of their number have disappeared or met unexplained deaths, all from an unseen enemy."

Audreeda then opined that "without this action Pootini would have brought the mountain region into her empire and would probably have overwhelmed Edgar's villages, threatening the whole of the Northlands."

Our march north continued without major incident. At first we travelled through good farming country. Here the population is small and sparsely distributed. Much of the land is still wooded with relatively small farmsteads dotted about. Farming is mixed with crops and cattle pasture operated in a rotation system. There are only a few villages, and before Pootini's invasion the people lived peaceably and kept very much to themselves, bar a small amount of trading with their immediate eastern neighbours and across the border with the transmarch region of the Isla Marches.

Pootini's arrival was not welcome but the people had no means to resist. As a consequence we were welcomed. Doubly so, because of my insistence that our troops pay for whatever supplies we take from the local farms. Pootini's lot were resented for their arrogance and blatant theft of produce in the guise of 'taxation to pay for your defence'.

After about 64 imiles we reached a mountainous region (not the one mentioned by Audreeda). These mountains cover an area equivalent to a square of side 96 imiles (Brinda's calculation) just South of Pootini's stronghold. The north-westernmost tip of the mountains being about nine imiles from the southern edge of the low tide beach adjoining the island of Prush.

Crossing these mountains was slow going. It had been raining every phase and we had to be on the look-out for potential ambush. The region is virtually unpopulated. Such locals we encountered are semi-nomadic, shepherding flocks of fairly wild sheep and goats, and in the lower forested slopes, pigs.

I mention these because of an encounter with a friendly swineherd. I was introduced to a most delicious confection. She called it a Pork Pie. It was a recipe from her grandmother, batch-baked when in camp and then carried for easy-to-eat sustenance while following the foraging pigs through the forests. The pie filling is made from minced meat from the fattier or less easy cuts of meat like the head and belly, mixed with herbs, wild onion and garlic. Unusually, the pastry is made with hot (almost boiling) water and, after cooking, some jelly made from boiling pig's trotters is added. The pies are left to cool and eaten cold. I have have never tasted anything better in my whole life. I determined to teach Daubey how to make them when I return to Elmhouse. The whole Pootini campaign is worthwhile just for this discovery!

Fortunately we only had a couple of brushes with the enemy in the mountain passes. One was just a chance encounter with a small patrol that was soon vanquished. The other was a more serious ambush attempt which my scouts had managed to detect. As a result we were able to turn the tables on the would be ambush, which consisted of a battalion force of sixty-four foot soldiers hidden on either side of a narrow pass, reinforced by sixteen horsewomen, waiting round a corner ready to swoop on our anticipated retreat.

It was not to be. My troops were well-prepared and in the mêlée we killed over half of the infantry (36 of the 64) and took the rest prisoner. Most of the horsewomen got away, with us killing one and taking one prisoner after one of our crossbows shot her horse from under her. Our losses came to just four killed and three wounded. Of the twenty-nine prisoners, twenty were forced conscripts from the subject communities who were happy to swap sides and join my army. The remaining nine were placed under guard and made to undertake domestic tasks in support of our logistics.

Twin Worlds III

Thus it was with a strong force that I emerged from the mountains into Pootini's heartlands. From the captive officer who had commanded our would-be ambushers I learnt that the main enemy force was concentrating some thirty imiles to the North-East while Pootini herself remained in her fortress on Prush, which was heavily fortified and deemed impregnable. In this way I learned about Pootini's use of body-doubles. I was assured that I would encounter yet another with the main army.

"You see," said the officer "Our dear leader is basically a coward, afraid of the assassin lurking in the corner and trusting almost no-one. She refuses to leave the security of her stronghold and avoids taking risks with her person. Unusually, the double you killed was also female, making the deception hard to detect. In most cases she has had to employ castrated men in these roles, on account of her diminutive stature meaning that the pool of potential female doubles is very small."

"Really!" I riposted, "I'd heard rumour she was short — suffering from small woman syndrome — according to the scuttlebutt in the Marches, but I'd sort of dismissed that as mere propaganda."

"Oh no, it's true enough. I've not actually met her, but I gather she's actually under six foot four (thumbs)[15] and most definitely suffers from small woman syndrome. She exercises a lot and is very strong and muscular for her size. Here, I have a picture taken from an engraving, which is distributed to all senior officers and officials in the empire. I tell you it's a major challenge to find suitable candidates for body-doubles. They need to be under six foot five and capable of matching her fitness."

---

15 6'6", tall for an Earthman, unbelievably short for a Duplosian woman, who average 7'6".

"Interesting, very muscular, and I see she is bare-chested and has very small tits, but she looks to be of normal height, judging by the horse."

"The picture is meant to be deceptive, the horse is in fact also small. She refuses to be pictured alongside other people. All paintings of her depict her in the foreground and any others present are always shown at a distance in the background. She tries to leave the impression that she is a great war-leader when in fact she has never risked herself anywhere near a battlefield."

On hearing this, I felt nothing but contempt for this enemy. At least Thay is worthy of respect. Although we could serve as each other's perfect body doubles, neither of us would ever stoop to such a cowardly act as Pootini. How could such a person have ever risen to a position of leadership?

I decided to leave Pootini to skulk in her island rathole for the time being and devoted my attentions to her army here on the mainland.

After a phase rest to recuperate from the mountain-crossing we continued our advance, now to the north-east. We were in hostile territory but encountered no significant opposition and no more than sullen acceptance from the local population. However, even here I insisted on paying for whatever supplies we required (although I gave no choice and would not haggle — my price was my price. It was fair by normal peacetime values and purchase was compulsory). The populace knew this was better than they would normally expect and I heard no more than the odd grumble. Hell, a couple of years ago, if I'd been on an old-fashioned punitive raid, I'd have had whatever I wanted with no payment and taken the people back to the Theocracy in chains as slaves. I'm not saying that a few men didn't get raped, but however much I discouraged such behaviour (and I did); there's no getting away from that fact that soldiers get lusty and will satisfy those lusts. That's how it's always been and, I suspect, always will be.

The army that I was now deploying amounted to over 1024 fighting soldiers. Bigger than any force I had ever heard of in Isla's history. Yet my estimate of the opposition was that they were even more numerous. On the other hand my troops were well-armed and centred on a highly disciplined and trained core. We ought to triumph easily. I sent one of our nine captives to the opposing General with a demand for surrender.

The response was evil but clear. One of their catapults (they had four) fired a missile into our midst. On examination, the missile was the severed head of the messenger. I could scarcely believe such savagery. This was one of their own women, one who had remained loyal to Pootini and refused to desert into my army. How could anyone engage in such savagery?

I split my van into three phalanxes, 256 in the centre and 128 on each flank. Behind them rode 32 chariots and my own mounted headquarters. These were followed by a number of skirmishers and two further phalanxes in the rear.

For the first time, I learnt what damage a catapult can inflict on the tight formation of a phalanx. The enemy began her assault with a barrage from her catapults. Four massive boulders flew through the air, landing amongst our line of advance. Fortunately their aim was not very accurate, but even so the phalanx on the right flank received a direct hit on one side, killing several soldiers and causing a certain amount of panic in the others. It took a while to restore order but we did so in time to redeploy into a looser line for the next salvo some imins later. In all we suffered four salvo's (16 flying boulders) before our troops began to close with the enemy rendering further salvo's too dangerous for their own side.

The enemy sent several waves of poorly armed foot soldiers into our shield walls, and these poor saps perished in numbers, while failing to breach our lines. The enemy also sent horsewomen against us. Our defences held in the left and centre but the already depleted right phalanx was eventually breached by a massed attack from several horsewomen.

My soldiers fought bravely, but with their formation broken it looked like they would be easy pickings for the mounted enemy and the huge numbers of infantry that were now being sent in to the attack.

Suddenly, the air seemed to be filled with arrows. These missiles came from far to our right and smashed into our enemy with devastating effect on horse and rider, and then on the onrushing infantry. This gave us the opportunity to reform and reinforce, completely turning the tables. Shortly after that, our enemy's resolve broke, and in the ensuing rout we gained our victory, killing or capturing the entire opposing army.

Just who were our saviours? It became clear that they were much feared by the enemy. The captured General talked about the silent death that came to any of her patrols that ventured into the woods on the lower slopes of the hills on the Eastern flank of the battlefield. Surely the source was these same archers.

"The woods and mountains are deadly to us," she said. "Our soldiers just disappear. We sometimes come across the corpses but there are never survivors. Our enemy is never seen and we never find the weapons that kill us. Tophase is the first time they have appeared in open battle. The first time we have seen the arrows. Even tophase we have not seen the archers themselves. Do you not know your allies?"

I confessed we didn't, but kept my counsel as to my conclusions.

I discussed the matter with Brinda and Audreeda. Brinda had done some calculations based on our own experience with our ordinary bows and our more powerful crossbows. She reckoned that to gain the range and penetration that we observed, the arrows must have been propelled with a force similar to our crossbows, or perhaps a bit less would have been sufficient. Surely, she argued, they would have required a two person operation and, even with a generous estimate, at most be able to fire at a rate of 64 arrows per ihor. After all, our crossbows fired at a quarter that rate. Thus our observation would suggest something like something like 1024 archers involved, which is way more than the estimated strength of Edwin's force. I really had to learn more.

But in this I was frustrated. On the point of the surrender, an arrow had landed at my feet. There was a note attached. It was brief and to the point. "Tophase we are allies. But no-one from the Theocracy is welcome in our lands. One phase we will meet, I hope in friendship. But tophase is not that phase. Don't look for me. When the time comes, I will find you."

Well, certainly I did not want to face the wrong end of those arrows. And anyway I had more important business to attend to. I would just have to hope that it would not be too long before I met Edgar's people in friendship.

With the defeat of her army, Pootini's General surrendered on behalf of all the Rush territory on the mainland of Isla. Only the high-tide island of Prush was outside her jurisdiction.

We marched west to the coast and set up camp on the edge of the beach opposite Prush. We had captured six catapults, and these I set up ready to bombard the walls of Pootini's island fortress.

In the event we only fired a couple of salvos, twelve boulders in all, and these achieved very little damage. A few crossbow fire-bolts did a bit more but nothing major. I saw we were in for a long haul if Pootini chose to resist, as surely she would.

However, shortly after our second salvo of boulders a side gate opened and a deputation appeared waving a banner of truce. I let them cross the beach and approach my headquarters post.

Negotiations went on for a phase, but the outcome was satisfactory. The opposing delegation claimed that Pootini had been deposed and executed. Whether true or not, I never discovered. Sure they exhibited a body and decapitated head on the ramparts, but there was no way that I could tell that this was not yet another body double.

However, they accepted the total loss of most of their mainland territory, asking to retain a relatively small beachhead, extending no more than eight imiles inland more-or-less in an arc centred on the midpoint of the beach with endpoints at the ends of the beach at low tide. The precise boundary was to be determined by a commission to be led by Brinda, bearing in mind defensibility. To save the inevitable human cost of a protracted siege, I agreed to this. I also accepted eight female hostages to be held in Fort in the Isla Marches, and my captured General to be held in Oakbridge Abbey where I would place her in the protective custody of Wilda. Other members of the defeated armies would be allowed to choose between returning to Prush, or to their former homes in the former Rush empire under pain of death should they seek to reinstate that empire or introduce any political ties with Prush.

16
Cray takes a hand

Cray has come to see me. Unannounced, but that is her way. I suppose I have neglected my civic duties again, but in the school holidays I just want to be here with Thar. It's Mummy-Daughter time. I know Thar has to go to school, but she's my baby and I just want the two of us to be together here in my house by the sea, away from all the hustle and bustle of Rivermouth with all the intrusion of adult responsibilities.

Goddess, I still miss Arthay. How can any man have such a hold on me. I sometimes dream he is still here. In these fantasies he plays an almost equal role to me as we live as a family of just the three of us. A man who is almost an equal, a fantasy indeed, and furthermore caring for his own child. Surely if the Goddess had wanted men to care for or about children she would have given them tits so they could be useful. I'm really not myself any more. And now I'm going to have to face a lecture from Cray. Why should I even care? She's not my mother, she's my mother's cousin. She's not even my Goddess, she's bloody Shay's Goddess. And I'm 43 years old, big enough and ugly enough to look after myself. But yet I do care. I must just pull myself together and face her.

I finished brushing my hair, checked myself in the mirror, and sallied forth into my library where Cray had been shown by my housekeeper.

"Sorry to have kept you waiting, Cray, I'm afraid I was having a mid-mornphase zizz. Welcome to my not-so-humble abode."

"Well your man has made me comfortable and, as you see, given us a pot of tea and some rather delicious biscuits. Craya, sit up straight and don't look so glum or Thay will think you've forgotten your manners. Sorry about that, Thay, I've rather dragged Craya along with me tophase. For some reason she seems reluctant to see you."

"It's not that," Craya mumbled. " I'm always pleased to be with Thay, I'm just not comfortable with what you want to discuss."

"That's because you're a wimp. Thay, it is more than time that you came out of your sulks, and resumed your place in society. I've recently returned from a visit to your sister and I am concerned at the way that a North-South divide is developing within the Theocracy."

"I don't give a damn about Shay. She can do what she likes as long as she stays as far away from me as possible. If that means her holing up in the North that's fine by me."

"Well, you jolly well should give a damn." Cray was starting to get exasperated. "You should be bigger than that. This must not be about you and Shay. The whole future of the Theocracy is at stake. If things continue on the current path, the Theocracy could split and life as we know it would change irrevocably.

Listen, Shay's power in the North is almost total. Apart from some unimportant opposition from Midborough, she has brought the entire northern half of the Theocracy together under her leadership. She is dealing independently with the northern wild lands and the Isla Marches without any reference to the authorities in Rivermouth. She has even got most of the northern temples in thrall. Although she hasn't taken any overt steps towards an open split, the logical result of her actions will be a rejection of the Theocracy and the delicate balance that we have both between secular and temple interests and between the various political families and power structures."

"So what if Shay rules the North", I responded, "It was always a source of petty squabbles. Surely some order wouldn't come amiss."

"This isn't just 'some order'. It is a complete unification and centralisation of power. Just look at how Shay has blocked the slave raiding and closed the slave market in Knot. The northern Wapentakes will speak with one voice, while here in the South we will continue to be divided and will end up in a constant state of upheaval."

"Well what do you want me to do, somehow unify the South. I do have a lot of influence in the south-East and should be able to control a few of the regional Wapentakes. Obviously Chalcliff is mine and South Coast East. Then Craya there will ensure I get full support from Rivermouth South and Honeyfield, and with that I doubt anyone in the south-East would challenge us."

"No Thay, that is precisely what I don't want to see, but greatly fear. The only outcome of such a move would be massive civil war with such mayhem and destruction that we would be knocked back to the level of the wild lands. You need to come back to Rivermouth, take your rightful place as a one of Isla's elite and establish a working compromise with Shay to ensure the unity of the Theocracy."

"I disagree," Craya interjected. "We are strong enough to defeat Shay. Of course we need Thay to lead us, but we can field a strong army if necessary. I have expanded the militia in Honeyfield and we train every period without fail. I've also developed strong ties with my neighbours in Mid-River and Cattlebridge who would be very much on our side. Cattlebridge, especially, is furious about the loss of the northern slave trade. I'm sure Thay could raise substantial levees from Downs, Estuary and South Cape to supplement her militias from Chalcliff and South Coast East. We could assemble the mightiest army the Theocracy has ever seen and absolutely crush Shay and her northern rabble. What I think we should do is assemble such an army and march firstly to Midborough, where we would be welcome. Then we would see if Shay dare to oppose us as we challenge her slave-raiding ban."

"If you can't talk sense, don't say anything." Cray turned on her daughter. "You really are the limit and have no diplomatic sense whatsoever. I blame that misbegotten woman that Thay foisted on you, always dropping poison in your ear. Thay, why in the name of Isla did you have to have anything to do with that evil creature?"

"You know very well, " I responded wearily, "She incurred life-changing injuries when Shay attacked her. I was responsible and couldn't just abandon her, despite her being a double traitor, first to me and then to Shay."

"Humph, she's an evil bitch who only got her just desserts. But this is a digression from what I have to say. Your war with Shay must end. You are both grown women. Each of you is obscenely rich and no longer needs to compete for your mother's attention and inheritance. You also each have lovely daughters who could and should be friends. They are both in the enviable position of being sisters without the burden of competition to divide them. Shar is a delightful child, whose company I very much enjoyed, just as I do Thar's. They could be the force to reconcile you and your sister."

We were interrupted by a loud squeal from behind an armchair. "I've got a sister!?"

I turned on the source of the squeal. "Thar, what are you doing hiding in that corner. You shouldn't be eavesdropping on the conversation of your elders and betters. Go to your rooms immediately. You are far too young to be exposed to political discussions."

"I didn't mean any harm, Mummy, I was just looking at some books when Auntie Cray came in and I didn't want to disturb you." Thar mumbled as she slunk out of the library."

"Oh Goddess, now I'm going to have to explain things I didn't want to until she was much older. I really don't know what to do. Look Cray, I appreciate your concern but I'm just not ready to commit to the next course of action. I'll be back in Rivermouth for the new school term and I promise I'll come and see you and thrash things out. Just don't get your hopes too high. It's not that I want to plunge the Theocracy into civil war but I just can't see myself entering into any sort of face to face negotiations with Shay, even if she were willing, which I doubt."

"Craya, I do appreciate your support in all this. You are and have always been my loyal friend. When I come back to

Rivermouth, perhaps we could look up an attractive man and enjoy a session together. Anyway, I'm sure you're right to train and strengthen your militia, but we must all hope that military action will be unnecessary. And you should take care not to heed that bloody surgeon too much. She may not be as evil as your mother maintains. However, she has a treacherous heart and her judgement is not to be trusted, especially where Shay or I are concerned."

My guests stayed for a phase before returning to Rivermouth. We didn't continue any political discussions, but instead concentrated on business and family matters. I did have to endure anecdotes about Shar's antics which I found painful. Deep down, I know it is wrong for me to visit the crimes of her mother on a child who sounds to be so like my own darling Thar, but I can't help my feelings and would so much rather ignore Shar's existence. As expected Thar quizzed me about it and I was extremely uncomfortable telling her about the feud between me and my sister and the appalling history of the begetting of the two girls — sister-cousins yet destined to remain strangers to each other.

The more interesting subject to come up from Cray's unwelcome excursion to Elmhouse was news of Shay's artificial rivers. Even though I don't want to hear about Shay's doings, I do realise that some things are important for me to know. Of course I knew that some artificial water courses had been dug in the Lesser delta region and even that some of these were navigable, but I hadn't thought about how it could be possible to use these established drainage techniques to extend the natural navigation of the major rivers. I'm NOT going to Elmhouse to see these wonders for myself but I can readily appreciate how a connection between the Lesser and Second rivers has consolidated Shay's trade monopoly and increased both her personal wealth and influence throughout the regions bordering her waterways. Accordingly I think I can understand how she has managed to control the borders with the northern wild lands, overcome opposition in Knot and prevent slave raids into those lands.

I've got a sister! Is it true? Why hasn't Mummy told me? She knows I want a real person to play with and go on adventures with. I'm going to believe it. I have a real live sister called Shar and if I can't see her for real I'll imagine her. I don't need my old imaginary friend. I'll say goodbye to her this very phase and instead I'll imagine Shar. Even if Mummy doesn't like it and won't tell me anything, I'll ask Auntie Cray. She's really met Shar and will answer my questions when Mummy isn't around. I'm often at her house after school when Mummy is working so I'll have lots of opportunities. Yes, that's what I'll do. I won't pester Mummy too much, just ask her politely, and then I'll feel free to ask Auntie Cray anything I like.

Two phases later

Well, I asked Mummy about Shar. She was a bit evasive but did admit that we are sister-cousins, which makes us closer than ordinary half-sisters, and in our special case we must be as close as full-sisters. You know, girls who have both the same Mummy and Father.

Mummy did waffle on a bit about some really boring and disgusting stuff about where babies come from. It involves working out just the right timing and then making a man do something very rude with you. I suppose that's why men have to be slaves. If they were free, they would surely refuse to co-operate. I know men don't have tits like grown up women, but apparently they have dangly bits between their legs and we women can make them put these inside our bottoms and then somehow a baby can get started. I told you it sounded most disgusting. Poor men, we can be so cruel. Anyway Mummy used to own a very special man called Arthay who had been given to her by her Mummy when she, my Mummy that is, became grown up. Mummy has a real sister called Shay. They are actually twins and when they were little were impossible to tell apart unless you knew them very well indeed. When they grew older they always dressed differently and did their hair in different ways so there was no confusion. But really they are still very much alike to look at. Anyway they were always competing with each other to gain my Grandma's favour and they became enemies.

Finally, Mummy said, it all came to a head when Grandma died. She had been cross that Mummy hadn't made Arthay give her a daughter and so gave her Elmhouse estate to Shay. That's up north where I've never been and Shay is making lots of money from river transport on the Lesser and Second Rivers up there; just like Mummy does on the Great River. Well, Shay tricked Arthay into giving her a baby, who is Shar, just to upset my Mummy. I get a bit confused over what happened next but Mummy made Arthay give her me and Arthay then drowned in the strait quite close to where we live. Now Mummy and Shay won't speak to each other and won't let me and Shar meet.

That's the story as far as I can tell. It means that Shar and I have the same father which makes us sisters, even if that's not what we usually mean by the name. Also because our Mummies are sisters, even if they don't want to be, we are cousins in the normal sense. That means we are sister-cousins. But more because our Mummies are twins that look the same, it's almost like we do have the same Mummy in some sense—just like full sisters.

Does all that make sense? I'm not sure that I can really get my head around it. What I do understand and will act on is that Shar is my sister and that we should be allowed to be friends because we don't have to fight over who gets our Mummy's property. I'm going to find out all I can about Shar and imagine doing things with her. Perhaps when I grow up I'll be able to meet her and we can become proper friends.

What a time I've had. I'm almost relieved to be back in Rivermouth. Thar's at school at the moment and I'm picking up the threads of my various business interests. Craya means well and is fiercely loyal to my interests but just isn't very competent when in comes to business, so I have a lot to do.

I really made a mess of explaining things to Thar. I suppose she is a bit young to learn about adult relationships but actually lots of girls growing up in the countryside learn from a very young age by watching animals. And in poorer families where they don't have the living space that we enjoy, it must be impossible to avoid hearing or even seeing your mother satisfying her sexual needs. So I wasn't prepared for Thar's reaction. Oh well, what's done is done.

What really messes my head is that Thar has now abandoned her erstwhile imaginary friend and replaced her with an imaginary Shar. Not that I was that taken by the imaginary friend either, but I did understand her loneliness. I had hoped that school would help her form real friendships and I suppose that eventually she would have grown out of the imaginary one. However, this new obsession with a sister is much more worrying. Quite apart from the distress it causes me for all the obvious reasons, it can't be good for her and will surely impact on her relationships in the real world.

On our return to Rivermouth, I decided to break the journey to call on my old schoolfriend, Cora, who has a small estate overlooking the town of Corona in the Downs region. I have rather neglected her of late, which is really bad of me. She does tend to be a bit needy, and, while I've been grieving so much at the loss of Arthay I have found it difficult to maintain the friendship.

It's complicated, but I'm conflicted. I have a clear duty to Clara, her child, who is my Goddess-daughter. However, Arthay was also the child's father and even though that was through my deliberate intention, I now find myself with mixed emotions when I see her.

Part of my problem is that I hadn't wanted Arthay to know that this was his own daughter. Not that that matters in our society, where generally men have no inkling of whether or not they father a child. However, and this is unusual, I did want Arthay to know about any child I had by him, in a sort of exclusive sense. Following the tragic events that led to his loss there is really no reason for me to be so coy about my Goddess daughter, but I am. Maybe one phase I will be prepared to tell Thar that she and Clara are half-sisters, but that phase is not yet. Nevertheless, I hope to mitigate Thar's current obsession with Shar by encouraging her to be friends with Clara.

The visit went reasonably well. Cora was pleased to see me and we had a very pleasant time reminiscing, having drunk rather too much of her excellent wine. Cora showed herself to be very understanding of my pain. She reminded me that like most of us, Clara had no knowledge of her paternity and assured me that she would not inform her of her relationship to Thar without my permission.

"After all", she said, "by custom, we don't really consider a shared father as implying any sort of relationship bond in the way we would for girls with the same mother. Furthermore, since it's actually quite usual for friends to share the pleasures of a man, our situation is not uncommon. There must be many a woman who is Goddess to the daughter of a friend and the father of her own daughter without either mother thinking anything of it or either daughter being aware of any blood relationship."

As for the girls, they played together well enough for children with a three year age gap. Clara had obviously been enjoined to be on her best behaviour and did her best to be kind to Thar. In her turn, Thar began to come out of her shell, overcoming her natural shyness, in response to Clara's overtures of friendship. It was a joy to me to hear her laughter as Clara pushed her on a swing, teaching her to maintain the motion by moving her legs and body and then how to start the swinging herself. I must install a swing at home. I have hopes that in the years to come this relationship will blossom. Maybe Clara might even be the one to initiate Thar into the joys of sex. Who knows?

Being polite, Cora offered one of her men for either a shared or solo session. This was only to be expected, but I really wasn't in the mood, and by her body-language, I didn't think Cora was either. The wine made us both more honest and open with each other and thus it was a relief for us both when I suggested we just had a cosy time together without needing the intervention of sex.

I only had a slight hangover after all that wine, and after a good breakfast Cora gave me a tour of her vineyard. Her estate is relatively modest with just two farms, one of which she rents out. About five years ago she tried growing grapes as an experiment and now has a flourishing vineyard on a south-facing slope. Apparently the vines like the chalky soil of the downs and produce flavoursome grapes for making white wine. This is the third year of her wine production, and she hopes to start selling it to a wider customer base than her existing small outlet in Corona. She pressed a case on me to take to Rivermouth because "the wine sold there is rubbish, just the dregs of production from the South Coast vineyards."

I was delighted to accept the gift. I also saw a good business opportunity. I offered to promote her wine to acquaintances in Rivermouth and we agreed a joint venture which promises much mutual benefit.

After that, we arrived in Rivermouth rather later than planned and consequently I had to rush about a bit to get Thar to bed and then make everything ready for her school. I was tired and soon ready for bed myself. On the other hand I felt more contented than I had for a long time. Facing the future was less daunting than it had been the phase before.

17
Control of the Borders

My victory over Pootini was complete. In the process I had also obtained unanimous approval for the ban on slave-raiding (excepting Midborough — but they don't count) and various agreements on cross-border trade and even a certain amount of migration.

I suppose I should have known, but I was not prepared for the amount of extra work and bureaucracy that ensued. It soon became evident that we needed some sort of control over the cross-border traffic.

Previously there hadn't been anything to regulate. As I had discovered from Audreeda, there was a certain amount of comings and goings in the Lesser Coast region, rather more than I or the Wapentake were aware of. On the other hand, the River border was pretty impervious. The northern tribes there were wary of the Theocracy and avoided contact whenever possible. Until I had built a few bridges, the only land crossing point was at Knot-on-Lesser, which was strongly guarded and used mainly for the slave trade. The citizens of Knot and their northern neighbours view each other with a great deal of suspicion and distrust. Further up and downstream from Knot, there were a handful of boat owners that were prepared to offer some kind of ferry service. However, crossings were rare.

West of the river the border is more open, but even so there was little crossing in either direction apart from the raiders. The sparse population kept alert to the presence of strangers and were ever on the watch for cattle raiding parties from the north. Likewise the northern border tribes were wary of the slavers and generally kept a low profile. They remained circumspect in any dealings with the Theocracy.

Now all that is changing and we have begun to experience more open contact all along the land border and at river crossings. Some in the tribes are beginning to complain about 'tourists' while here in the Theocracy we have various complaints about northerners 'stealing our jobs by undercutting wages' and putting other pressures on Theocratic society. Several Wapentakes have also expressed concern about not having any idea as to who and how many are entering or leaving our territory.

I had to act to get things back under control. I had given a thumb and been taken for an imile! In the end my solution has been 'Bureaucracy'. The idea of me instigating that is enough to make my friends laugh .

However, it is not to be helped. It wasn't entirely plain sailing, I wasn't able to impose the controls by myself.[16] I obtained the

16 Actually, that is pretty much what Shay did do. Nobody was going to oppose her.

agreement of the main border tribes and presented the solution for ratification by the relevant Wapentakes.

All official crossing points are guarded. This includes all bridges and major ferries over the Lesser, and anyone crossing the border in either direction has to have a passport, explaining who they are, where they were born and any other relevant details. These passports can be issued in various centres in the border regions, but also at the crossing points themselves. This way we are able to keep records on just who is and who isn't present in the Theocracy.

Anyone crossing elsewhere into the Theocracy is required to present themselves within one phase of arrival to have appropriate documentation inspected or issued. Any northerner found in the Theocracy without documentation will be returned across the border.

The northern tribes set their own rules for visitors but generally they expect visitors to make themselves known and be subject to any local regulation. Our passports are accepted as evidence of bona fides. At first only a very few northerners could read them, but that is changing as literacy spreads.

By now we have freed all non-penal female slaves within the eight Wapentake regions closest to the border. The exceptions among the council of the north being Midborough, West Bank and Upper Great River. Some of the freed women have wanted to return to their erstwhile homes in the north or west, but others like Wilja have made their lives here and wish to stay. Actually, Wilda has promised to escort Wilja to visit her former home once affairs have settled down. Maybe next year. Wilja would like to see her sister Wena and Wilda's father Edgar again, while remaining resident at Oakbridge.

All the effort I am having to put into the politics has detracted from my ability to keep on top of all my other concerns. Fortunately I can trust Brinda completely with the canal construction, and also with ensuring that the workforce keeps up their military training.

Back in Lesser Coast, things have slipped a bit. My team of blacksmiths are making progress with steel production, but rather more slowly than I would like. They are more-or-less keeping up with basic weapons production, swords and shields and so on; and, most importantly, pike heads, but the more innovative weaponry is behind schedule. Also the progress with steel rails and armour for horses is even slower.

I suppose I shouldn't really complain. I can be a somewhat exacting task-mistress, and some of the designs that Brinda and I have come up with are proving quite challenging. I guess I am lucky that Thay appears to be reluctant to move against me. Surely she will do so before too long. My spies in Rivermouth report that many of the more powerful southern families view my ban on slave-raiding as a provocation. My cousin Craya, in particular, is being vocal in her attacks on me. Cray, as ever, is trying to calm things down, but I don't think she will succeed. It's a good thing that Craya is such an incompetent wimp. Unless Thay takes positive control, Craya's bound to make a mess of things for her. Surely I must be on borrowed time and will soon reach a crisis point.

Bottom of my priority list seems to be Shar. I know I'm neglecting her and relying too much on Valray and Wilda. Like me in my childhood, Shar is well on top of her schoolwork and I have no worries on that score. Wilda certainly maintains a watch on her progress and ensures she is sufficiently challenged on the work front. It's outside school that I'm concerned. Valray gives her a lot of love, which is good, but she is too indulgent and Shar can twist her round her little finger. Some of the language that Shar comes our with sometimes indicates that she is running just a bit wild and spending too much time with some of the more licentious among the canal workers.

18
A Bad Mother

I was quite shocked the other phase. I'd been away sorting out some problems in Steele and, needing to clear my head before showing up at home, was taking a walk along the riverside when I heard Shar's voice in the distance singing an extremely bawdy chorus with great gusto, "We're gonna rub your bumps while you suck our tits, we're gonna shag you all to bits." She then came skipping round a bend, collapsing into giggles when she saw me. I sincerely hope she doesn't understand what she was singing, 'though I fear she does!

"I didn't know you were here, Mummy."

"So I gather," I riposted. "That song is most unsuitable and unladylike."

"Oh, it's just something that the phalanx-ball teams sing in the bath after a game. I don't know all the words but I know the chorus. And it makes the men go as red as a beetroot, especially when the girls point at their wobbly bits and make as if to grab them. It's all very funny. Harmless banter is what they say if the men get upset."

"And just what are you doing, to witness such goings on?"

"Oh, sometimes I get to go in the bath too, they are all very kind to me and I splash about and enjoy myself. When am I going to grow tits? And will I also grow hair round my fanny? Some of the phalanx girls have quite a bush on them, it's no wonder they always seem to have an itch there. Oh, and why don't we have cocks like the men? They seem much more useful for peeing, especially if you've got all that hair in the way."

Oh Goddess, I am such a bad mother. Shar's still only a young child, and is so neglected that she's mixing in the most unsuitable company and learning things that are totally inappropriate for her age. I was also very much a loner at her age and did all sorts of things that my mother had no idea of, but I don't recall being so sexualised as a mere infant. Sure, I did start early, and my behaviour in my early teens would (I think) have appalled my mother, but I had at least reached puberty before I took an interest in such matters.

Looking back I don't think I responded very well, but I was completely gobsmacked my my daughter's questions.

"Shar, go home at once", I screamed, "I'll speak to you later, when I've had a chance to calm down. You leave me absolutely speechless. I really don't know what to do with you. You have grown wild beyond belief and things need to change. Go, quickly, before I forget my principles and give you the smacking you undoubtedly deserve."

Shar scurried off, bursting into tears as she went. "I didn't mean to upset you, Mummy, I was only asking questions because I wanted to know and I love you and thought you would help me understand." Her words creeping out between sobs as she receded along the tow path.

I wasn't that long in following her home. I'd rather lost my appetite for the walk. However, it had been a while since I had eaten and I didn't want to confront Shar with a rumbling stomach, so I sat down for dinner before summoning her to the library.

During dinner, I had managed to calm down a bit and marshal my thoughts for what I feared would be a most uncomfortable conversation. Just how do you discuss sex with a seven year-old? What does she know, and what half-truths has she picked up from the great unwashed. Actually not so much unwashed, since it appears she has been getting her education in these matters through wallowing in a communal bath with the lowest orders of society. I'm pretty sure I hadn't even seen a naked man at her age, let alone looked on while a pile of randy women disported themselves while pointing at the male genitalia.

"Right Shar," I began. "Let's sit down in the comfy chairs, because I've got a lot to say to you that makes me feel quite uncomfortable. You really are far too young for all this, as it's more appropriate for your teens, but since you've been mixing in such dubious company where you hear and see things you shouldn't, I'm going to have to swallow my reservations. What do you know about how babies are made?"

"Oh, that's no secret, I've helped Grandma Valray in lambing season, so I know how the baby lambs grow in their mummies' tummies and come out through their fannies. I help to clean up the lambs and give bottles to them when their mummies can't feed them, usually when there are triplets. I've also been around when the rams are put to the sheep in the first place. The rams chase after the sheep and when they catch one they jump up and stick their cock right into the sheep's back end. That's what we want them to do as it's what puts the lamb there."

The joys of a country upbringing!

"Oh, I see," Shar went on, "I just hadn't thought of how it might work for people." (Shar is definitely NOT stupid). "The shepherd always speaks to the rams and says something like 'go and scratch their itches for them'. So that's it, is it, the girls fannies itch when they want a man to give them a baby. But what I've sometimes heard them say isn't 'I want a baby' but 'I need a bloody good fuck', and most of the women seem to want this most phases, but they don't seem to have much luck in getting babies. I'm still puzzled."

"They say that to you!" I was more shocked than ever.

"No, not to me, but to each other, I think they don't know I have overheard them. It's usually just between two of them and then quite often they go and whisper to a man and take him off somewhere out of the way. I'm sure they don't want me to know what they're up to, in case I snitch on them, but I wouldn't do that. I'm not a sneak. Anyway, if they see me trying to follow they quickly shoo me away."

"And have you followed and seen what they do?" I was curious despite being totally appalled.

"Not usually, but I have occasionally seen a bit at a distance. I've seen them pull the man's clothes off and undress themselves, and then jump up and down a bit. But I haven't really seen very much, they all seem to want to be private when they're doing this. Perhaps because they're naked, but they don't seem to mind that when we're all in the bath. Grown-ups are so strange."

Well, after these revelations, I was able to present the more salient facts. I told her that this was indeed the mechanism for starting babies, but that it didn't have to always result in pregnancy. You had to get the timing right for that, which is indeed what the shepherd does for the sheep. I explained that while the farmer needs the sheep to have lambs every spring, people are not so rigid in the timing or frequency of having babies, but our bodies are ready throughout the year. I also explained that when you grow up you find you need to indulge in sex quite often and that the act itself is very pleasurable, especially for women. Men enjoy it too, but don't need it in quite the same way and can get hurt if made to do it too often. This is why it's women who take the leading role and are by far the more demanding. I then tied this into the whole practice of ownership of men and my campaign against such slavery.

"Finally to answer your earliest questions, you will grow tits eventually, usually at about thirteen years old. Hair will also grow around your vulva (the proper word for fanny) at about the same time and these are two outward signs that you are getting ready to join the adult world, sexually speaking. There are also other changes going on inside you that I won't talk about now but will do when you are a bit older, and in good time before they actually start to happen."

"OK, I suppose I'll just have to wait then, but does that mean I'll be properly grown up when I'm thirteen?"

"No it doesn't", I said emphatically. "What it means is that you will be physically able to bear children, but you will still yourself be a child with much more development both physically and mentally required before you are ready to assume adult responsibilities. Indeed, according to law, you will not be fully adult until you come of age at twenty-four."

"But does that mean I'm going to get itches when I'm thirteen but have to wait until I'm twenty-four before I can scratch them. That sounds unbearable."

"Oh dear, have you been listening to me. It's not a real itch like when you get bitten by a mosquito. And it isn't a real scratch that you need to alleviate it. You will start to experience sexual desires after your body has finished developing. We all do. And you won't need to wait until your fully grown. Before the time comes I will give you a much more complete talk than is appropriate at your present age. You'll also learn more in school. Then you will undoubtedly find someone to help you have your first experience with a man and then, while avoiding the complication of becoming pregnant too young, you will be able to enjoy pleasurable times when the occasion is right."

"Will you be with me to help the first time?"

"That's a good question. The answer is probably no, unless you really want me there. In olden times it was quite common for a girl's mother to makes all the arrangements and supervise the occasion, usually when the girl reached sixteen, but that tradition has long been obsolete. Usually nowaphase it's something you do with a more experienced friend of your own generation."

"Auntie Cray told me that your Mummy had bought Arval as a present for Thay on your twenty-fourth birthphase and that's what set you off against each other. Is that usual, and will you buy me a man when I'm twenty-four?"

"You are now making me uncomfortable again. I don't want to be reminded about all that but I suppose you deserve to be told. Yes Chay did buy Arval for Thay, and I was very upset. Again, this custom is quite rare now, and where it does survive is very much confined to upper class families like ours. Looking back dispassionately (which is something I find very hard) I don't think Chay had set out with the intention of buying a man for either of us. However, Arval was an exceptional young man and I can understand why she snapped him up when the opportunity arose. My relationship with both Chay and Thay was already bad and what ensued was pretty inevitable. I took it particularly badly because it signalled that Chay had irrevocably decided that Thay would be the principal heiress. Again, I suppose this was inevitable, I was every bit as worthy as Thay, but of itself that wouldn't matter. Thay is older by half an ihor and that meant that my only chance was if Thay proved to be unworthy, which wasn't going to happen.

When it comes down to it, the tradition of giving a man in this way is a way of the mother selecting the father of her future grandchildren. Twenty-four is a good age to have your first baby and it does appear that when daughters reach that stage, their mothers start aching for a grandchild, who they will then dote on and spoil in they way that Valray spoils you. In past times mothers would even go to the extreme of being there to supervise their daughter getting pregnant by the chosen man. Actually this seems quite disgusting to me.

Anyway in your turn, I will not buy you a man at twenty-four or any other age. As you know, I have become implacably opposed to the whole idea of men being the property of women. I don't have the power to prevent it, but I have made a start. I have introduced laws to allow men to be free of ownership in most of the northern Wapentakes and I have freed all the men that were formerly under my ownership. So, I will not buy anyone for you or anyone else. On the other hand, I'm sure that when the time comes I'll nag you for a grandchild and I expect I'll make constructive suggestions as to who might be a suitable father. On the other hand if you are a worthy daughter, you will make up your own mind, independently of any advice that I might give."

"OK Mummy, thank-you for answering my questions. Can I go now, Daubey has promised me a treat before bedtime."

"Daubey is someone else who spoils you. Before you go I must remind you that some of your language is inappropriate and you must stop using it. A cock is a slang term when used for the male organ. The proper word is penis, and you shouldn't have much cause to mention it anyway. Also I do not want to hear of you using the words 'shag, fuck or bloody'. These are inappropriate for children of our class and will rightly get you in trouble at school or even with those who dote on you so much at home. Likewise the singing of bawdy songs, and indeed your mixing with the common soldiers and workers on our canal project. In future you must always be accompanied by a responsible adult when visiting such company. I will make appropriate arrangements. I also think the time has come for you to board at school in the regular way. I shall arrange this with Auntie Wilda."

Shar pouted.

"Do you understand, young lady?"

"Yes Mummy," at that Shar left the library sulkily. Once outside the door she ran off to the kitchen to find Daubey.

I sank into my armchair and pondered. If Cray is to be believed, Thay and Thar exhibit the opposite problem. Thay is far too protective of her daughter who has become very clingy and is much too quiet. Of course, I've never met my niece, nor do I want to, but I have seen her in the distance on some of my occasional visits to Rivermouth. She does indeed resemble Shar very closely. After all, I suppose that biologically they are full sisters of the same age, effectively sororal twins. As far as I can tell they are much the same height, tall for their age, and Thar is also bright academically, albeit behind Shar because of Thay delaying her schooling, while Shar's has been accelerated. I suppose it's going to be inevitable that they will meet one phase when they are adult. I hope that phase is far off. Shar knows of Thar's existence, thanks to Cray, but at least she doesn't plague me with questions. I suppose she knows my antipathy and acts accordingly.

Whoops! I think I've messed up big time. Mummy is distinctly unhappy and I'm going to have to keep a low profile for a bit.

Mummy did bore on a bit over this sex stuff. I'm not sure I understand it. It seems to cause an awful lot of trouble for us people. Sheep are much more sensible about it, even though they are so stupid most of the time. I mean, I know babies are important, but there really should be a better way than forcing men to do rude things all the time, especially when you don't actually want to get a baby in your tummy. It seems to me that men are very tolerant, but you can see that they get quite distressed when women are so rude to them in front of everyone. You know, when some of the women get a bit drunk and make comments about a man's cock (or should I say penis to avoid offending Mum — No I won't, she's not going to read this after all so I can use the rude words). Even worse, sometimes women go so far as to grab hold of a man's bits and say things like, "make it bigger for me". That tends to make men blush and try to hide it behind their hands. It seems unfair to me, is it their fault if they are not big enough for some drunken woman? Women have different sizes of tits, so I suppose men will have different sizes of cocks. When I grow up I'll not be so rude. I think we'd all be better off if we only ask men for sex when we actually want to start a baby.

I don't really mind having to do regular boarding at school. It was going to happen before too long anyway, and a few of my friends are also about to start boarding. I'll miss coming home at period-ends but I'm bound to have fun things to do at school and exeats for the youngest girls happen every two periods anyway.

It will be a bore having to be 'escorted' to see phalanx ball games, and not to be able to join in the fun; but someone's bound to report me if I turn up where I shouldn't, once they've been told about Mummy's new rules. And I guess I'll have to be careful about what I say when Mummy might overhear. I wonder if Thar has similar problems with her Mummy. I'd like to meet her and compare our lives, but there's not much chance of that.

I'd also like to go to Rivermouth, it sounds like it's a very exciting place. I suppose I'm just going to have to wait until I'm grown-up. Of course, Mummy goes there sometimes, but she avoids it as much as possible because she doesn't want to see her sister or Thar. It seems so unfair that, just because Mummy and Auntie Thay don't like each other, I'm not allowed to see my sister. Because, like-it-or-not, Mummy has to understand that Thar is MY sister and I want to be able to play with her. I wonder what she knows about me. Perhaps when I'm away at school I might find some way of getting a letter to her without either of our Mummies knowing. Perhaps Auntie Cray might help. When she visited us here, she told me that she wished Mummy and Auntie Thay would stop their ridiculous feud. After all, she said, what's past is past and they no longer have to compete over an inheritance. Also, nothing they can do will change what happened to my father or bring him back.

Yes, that's what I'll do. When I've got some free time at period-end in school, I'll write to Thar and put the letter safely inside one to Auntie Cray and ask Auntie Wilda to send it for me. No-one will object to me writing to Auntie Cray and I know that she sees Thar sometimes.

19
Edwin's Vision

My mother is dying. She hasn't really recovered since my father died last year. Although she has urged me to go, I can't leave her to die alone. As long as she lives I must stay here. I have promised this to her and to my Goddess.

It was some years ago now at midsummer. I was alone in the western hills, camped by a high tarn. I had been out hunting for deer with two of my friends. This was shortly before I took over from my father as war-leader. That sounds a bit grand, but it was the title he had been given. In reality, most of the time, I led a small band of archers, but more of that later.

I had sent the others back with the fine stag we had shot. Mine was the arrow that found its mark, and the antlers would belong to me, but the meat would feed our village while the other parts of the beast would all be made use of in various artefacts. I wanted some time alone to ponder the responsibilities that would soon be mine. Geos hung large and full in the sky above the tarn bringing its light with it. I had stripped off and was wading into the icy, refreshing water when suddenly a storm blew up. Such short-lived but violent storms can come without warning in these high moors. Under a flash of lightening I saw her. A vision of the Goddess sprang up in the middle of the tarn, gleaming with light that brightened the entire sky.

I fell to my knees in the water. I would have drowned and passed to meet her, but something told me to rise up, for I had work to do and a destiny to fulfil. I clambered out of the tarn and returned to my bedroll where I fell into a deep slumber and dreamt.

When dawn broke I awoke and rose. Remembering my experience, I raised a cairn as an altar to my Goddess. A skein of geese flew overhead. I drew my bow and shot the leading bird who fell right on the peak of the altar. There I offered her in sacrifice and vowed my service and fidelity.

I don't know how, but I knew that one phase I would meet my Goddess in the flesh. Until that phase, I would remain celibate, no matter what. It hasn't been easy. Conquering my natural desires has not been too hard, but even here in the enlightened community of our linked villages, men are expected to serve the sexual needs of women. I am unusually big for a man, like my father before me. Although I blush to say so, I am proportionately well-endowed and hence had previously always been in much demand. Despite my making my new allegiance clear, I have to rebuff many importunities. Fortunately my inherited status has helped me, and I have enjoyed the support both of my father and, more significantly, my mother in keeping my resolve.

Decades ago, my father had organised resistance to the raids on our communities emanating from the southern Theocracy. He had himself been captured and raped. He had also lost the love of his life, my aunt Wilja, my mother's beloved sister who was heavily pregnant. My father had managed to escape but has been racked with guilt that he had been unable to rescue my aunt. He found consolation with my mother and as far as I am aware has resisted all others for the rest of his life. Thereafter he devoted his life to the defence firstly of our village and then to the other four villages that have become linked in alliance. His efforts resulted in his unique appointment as war-leader, despite the disadvantages of his sex.

Among his many military achievements, Edgar perfected the design and use of the longbow, turning archery from a minor hunting tool to the powerful weapon that it has become. I have been the beneficiary of his invention and in my youth spent many ihors practising my technique and perfecting my skill. As of now I have become the most accomplished archer in the five villages, and thus in all the Northlands.

In recent years we have learnt of the activities of the lady Shay of the Theocracy. After the raid that took my aunt, my father vowed that no woman from the Theocracy would again set foot in our territory as long as he lived. That vow has been kept, but it has been apparent to us all that the time would come when we would want to deal with Shay. It is clear that she represents a change in our relationship with our neighbours with her promise to end the raids that provoke our hostility.

Although our five villages are fairly self contained as a community, we are nor entirely isolated from our neighbours and remain welcoming to travellers from other communities in the northern regions. Thus we learnt of Shay's dealings with several of our southern and eastern neighbours, and received a visit from Audreeda from the south-eastern coastal community. I was away at the time of this visit but learned of the details later. Audreeda is unusual in that she has spent time living incognito inside the Theocracy itself and is unusually familiar with its customs and politics, and can even read and write. She is also friends with the lady Shay. Part of her mission to us was to sound out our willingness to receive a visit from the great lady herself.

My mother made it clear that while my father still lived, nobody from the Theocracy would be welcome, but held out the prospect that in due course a reconciliation might be possible. Audreeda gave her assurance that Shay, at least, would respect our prohibition but would also be open to engage with us when we were ready. She also was able to give us the news that my aunt Wilja was still alive and that her child, my sister-cousin, held a powerful position in the Theocracy as Abbess of Oakbridge. She had taken the name Wilda in honour of her heritage and was closely allied to Shay herself. I promised my mother that when the time was right I would travel to the Theocracy and seek them both out.

As things turned out, it was not long before I would set eyes on Shay myself, although I chose not to meet her at that time. Even at a distance I could see that she was an uncommonly handsome woman, indeed striking is perhaps the most appropriate term. She is tall, even for a woman, taller than me. Remember I am an exceptionally tall man. She is about seven years my senior, and if I were not committed to the Goddess of my vision, I could easily fall under her spell. I will have to be very careful when eventually I do meet her!

Two further events occurred that were to change my life for ever. Just a few years ago, the north-west was in turmoil. Our villages had begun to experience an influx of refugees from the south and west. These refugees told of an invasion from the far west with a cruel army taking over the lands and putting to death all those who stood in their way. The leader of the invaders was called Pootini and her name was spoken with fear in the eyes and mouths of those fleeing before her.

The moors immediately to the west of our villages are virtually uninhabited and served as a buffer between us and Pootini's domains, but it was clear that, left undefended, they would not remain as a barrier to her ambitions. My father was already unfit for the travail of campaigning in such hostile country and I was appointed to lead a force of Archers, some thirty-two of us, into the mountains to wage a resistive campaign to discourage Pootini's westward expansion by that route.

I felt the responsibility of this command keenly and before we set forth, I went alone to my holy tarn to meditate and commune with my Goddess. The other life-changing event occurred after I had spent the night at the tarn.

As dawn broke, I woke and climbed out of my sleeping roll and entered the tarn to refresh myself. When I turned to walk out of the water I found myself faced with a woman pointing an arrow straight at me, or rather, straight at my genitals. Extraordinarily, she was holding a longbow very like my own. I say extraordinarily because the longbow is a man's weapon.

"I might have taken you for be one of Zoni's followers, except surely you are too young. It is over a quarter of a century since Zoni was expelled and neither she nor her followers have been heard of since. It has long been assumed that they had all died out."

She answered, "any reports of the demise of our community are much exaggerated. We are Mazons, Zoni's people and she is very much alive. My sister there and I are daughters of one of her original followers, born not long after the expulsion from your villages. We have kept clear of you ever since, living in these moors and mountains. You are not welcome in our territory any more than we are in yours."

Looking beyond my captor's shoulder I could see another similarly clad and armed woman some fifty strides away. Presumably her sister. "This tarn is a holy place to me, where I experienced a life-changing vision of the Goddess, and I come here to meditate. I am Edwin, son of Wena and Edgar of the five villages. We are concerned about the reports of hostile activity from someone called Pootini to the west of these mountains and I have been appointed to resist her Eastwards encroachment. I have no quarrel with you or Zoni. I was but ten years old when she was expelled. I know little about it but I gathered she was considered a bad influence, eschewing sexual relations with men in favour of other women. If that is indeed the case how did your birth come about. As far as I am aware no men accompanied her into exile."

"Ah! so that's the storyline is it. Actually the reality is more complicated. It is true that Zoni herself is exclusively homosexual and that she was charged with corrupting public morals. However the charges against her did not really relate to her sexual preferences. After all, almost all women enjoy an element of same sex dalliance as part of our rounded sex lives. In our community, men still have a role to play, albeit somewhat diminished compared to what I understand is the case in your five villages. So we have had some children born among us."

"Right, I think I see, but Zoni didn't take men into exile with her and er, excuse me if I'm rude, surely there are other complications." I blushed and pointed at her bow."

She laughed. "Well, just because we kept away from your villages, didn't mean we remained totally isolated. We have learned from the Theocracy and raided our Eastern and Northern neighbours for slaves, both men and women, but principally such men as we require. I'm afraid we don't treat them very well, worse than in the Theocracy, as I fear you may discover. Also a few of our number don't aspire to be warriors, while for those that do, slave women look after our babies."

"What do you want with me? And do you have to point that arrow like that? It makes me nervous. Also I'm getting cold standing around dripping wet."

"What do we want? Simple really, I'm under orders to bring you to Zoni. I'd prefer to leave you intact, but if necessary this arrow will castrate you, and while you are doubled up in pain, we'll tie you up and force to to come with us. Your choice, co-operate and come quietly, or otherwise. Who knows, I may even reward you by letting you impregnate me one phase."

I wasn't in a position to argue. I was allowed to get dressed and pack up my belongings, even my weapons. A halter was put about my neck and a blindfold around my eyes. I was then led by what I suspect was a circuitous route to my captors' encampment, my progress being hurried by tugs on the halter and prods in my back from a spear or arrow, I don't know which.

20
Zoni

After about two ihors brisk walking, I was brought to a halt and the blindfold was removed.

I found myself in a wooded valley, with a number of tents, wigwams really, interspersed among the trees. I didn't have much chance to look around before being hustled into one of these wigwams. However, I did notice a number of people scurrying about the place engaged in various activities. I couldn't help but notice that all the men were either like me being led via a halter around their neck or else walking with their legs shackled by a short rope joining their ankles together. Clearly, they were not trusted to have independent movement.

"Well, you must be Edgar's son, you have his look about you. I vaguely recall you as a boy. I am Zoni and the leader of this warrior band."

The woman that was Zoni was showing her age. She must be about sixty, I thought. She was muscular and looked to be fit, but she was thin and her skin was loose and wrinkled. It was clear that she had suffered a hard life in these inhospitable regions. I cleared my throat and spoke defiantly. "Yes, I am Edwin, son of Edgar and Wena of the five villages. I have been brought here against my will and demand to know why I have been so ill-treated. I have done nothing to harm you, nor have I intruded on your people. Yet I was disturbed in my rituals and dragged here like a common criminal."

Zoni stood up and approached me. "You," she said, "you hail from the community that expelled me and my followers for no reason but that we wished to follow a warrior life-style, using the very weapon that you yourself bear. In the years since we departed into this exile, we have made our own community. Our life isn't easy but we are free. In all these years we have deliberately avoided contact with your villages and kept clear of your territory. It is only natural that we regard your arrival within our hunting grounds as a hostile act. My warriors were right to apprehend you and bring you here. You have not been mistreated, at least not yet. What happens later will depend on this meeting. Your blindfolding was purely a matter of taking proper precautions to preserve the secrecy of the location of our present encampment."

Although a couple of others were present, what followed was really a dialogue between myself and Zoni. During this I explained the concerns about Pootini and the mission I had to prevent her incursion over the moors.

Unsurprisingly, Zoni was also concerned about Pootini and had indeed already had some skirmishes with her armies. Some of the men and women that were shackled within the encampment were prisoners captured during these skirmishes. It became apparent to us both that we could become allies in our endeavours. Zoni seemed to have a relatively open mind to this, partly, it seems, because she has some genuine respect for both my parents. Her companions were dubious. They reminded her that their community relied on secrecy and, as was their normal custom, nobody who discovered them could ever be allowed to return to their erstwhile homes.

During the course of our negotiations, I learnt quite a lot of details about this warrior community. My own community, the five villages, had passed a law declaring the longbow to be for men only and banning women from taking up the weapon in the future. There are good practical reasons for this. Zoni and her band of followers had already taken up the weapon, and their continued archery would have been tolerated as long as they stopped encouraging others to join them. However, they had rebelled and refused to promise to cease further recruitment to their ranks, hence the exile.

Zoni herself, and several of her followers had sexual attraction only to women. But there were some who also enjoyed men, and even some of those who didn't would have liked a daughter. For this reason, shortly after exile, they raided other communities for men, but never from the five villages. They also took some women to employ as wet-nurses, as feeding their babies was incompatible with their lifestyle — as Zoni put it to me. They called themselves Mazons (Zoni's people) and led semi-nomadic lives hunting in the moorlands. They couldn't risk their captives escaping and thus held them in rather constricted conditions. On the other hand children born to the community were raised in freedom.

I heard much to shock me, but I understood their necessity. However, I realised I would have much to do to talk my way out of sharing the fate of their captives.

As I have said already, I was lucky that Zoni exercised the ultimate authority and was prepared to trust me. I made solemn undertakings never to divulge their whereabouts, or lead outsiders to their encampments. If I were to find myself in need of meeting them in the future, I promised to visit them alone.

We agreed on a division of effort in our mission against Pootini. My men would operate in the more southerly area while the Mazons would patrol the northern parts. Neither of us could field sufficient numbers to secure the border alone. Indeed even with the effective doubling of forces that the agreement gave us we knew we would be hard pushed to act as a credible deterrent to our enemy.

In the event, our military co-operation went well. Our weapons allowed us to operate at quite a distance from our targets, and both my men and the Mazons operated largely unseen. The Mazons would occasionally take captives. But we never did, having no facilities to deal with them. On the rare occasions when we found ourselves with a live prisoner I was able to arrange their transfer to one of the Mazon warriors. Of course this gave me some sleepless times but such are the exigencies of guerrilla warfare, and needs must.

Our campaign was successful. Pootini's soldiers became terrified of venturing into the moorlands. Too many of those that did so never returned, and their bodies were seldom found. The rumours went out that the moors were inhabited by supernatural beings who would devour the bodies and souls of any who entered their domains. We did nothing to discourage such myths. However, while we prevented Pootini from invading through the western mountains, we were able to do nothing to end her empire. There was no end game in sight and our commitment seemed to be never ending.

Then at last Shay led an army from the Theocracy and Isla Marches to tackle Pootini head on. We and the Mazons contributed to the battle by holding her Eastern flank. In the aftermath of her victory, I was in a tree close to her camp and saw her quite clearly. I don't know why, but it seemed clear to me that the time had not yet arrived for me to meet her. At that time I was not very literate but my mother had learnt something of the writing and together we had prepared a note for such an eventuality. I can't explain exactly how or why, but I had had some prescience of such a need. I attached the note to my favourite arrow and fired it to land close to her feet. She would now know of my existence, and that one phase I would seek her out.

As my mother's life ebbs away, I know that phase will soon be upon me.

21
An Illicit Correspondence

Dear Auntie Cray

I've now been sent to board at school in the regular way, not just living with Auntie Wilda as before, because Mummy says I'm getting too friendly with the workers and need to learn more ladylike ways. I miss going to watch the work and games but I suppose I was bound to be sent to board sooner or later. Anyway, this means I have time to write to you after I have written my usual letter home to Mummy.

When you were with us you told me about my sister-cousin Thar and I would really like to get to know her. Mummy won't talk to me about her because of the thing she has with her sister, and I don't want to upset her so need to keep my interest secret. You said you saw Thar quite often and also that you wished my Mummy and Auntie Thay would see the good in each other and stop their fighting. Well, as far as I can see, that's not going to happen any time soon. I don't want to have to wait until I am grown up to learn more about Thar and I don't see why we should have to be enemies just because of our Mummies' problems.

I've written a letter to Thar which I hope you will be able to give her. I really hope we can be friends and that she will want to write back to me. If she does write, can you send her letters to me at school. Nobody will object to me getting letters coming from you.

Love From

Shar

Dear Thar

I hope you don't mind me writing to you out of the blue. I've so wanted to do so ever since Auntie Cray told me about you. She said we were very alike — and when she visited us she even called me Thar by mistake a couple of times. Fortunately my Mummy wasn't around at the time. She would have had a fit!

I've got myself in lots of trouble when Mummy caught me singing a rude song that I'd learnt from some of the workers here. After a hard phase working in muddy conditions they often have a big bath together and sometimes they let me join them. They tend to sing rude songs and use language that Mummy says is unladylike, although I have heard her use some of the bad words herself when she thinks I can't hear her. Also some of the workers are men and they get teased about their naughty bits and Mummy was very shocked that I was in the bath with them all. Anyway, as a result I've been banned from wandering off too far on my own and also made to board properly at school. The good bit about that is I can write to Auntie Cray from school and enclose a letter for you.

Perhaps I should start by telling you a bit about myself. I am seven years old, the same as you, Auntie Cray says. I was born on the 17th phase of Spring in the year after Grandmother Chay and our Father died. I am big for my age, nearly 5 feet and 6 thumbs tall. My eyes are blue and my hair is fairish - not quite blonde but not really brown. Auntie Wilda says I'm doing well at schoolwork and I'm in a class for nine year olds. I enjoy reading and sums. I sometimes talk with Auntie Brinda about quite complicated sums. Mummy says I have to be a bit careful because ways of doing some difficult sums are supposed to be secret.

I forgot, you probably don't know about Aunties Wilda and Brinda. Auntie Brinda is not really my Auntie but she is a friend of Mummy's who is in charge of all of the canal works. Mummy says she is the best Engineer in the Theocracy. But Auntie Wilda is my real Auntie and yours too. She's my Goddess. She's also the Abbess of Oakbridge and so is really in charge of my school, although she doesn't do any regular teaching. She is on the Arch Convocation and does some important political stuff with Mummy that I don't understand. She is our Auntie because she is our father's half-sister. Our Grandma Valray captured Wilda's mother and father on a raid in the north, just before Wilda was born. Her father escaped, but not before he had given Valray a baby — who was our father. His name then being Arval, which is the name Mummy uses when talking about him. Auntie Wilda's mummy was made a slave at Oakbridge and worked in the kitchens but Wilda was free because she was born in the Theocracy. It's all very complicated and I don't think it's right for people to own other people—not even men. Mummy said she never used to even think about it until after our father drowned. Then she decided slavery was wrong now and she has persuaded everyone here to free all women slaves and even some of the men.

Gosh, I have been rabbiting on. I really hope you will reply to me. I do so want us to be friends — after all we are almost full sisters and we don't have to fight over an inheritance. But we need to be careful because of our Mummies. I'm not going to tell my Mummy that I am writing to you.

Love From your sister-cousin

Shar.

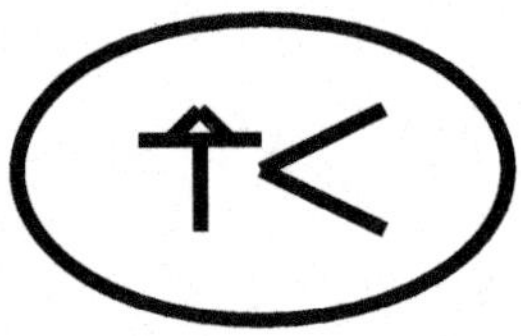

Dear Shar

How wonderful that we can write to each other and Auntie Cray has agreed to help us. I agree I don't want to tell my Mummy either. She would only get upset and then stop me somehow. I do love my Mummy very much but I so want you as a friend. Mummy never told me about you, I overheard Auntie Cray telling Mummy that she had met you and I got very cross that I hadn't even known you existed. I have spent most of my life here on the south coast. We have a very nice big house and there is lots of space for me to play but no other children to play with. I used to have an imaginary friend that I could talk to and do things with, but once I heard about you I said goodbye to her and instead have imagined you were with me to play, even though Mummy doesn't like it. Mummy really doesn't like me to be away from her. It's as if she's scared that someone will steal me or something. I started at school a bit later than most children, but I caught up with the work quickly enough as Mummy had already taught me to read and we have lots of books at home. My school is in Rivermouth, and in term time we live in Mummy's house there. After school, if Mummy is working I go to Auntie Cray's house until Mummy can come and get me or send one of her men with her carriage. I would like to ride on my pony but Mummy won't let me bring it to Rivermouth. She says it's much too dangerous for me to ride in town. Although I'm OK with the schoolwork, I'm a bit shy with the other children and don't have any special friends there. Because it's a town school we are only really there for lessons and don't have much opportunity to play together, and the other girls seem to be a bit wary of me because of Mummy being so important on the Wapentake. It seems unfair. I have become sort of friends with Clara who is Mummy's Goddess-daughter. Her mummy, Auntie Cora, was friends with my Mummy at school a long time ago. We've been to stay at her farm sometimes and Clara is kind to me, but she is three years older which seems a lot. She pushes me on her swing sometimes and has taught me how to swing my legs to work it myself. Your description of yourself does sound very like me. I'm just five phases younger than you. My birthphase is the 22nd of Spring. Auntie Cray says that our Mummies would be almost impossible to tell apart except that they do their hair differently and wear different styles and colours of clothing. She says they don't like to see each other but actually they do so every time they look in a mirror. I wish they weren't such enemies and we could be one happy family. It seems so stupid.

I can hear Mummy at the door so I'd better close now and give this to Auntie Cray.

Love from your sister-cousin

Thar

22
Politics & Progress
Dateline 18-25 Spring Year 1[17]

Matters haven't stood still while I was busy fighting Pootini. A year or so after her defeat I was invited to Fort to discuss the future relationship between the Theocracy and the Marches. In late Spring that year I took up the invitation.

As had become clear in our previous encounters, the Earl is progressive in her thinking and my reception in Fort was welcoming. The Earl has no difficulty in supporting my slave-raiding ban which she says will be of great help in improving cross-border relations. She quizzed me on the prospects for closer integration of the Marches into the Theocracy. While the Temple at Fort has some differences with the orthodoxy of Rivermouth, they are of a minor nature, and no greater than the variations that occur between the major religious centres within the Theocracy. For example they are more liberal than The Great Temple or Midborough Abbey but more conservative than

17 The rest of this book all occurs in what will much later be known as Year 1, the year following the first contact between the peoples of the planets Duplos and Geos. But as yet this contact, and the concept of numbering years is unknown on Isla. The rest of the date refers to phases and 'Selenths' (seasons). Thus 25 Spring is the 25th phase of spring 25-27 April in Earth terms. A phase is one Duplos rotation and is 3 Earth days long.

Oakbridge Abbey, so the possible objections from the Arch Convocation should be manageable.

On secular matters the Earl is very much in agreement with the consensus that we (barring Midborough) have reached in the Council of the North. For my part I welcomed her initiative and have promised to do what I can to help. I decided that my first step should be to call a meeting of the Council of the North where I'm sure I can have the Marches and Fort Temple admitted as full members. Then, with the backing of our northern coalition, I can present the case to the Superior Wapentake while Wilda can do the same in the Arch Convocation. We might have to do a bit of slight of hand to get approval but I think we can manage it, essentially by playing one off against the other. "Divide and conquer, old girl," I said. The Earl laughed and slapped me on the back.

After that I decided to call in on West Bank and I was off to Westmarch Abbey to schmooze with the West-Bankers. West Bank have always been nervous of my initiatives on slavery and have tended to line up with Midborough in opposition to my plans. However, since Pootini's war they have become more tolerant of my position. Furthermore Westmarch Abbey itself is more liberal than its secular Hundred, and enjoys good relations with its neighbours in Fort and Oakbridge.

Thus I was optimistic of gaining support for closer union with the Marches, and was not disappointed. I had hoped for some movement on the subject of slavery and actually got more than I expected, though less than I might have dreamed of. In truth, West Bank is not too bothered about the North. They rely on the Marches to keep them out of their hair. Thus they have agreed not only to accept my raiding ban but to actively support it.

Their sticking point is any thought of extending the ban to the Western Wild Lands. Apart from their economic interests in the trade, which are considerable, they also rely on the fear of punitive slave raids to help keep their wild neighbours under control. Whereas in normal times, the incidence of cross border conflict is relatively rare in the north, such problems are common in the west.

West Bank is very much a pastoral community. There are no towns but several large livestock farms which are difficult to defend. The wild lands to the west are much less productive and thus the rich cattle farms are a tempting target for raiding. The West Bank farmers need the assurance that such raids will be punished severely. Enslavement and transportation to distant lands in the South East are considered an essential deterrent.

While I remain implacably opposed to slavery as an institution, I can sympathise with the West-Bankers' plight. Obviously I've had to compromise here. I've salvaged my conscience with a formal agreement that all such raids will be punitive against actual incursions and that (at least on paper — I'm not a fool) the onward sale of captives will be to institutions or enterprises as labour, not as objects to be owned and abused by individuals.

The West Bank Hundred has also agreed to order the freeing of all female slaves of Northern origin, and also such of Western origin as are prepared to give a solemn undertaking not to return to the Western Wild Lands. They've also agreed to commute all whole-life penal servitude sentences to a fixed term, and in future only use fixed term sentences in their penal code, bringing them into line with most of the Northern Wapentakes. Finally, while they would not force anyone to emancipate their men, they will fall into line with most other Northern Wapentakes and allow for the emancipation of men within their Hundred and to respect the rights of free men from other parts of the Theocracy.

In all reason, I could not have asked for more. Apart from the fudge over the Western Wild lands, this package is actually rather more than enacted by some of our other constituencies.

23
Council of the North in Knot
Dateline 26-28 Summer

I now have a good set of objectives for the up-coming Council of the North. These will be:

a. Permanent admission of the Isla Marches and Fort Temple as full members of the Council of the North with complete open borders between the Marches and its Theocracy neighbours.

b. To propose and support motions in the Superior Wapentake and Arch Convocation to unify the Isla Marches with the Theocracy with consequent enlargement of these two bodies to include a Lay representative from the Marches and the Chief Priestess of Fort Temple respectively.

c. To rationalise the various rules concerning slavery along the lines agreed with West Bank. Thus all Hundreds and Wapentakes in the North would have to comply with the following:

(i) Raiding parties to the North to be banned from passing through the region, with any captured slave, male or female, to be returned to their homes at the expense of the raiders.

(ii) All non-convict female slaves to be freed. Northerners to be allowed to return across the border if they so wish but Westerners to be required to undertake to remain within the Theocracy. Former owners to be required to offer employment where practicable.

(iii) Owners of male slaves to be entitled (and encouraged) to give them their freedom as for females.

(iv) The freedom of such emancipated males to be recognised throughout the region with no threat of re-enslavement or deportation to regions outside the jurisdiction of this Council.

(v) Punitive slavery for those convicted of crimes to be re-termed as penal servitude with official supervision from the lay or temple authorities, rather than being under private ownership. The servitude being for labour only. For example someone serving such a sentence would be entitled to refuse demands for sex.

(vi) All future penal servitude to be for a fixed term as determined by the court on conviction. Any existing whole-life sentences to be reviewed and replaced by a fixed term. The review should start with those who have already served the longest times.

(vi) A propos the above. All penal slaves who have already served more than five years must have their sentence reviewed within one year, and all others within two years.

d. The system of passports for the control of immigration and cross-border movement to be extended throughout the region. A new service to be headquartered in Knot-on-Lesser to be established to oversee the development of this system. For males, passports should include their status as free or enslaved, with details of the owner for the latter. For children, the details of their parent or guardian should be included.

It was well into the Summer before I could get all the various representatives together for the Council of the North but eventually I set off from Elmhouse for Knot for the meeting. Ever since I opened the link to the Second River, Knot has prospered.

As I write, the population has risen to over 2048 and is still growing. I am no longer a pariah in the town but am much feted by the Town Council and the College alike.

We held our meeting in a brand new hall in the Isla-of-the-Knotted-Bends College. They have a new Chief Priestess who is much more liberal than her predecessor and is fast developing their educational mission. They are no longer limiting their teaching to training priestesses, but are evolving a much wider curriculum taking students between the ages of 16 and 18 from a lay background with no intention of becoming priestesses or theologians. I am very impressed by what they have achieved in a short time. Maybe Shar should complete her education there. Maybe even one phase they might educate boys alongside the girls. However, that is a step too far for the time being.

The Council went very smoothly. No doubt this was assisted by Midborough's decision to boycott the meeting.

Obviously, there was heated discussion over points of detail, but my intentions were understood and supported. With only minor amendments by way of clarification and guidance to the courts and others to be involved in enforcement, all my objectives were met.

Getting West Bank onside earlier had been crucial. Not only did they not cause me any trouble, but their acceptance of the slavery measures served as a powerful example to others that might have remained uncertain. Everything passed unanimously and all the representatives to the Superior Wapentake and Arch Convocation have been mandated to support our line in their respective bodies.

In legal terms this mandate (and the other agreements reached) also apply to Midborough, but in practise I am well aware that they will not comply. On the other hand they will look very silly and get no sympathy from any wavering representatives from the South.

Immediately following the Council, Wilda and I set out for Rivermouth. Well not quite immediately. We enjoyed or endured a round of civic receptions first. Knot was doing what it could to make itself the permanent home of the council. Something else that will enrage Midborough once the present crisis is over.

And we didn't travel directly. I needed to attend to some of my other interests first.

Dateline: 30 Summer

First stop was a side trip to Steele. We spent a couple of phases staying in my house outside Barton, but my business was in Steele. Progress with weapons is coming on. We have four refurbished catapults captured from Pootini. The others having been stripped for parts. In addition we also have four more of an improved design. These are fully operational and yet two more are under construction. These six catapults are modified from the original designs as used by Pootini's forces at Fort. The new designs can take heavier loads and be worked more quickly, accurately and over a longer range. The new firing rate is pretty well double that achieved by Pootini, over one and a half times the range and with bigger loads. I was shown a stockpile of rocks and this was supplemented by some iron balls about a foot in diameter. These will be incredibly destructive against walled fortifications or buildings. I can only imagine the panic if one of these balls lands on a packed phalanx.

"What about transporting them to a battlefield", I asked.

"Ah!" replied the blacksmith, "See here."

He lead me to a long shed. Inside was a low flat trailer standing on iron rails. "We manhandle the engine on to this trailer. Then two shire horses can pull it along the rails which lead to the canal jetty. There we have a specially constructed boat which also has a railway to enable us to load the engine on it. Then as long as your battlefield is on the waterway system, we're done. At the other end, it will be more laborious if you don't have the infrastructure but at least we have portable rails to allow us to disembark the engine. Moving it by road will require changing the wheels and then a team of about six horses can manage it."

The completion of stockpiles of other armaments have also proceeded well. We have sixteen crossbows, enormous numbers of swords, pike-heads, shields and knives as well as steel helmets and chain mail. On top of that he had completed head and shoulder armour for thirty two horses.

We are ready. I can field a larger, better-equipped and more disciplined army that has ever been seen in History. Thay is toast. I gave the order to start shipping the hardware to Midborough.

Dateline: 2-8 Autumn

Our next port of call was Midborough, or rather the terminus of our canal works a few hundred strides north-east of the town, but still within the jurisdiction of Midborough Rural. This is the first time I have been able to undertake the journey entirely by boat. The final works had been completed and the water let in to the last section of canal while we were busy in Knot.

I was met by Brinda. She was supervising the laying of rails from a specially constructed wharf in readiness for the arrival of the catapults.

I brought her up to date with the Council meeting and what I had seen in Steele, although she was well aware of the latter.

"I don't think it will be long now," I said. "We've got full agreement on all my objectives and I can't see Thay rolling over for me to tickle her tummy."

Brinda scratched her chin and spoke slowly and deliberately. "I don't know about Thay, she is still being reclusive and, I'm told, spending most of her time on her estate with her daughter. She only comes to Rivermouth for the school term and then works mainly on her business affairs. Maybe the threat of our connection to the Great River will be her trigger. It's Craya that you need to watch, her and that ex-surgeon dripping poisonous words into her ear. I know for a fact that Cray is unhappy about the way things are developing."

"Yeah, well Cray is always trying to broker peace between us so she won't like her daughter stoking the fire. It's a pity it wasn't Craya that drowned all those years ago. Crayza was ever my friend, and I loved her too."

"Is that so? However, it's Craya you are facing. She's training quite any army in the fields outside Honeyfield. She has the full Honeyfield and Cattlebridge militias under her direct command and has supplementary forces contributed by Rivermouth, Mid-River and Estuary. I've also heard that there are other units committed from the remaining South-Eastern Hundreds."

"If it's Craya we face, it will be a breeze, like taking candy from a baby." She's a coward herself and has none of the qualities needed to command a fighting army. We will outnumber her, out-equip her and out-manoeuvre her. If we have to face Thay, we will have a fight on our hands despite our material advantages, but dealing with Craya is child's play. We could leave it to Shar!"

"Who you are neglecting terribly."

"Yes, don't think I don't know it. I'm a terrible mother as I have been brought to realise through recent events. I vow that I will make it up to her when this war is over."

"This undeclared war. I'm committed to you, Shay, but I'm not entirely comfortable about our chosen path."

"It is inevitable and we must make preparations. I want us to tour the area now to establish our positions for the forthcoming battle for Midborough."

Brinda, Wilda and I then rode around the neighbourhood where I pointed out the various defensive features we would exploit.

"As I see it our only real danger now is if Midborough were to risk a pre-emptive strike while we are still weak on the ground. However, I don't think they'll do that because they will see the risks to themselves without perceiving the danger of us building up our strength. Most of our forces are currently encamped on either side of the Lesser outside Knot, and our material is still stockpiled in Steele. I have given orders to start moving the latter, mainly to our encampments outside Knot but with the heavier weaponry to continue on here. I want you to prepare to accept the first wave of 256 troops that will give you sufficient force to resist any attempt to break out of Midborough. The rest of our army should then follow on later."

"And when do you expect that to be?", queried Brinda.

"The next step is for Wilda and me to do our business in Rivermouth. I will then return here and when I arrive will be time to order up the main force. Wilda will travel to Elmhouse and fetch Shar and Valray. I don't want them left where they might be taken hostage. I can defend them better here."

Wilda and Brinda both shook their heads. They were naturally concerned about bringing a child to a battlefield. I had to jolly them up. "Don't look so glum, Shar will be safe enough with us. We will certainly defeat Midborough and any army led by Craya. The worst that can happen is that Thay will take charge and even then our weapons, numbers and fighting tactics will ensure victory."

"And if you're wrong?"

"I'm not, the pikes alone will win it for us. In any case, Thay will destroy me but she won't harm Shar. Craya would, but Craya won't win."

We spent several phases planning our deployment to the East of Midborough. This would mean crossing the boundary from Midborough Rural in order to lay rails to facilitate bringing our catapults within range of the North and East gates to the walled town. Brinda would start the works just as soon as the extra 256 soldiers arrived from Knot. Wilda and I then took an unusual route to Rivermouth. We rode to the new canal terminus to the South of Midborough and travelled by boat along its twenty-three imile length through Midborough Rural and Central to the current end of works just short of the Cattlebridge boundary. Our horses were walked alongside by a patrol of soldiers. This was the first time I had been on this new section of canal, just awaiting the outcome of the forthcoming fighting before making the final connections through Midborough and Cattlebridge to link to the Great River.

24
Omens & Portents

Dateline: 8 Autumn

I don't know when it started, but for some time now, people have noticed strange new stars in the eastern sky. The superstitious have been claiming that these are portents of things to come. The Goddess will return. Maybe Nepa will finally inundate the island. Or perhaps Lana or Isla will triumph and return to reclaim all the land and close the strait, or that we will all perish in a calamitous war. Anyway, we are called to repent and renew our faith in the Goddess and follow her ways as of old.

What a load of tosh. Goddesses are a myth to keep the peasants in their place and allow us, the natural rulers, to continue to enjoy our privileged existence. I know I benefit personally. I must now be the richest woman in all of Isla, but that doesn't mean that the system is right. I can't explain the new stars or lights in the sky but I'm sure that portents and omens and Goddesses have nothing to do with the case.

On the other hand war is now inevitable. Midborough is causing me some major headaches and I'm going to have to intervene militarily which is surely bound to provoke a response from my sister down in Rivermouth. But stars foretelling catastrophe! No way.

More intriguing than the lights in the sky are the strange birds. I've not noticed any in Elmhouse or in the Northlands, but in the last few periods since late Summer, they have been prevalent around Barton and the Lesser delta region, and also around our canal works outside Midborough.

These birds often seem to hover near our works just out of reach and seem to take an unusual interest in what we are doing. One even entered some of the work sheds in Steele and appeared to be watching activities, almost as if they were spying on us. The chief blacksmith nearly caught it, but unfortunately it got away, flying at an incredible speed to do so.

Of course, there have always been birds flying around but these do seem different. Usually we just see birds flying past or obviously foraging, nest building etcetera. We don't usually see them looking like they are watching us, yet it seems that we are now being watched even from high above.

The superstitious think these birds are also omens, or messengers or even manifestations of the Goddesses. Some of the more fanciful stories going round just beggar belief. Yet even I have to accept that they are strange. And it's not just here. Travellers from the south are also telling similar tales with claims that the birds are definitely coming across the strait from the continent. We have always been told that the continent is uninhabited, but it is obvious that birds do fly across the strait. After all, it can't be very wide. I guess just a few imiles along the narrow stretch near Thay's house.

Apart from their apparent interest in our goings-on, the other strange thing about them is the sort of whirring noise that they make, this is quite unlike any normal birds. It is all very puzzling. Audreeda has a theory that they are exhibiting intelligence and are gathering information about us. Maybe, she says, there is other intelligent life on the continent and they are directing these birds in preparation for crossing over here. To me this seems too fanciful a notion to entertain, but I do have a great deal of respect for Audreeda's intellect and perhaps I shouldn't be too ready to dismiss her speculations.

I've also talked to Brinda about the phenomena and she is as puzzled as I am. She has seen some of the birds from quite close up as they have taken quite an interest in the canals, seemingly inspecting the various constructions quite closely. One attempt to catch one ended up with Brinda falling headlong into a lock. Fortunately it was full at the time and she took no hurt. Just suffered a soaking and some sarcastic comments from the workforce.

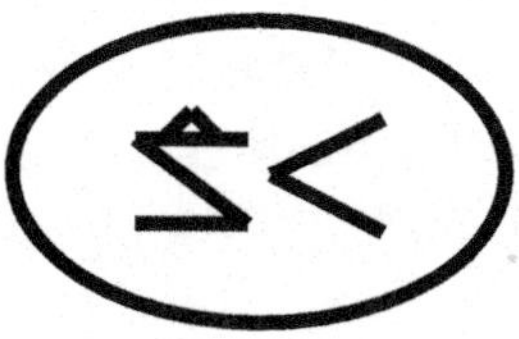

Dear Thar

Thank-you so much for your reply to my letter. I'm really happy that we are going to be friends, despite our Mummies. I'm quite envious of you spending so much time with your Mummy. Mine is always so busy that she leaves me very much to my own devices, and the care of others. It's not that I am neglected. Grandma Valray spends lots of time with me and I have lots of fun around her farm and down by the river. Then when I'm at home Daubey, that's Mummy's housekeeper, and the other staff go to a lot of trouble to keep me amused as well as feeding me goodies like cakes and tarts and stuff. Even at school, when not in lessons, Auntie Wilda goes out of her way to be kind to me, even though she has all sorts of important things to attend to in the Abbey. But somehow time with Mummy is different and I love it when she has the time to do things with me, and not be distracted by her work and other cares.

Last year she was away for ages fighting a war with Pootini to help the people from the Isla Marches. I didn't really understand what was happening, and people kept pretending that nothing was amiss, but I could tell they were worried, and now I know more about how dangerous war is and that Mummy might have been killed or badly hurt.

Now she seems to be worrying about these strange birds that everyone's talking about. She's asked me to look out for them and tell her if I see any behaving strangely. Well, I haven't seen any here in Elmhouse or in Oakbridge. It sounds like it's all happening further East and South. Have you heard anything about them, or even better, have you seen any? It seems unfair that they are interested in everyone else but not us here in the north-west!

Well, I suppose I'd better stop and get on with my sums prep which I've sort of got bored with. I wish they'd give me more interesting sums, these additions and subtractions I've got to do are too easy and then I lose interest and make silly mistakes which makes the stupid priestess think I don't understand, when actually I understand perfectly — I'm just BORED.

Love From Shar (Please give my love to Auntie Cray)

Twin Worlds III

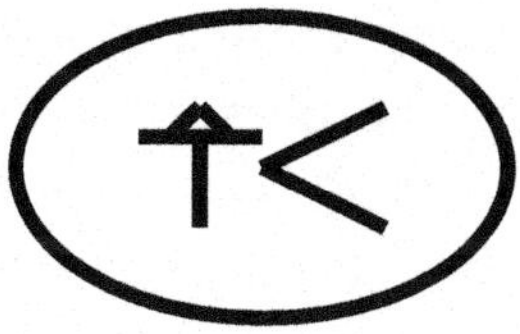

Dear Shar,

Gosh, I can't think what it's like to be left to my own devices. Mummy doesn't like me to go out of her sight. She had one of the men make me a lovely swing in a big tree next to the house and I spend a lot of time on it, but she can see me through her library window which her desk faces so she can watch over me while she does whatever it is she does with various papers. Even when I'm at Auntie Cray's, Mummy insists I'm never left alone and a footman accompanies me everywhere when we're in Rivermouth. Even here, I'm only allowed to ride with a groom present. I know it's because Mummy loves me so much, but that doesn't stop it being suffocating and irritating. I'd love to be able to run around a farm and mix with ordinary workers. I never hear bad words, except when Mummy thinks I'm not listening and is vexed with something your Mummy or that cripple who lives with Auntie Craya has done. I'd like to know songs with rude words like you do!

You ask about the birds. Well I see them quite a lot. They come from across the strait, and sometimes they hover quite close to me, but just out of my reach. It seems like they want to be friends with me but are too scared to actually come to my hand. They make a slight whirring noise when they fly or hover but they don't cheep or sing. Also I've never seen them try to catch a worm or act quite like normal birds.

In Rivermouth, one came very close to Auntie Cray and gave her a fright. She almost caught it and her hat fell off. It must have been quite funny to see. You might not know, but Auntie Cray is actually the most important person in the Theocracy. She is President of the Council as well as being the Speaker of the Superior Wapentake. It's beneath her dignity to be seen chasing a bird and losing her hat in the street! When I heard about it I split my sides laughing as I tried to imagine the scene. Mummy got quite cross and told me that I should show more respect. But she didn't use any rude words to me, like I'm sure most people would. It's unfair—after all I do go to school so I hear things in the playground and it can be embarrassing when you pretend to know what the other girls are saying but you don't because your Mummy tries to hide things from you.

Just thinking about something you said in your first letter. My Mummy would go ballistic if she discovered me joining grown-ups in a bath. I don't think anyone except Mummy and Aunties Cray and Craya have ever seen me undressed. Oh, and Auntie Cora and Clara when Clara and I had a bath together when we had got muddy playing in her farmyard. And I've NEVER seen a man or boy undressed. What are they like. Is is true that they have an extra finger between their legs which they use to scratch women who have an itch? That's what one of the girls at school said, but I don't know whether to believe her. I just pretended to know all about these things, but I don't and I daren't ask Mummy or Auntie Cray. But if you've been in a bath with men perhaps you do know the truth and can tell me.

Love from your sister-cousin Thar

25

An unexpected Ally

Dateline 18-19 Autumn

There was a knock on my door. A priestess poked her head round. "There are two men here who are asking to see you. Shall I let them in?"

I wasn't expecting anyone but maybe my daughter had sent them with a message. She's a very important person and is currently accompanying Lady Shay on some political business that I don't really understand, but until whatever it is is resolved, I have to be patient. Then my daughter will take me to my old home in the North to see my sister and my daughter's father. Perhaps this is news of when we can set out.

"Yes, send them in," I called.

I would have known him anywhere. Unless he was a ghost, the young man before me was the image of my Edgar, a bit older than when I had last seen him. He also had the look of Arval whom I had last seen as an 18 year old entering the service of Lady Chay. I didn't recognise his companion. Both men were tall and armed with a bow of length equal to their height, a quiver full of arrows and a sword at their side.

Tears came to my eyes. "You must be Edgar's son, you are the image of him. What brings you to see me after all these years?"

He answered me in an accent I remembered from long ago. "I am indeed Edgar's son by your sister Wena. I hice Edwin and was born thirty-two and seven years ago, after you had been captured. I promised my mother that I would seek you out. I also wish for a meeting with the Lady Shay and I am told you might be able to direct me to her."

I was all a-fluster. I rushed to him and hugged him close. "Then you are my nephew and brother-cousin to my daughter Wilda. She is away with Lady Shay at the moment. But first, how are my family, Edgar and dear Wena? I am so pleased he found consolation with her. We would have shared him if I hadn't been captured and you and Wilda would have grown up together."

"I'm sorry to have to tell you that both my parents are no longer with us. Edgar died just over a year ago after the war with Pootini. Wena and I were with him at the end. Wena became ill towards the end of last summer selenth and died not long after new year. While she lived I would not leave her. But now I have come south to fulfil my destiny."

My tears fell more rapidly. "I had so hoped to be reunited with them. My home is here now, but since Lady Shay opened the borders I planned to return for a visit. Wilda was going to take me once the current crisis in the Theocracy is resolved. Lady Shay has banned the slave trade, but has to suppress the opposition from the southern part of the Theocracy before it is completely safe for us to travel."

Edwin then told me that he knew about the slave trading ban which was how he and his companion had been able to come here openly, using the new-fangled passports. He has a band of bowmen waiting just north of the border and he plans to offer his services to Lady Shay for the battle that he is sure is to come.

I am a bit fearful about that. I hadn't realised that things had gone so far. No wonder Wilda was insistent on delaying our journey north. I lead a sheltered life here and Wilda is very protective of me.

I got the duty priestess to arrange food and accommodation for my guests. It helps when your daughter is the Abbess! I then had a message sent to Elmhouse and in the morrow we would set off there to find out more about Wilda and Lady Shay's whereabouts. I don't ride but there are always boats from Oakbridge going up the Street River. I would have no difficulty getting passage.

In the event I didn't go with them. Edwin and I had sat up late talking about family history, with me reminiscing my early life in the wild lands and describing my life and situation at Oakbridge. Apart from missing Wena and Edgar, I was able to assure him that my life was comfortable and happy. Also that I was now completely free, remaining at Oakbridge by choice. Edwin, in his turn gave me news of my homeland. I learnt how Edgar had brought the five villages together in alliance. How he had been made war leader and invented the longbow that Edwin himself has perfected.

He has dedicated himself to the service of a Goddess he encountered in a vision high in the moorlands. I'm not at all sure about this sort of religion. I know I'm part of a religious order myself, but we are so much more pragmatic about the Goddesses and a lot of the ritual and stuff is purely a matter of tradition and an attempt to explain our place in the world through metaphor. Or so Wilda tells me, and she should know, having studied these things deeply. However, I wish him luck and good fortune in his pursuit and hope he finds peace in his troubled mind.

I also learnt of Zoni's rebellion and exile. I knew her as a child and teenager. She was always a bit peculiar, brutal to a fault with a streak of cruelty. Nevertheless, I was shocked at some of the things Edwin told me about the Mazon society. It seems to me that it was all very well them being helpful allies in keeping Pootini at bay, but their treatment of captives appalled me. Nobody here keeps slaves permanently shackled; and I've never heard of women being forced to get pregnant in order to serve as a wet nurse for someone else's child. Nor have I heard of men being castrated when no longer wanted for sex and then being worked to death in the most dreadful conditions. I think we do need an expedition to sort them out; but no doubt Shay's new laws will forbid it.

Anyway I said my farewells to Edwin and his companion at the quayside as they set off for Elmhouse. They will be expected and I'm sure will be helped to find Lady Shay. At a personal level I am excited that Edwin will be able to meet his sister-cousin and I hope they will become close friends.

26
Rivermouth 2

Dateline: 10 - 18 Autumn

Wilda and I arrived at my apartment in Rivermouth late in the tenth phase of Autumn. It was a cold phase, but we were expected and my caretaker had lit a fire and ensured everything was comfortable for us. We were both tired from the journey and from having had quite an exhausting few phases in our encampment outside Midborough.

While I was making battlefield preparations with Brinda and some of my senior officers, Wilda had been talking to the workforce/troops attending to their spiritual needs and assuring them of the rightness of our cause in the eyes of the Goddess. The Great Temple at Rivermouth had got it wrong, she told the soldiers. Men might be the weaker sex, but firstly, that was no excuse to enslave them, and secondly, the Goddesses were so far above us mere mortals that in their eyes women and men are equal. Equal but different, each with their own part to play in the Goddess's great plan. Both are needed to continue the human race, and are equally important in doing so. Women had to be stronger to cope with the burden of childbirth, but were compensated through their greater pleasure from sex and the joy of their young children. Among the changes we should be bringing about through the emancipation of men should be the enhancement of male/female relations and mutual respect and the encouragement of male bonding with their children.

It was interesting to me that Wilda appeared to borrow some of her ideas from the monotheistic insights from Hild that I had brought back from my journeys in the north. I also noticed that Wilda tends to speak of the Goddess in the singular, and pays scant attention to the pantheon. I have to say that her theology has developed quite a long way from traditional doctrine and was well received by her auditors, both male and female.

Thus we stayed up for no more than a simple supper before seeking our beds for a long and refreshing sleep before facing the rigours of the Rivermouth political scene.

My first call was on Cray, now both the Speaker of the Superior Wapentake and President of the Council of the Theocracy.

I have no intention of asking the Wapentake to approve any of my new laws. I regard those as none of their business, and I will merely present them as a fait accompli and inform them of the implications for the regions of Isla outside the jurisdiction of the Council of the North. My formal business is to get recognition of the integration of the Isla Marches into the Theocracy through inviting their representatives to join the ruling institutions. Namely the SW itself and the Arch Convocation.

While I was seeing Cray, Wilda was meeting the leading clerics at the Great Temple. I mentioned this to Cray, and presented it as a done deal that Wilda was merely making the final arrangements for the Temple of Isla in Marsh at Fort to join the AC.

Cray does not enjoy very good relations with the Temple. Three years previously, they had pushed their opposition to her presidency as far as they could. They had finally to back down when faced by force majeure and the prospect of a serious rift between the two houses. As an aside, that is one of the few occasions when Thay and I were on the same side in a political show-down.

It is no secret that Cray wants to reduce the power of the temples. Again, this is a policy that both Thay and I support. However, I'm not above exploiting this for my own ends. In this case using the fear of an extra seat in the AC to persuade Cray to support enlargement of the SW to include the Isla Marches. Wilda was using the same tactics on the leaders of the two Rivermouth Temples, with similar success.

The formal meetings turned out as well as to be expected. The SW and AC both met on the nineteenth of Autumn and accepted our proposals for the inclusion of the Marches. In the SW only Midborough and Craya for Honeyfield voted against. Thay abstained along with her neighbour and close ally, the representative for South Coast East, and the representative for South Coast West who had made a rather rambling speech expressing concerns about the implications for her neighbouring regime in West Isla, but accepting that the constituencies bordering the Marches (West Bank, Oakbridge and Borders) were the experts on relations with the Marches. Wilda reported that the Temples were generally pleased to welcome Fort and the debate in the AC had been uncontroversial. The Council meeting the next phase merely rubber stamped the deals.

After that I dropped by bombshell. As I said, I wasn't asking for approval, merely presenting the position of the Northern Wapentakes as approved unanimously by those present in the Council of the North. The Mayor of Midborough was fuming. She realised that her boycott of the earlier meeting had backfired on her with not one northern Wapentake or Temple resisting or even abstaining. It made her look foolish, thereby undermining her position, even with those who held her views on slavery and the rights (or not!) of men. She declared that the raiding ban did not extend to Midborough and that raiding parties would be welcomed there. Similarly she announced that unowned men would not be recognised in her town. Even Thay laughed and shook her head.

But that was only a minor triumph. The real opposition was not silenced by the humiliation of Midborough. Leading the charge in expressing their anger was Craya. Thay sat quietly beside her and let her make the running. Craya declared the so-called Council of the North to be an unauthorised body with no constitutional power. As such it did not have the authority to impose the ban or to legislate for male freedom from female ownership. Accordingly she herself would lead a party to cross into the Wild Lands and take some slaves to demonstrate clearly that the ban had no force. Furthermore since, she claimed, the emancipation of men would challenge the whole fabric of society in the Theocracy she was sure that the Honeyfield Hundred would back her in legislating for the arrest and sale of any so-called free man caught in their jurisdiction. She then recommended all Wapentakes and Hundreds to legislate on similar lines.

I countered her complaint about the Council of the North by sidestepping the issue as irrelevant. Each constituent Wapentake had the legal right to enact the legislation to enforce both the trading ban and to enable emancipation. That had been done throughout the northern constituencies and any raiding party would be turned back. If such a party wished to cross into the northern wild lands, they would have to learn how to fly, or risk a sea voyage.

By this point the council discipline had broken down completely with my supporters banging tables and cheering me on, while opponents leapt to their feet and shook their fists at us, as Cray banged away on her gavel trying to restore order. "Order, order!", she cried but the council ignored her and broke up in pandemonium. Interestingly both Thay and I exhorted our respective followers to calm down and refrain from violence.

Well, I didn't want the fighting to start here in the council chamber. I had achieved what I wanted. Craya, at least, had taken the bait, even if Thay was showing a proper degree of restraint.

We left Rivermouth the following phase. I didn't want to face Cray at this juncture. I returned on horseback to our camp outside Midborough. I avoided the river and main road through Cattlebridge but instead rode through the sparsely populated Central countryside. Wilda accompanied me for the first part of the journey. We parted after about 48 imiles as she headed due west to Elmhouse to pick up Shar.

Our departure had not been entirely without incident. Someone (I suspect Craya) had whipped up a rent-a-crowd mob to demonstrate outside my apartment block. They were making lots of noise and waving placards saying things like 'Hands off our men', 'Down with Shay' and 'Split the traitor'. There was even one to make me laugh: 'Shay doesn't (give a) fuck'. It could have got quite ugly, but fortunately someone (I credit Cray) had called out the watch to keep the protesters away from the house and we were able to mount our horses and make our escape with the sounds of the crowd fading as we put distance between us and them.

27
Thay Wakes

Dateline: 21 Autumn

I don't hate Shay. I just don't want to see her or have anything to do with her. As far as I'm concerned, as long as she stays up North, I don't really care what she does. It's true that Arthay was special, and absolutely the equal of any woman. In practical terms he was pretty free when he was with me, and had it not been for the mess with Shay after Mum died, I'm sure we would now be living together on equal terms.

In a sense I'm glad to see that Shay also appreciates how special he was, but I do feel she is over the top in her reactions, ascribing to all men the status that I feel belonged to Arthay alone. OK, it isn't easy to justify slave-raiding in the wild lands. The people there may be barbarians, but that isn't really an excuse for us to assume ladyship over them, just because of myths promulgated by the Temples. So I guess I'm sort of with Shay, at least as far as discouraging non-punitive raiding. I also concede completely that it is a duty for women to treat their men well and fairly. But to go to the extreme of allowing men to live totally independently of women seems to go too far. Men are weaker and intellectually inferior. That is demonstrable fact. Arthay was just different. The exception that proves the rule. Policy and law cannot be moulded to suit one particular individual. Why doesn't Shay see that? I may not like her, but I do accept that she isn't stupid. I can't see how overturning centuries of tradition, not to mention smashing the natural order upon which all civilised society is based, will help either men or women.

I just want to live quietly on my estate, taking care of Thar and keeping Arthay alive in my heart. Every phase when I'm home I walk to the spot where he went over the cliff. I've set up a bench there and every Autumn I plant bulbs: snowdrops for winter, daffodils for spring and bluebells and tulips for later. I sit on his bench and think of him, losing myself in dreams of the three of us enjoying a happy family life. He would be as proud of HIS daughter as I am. There, I've said it. Thar is not just my daughter as society would dictate. She is equally his. I neither know nor care about other fathers. But my Arthay would have been a real parent who knew and loved his child. I can't let go of him or of my grief. If only I could put all the blame on Shay, but I can't. I played my part and am as consumed by guilt as by grief.

Yet I know I have other responsibilities. As bloody Cray keeps reminding me. I have a position to maintain; and with wealth and power comes responsibility and duty. And it's about time I woke up to mine. Well, yesterphase's performance in the Council must be the trigger to wake me up. I'm not at all sure that Craya is right to provoke Shay's reaction by launching her raiding party, but at least in public, I must support her. Craya has always been my closest ally. Even when we were children. She has her weaknesses, I know that only too well, but she has spent her whole life devoted to me and my interests. Her loyalty must not go unheeded or unrewarded.

The problem is that she sees things too much in black and white. She means well but her intellect is not strong. Her mind has also been poisoned by that blasted surgeon. How I wish I had never set eyes on her. She absolutely hates Shay — I have to concede, with good reason. But the constant drip of her poison into Craya's ear has caused the hatred to infect her too. Craya's attitude to Shay is no longer merely a reflection of my own; the support of a loyal friend and cousin. Now the hatred kindled in her heart colours all her actions and clouds her judgement so much that she sees only bad in all that Shay says or does.

I'm staying locked in my house tophase, and keeping Thar safely indoors too. No school for her. Against all good sense, Craya has organised a mass demonstration outside Shay's block. I'm very concerned that it could result in a riot that could spread right across Rivermouth. I was so worried after yesterphase's meeting when Craya told me of her intention that I alerted Cray to the danger. The last thing Cray wants is for her daughter to be embroiled in a riot and she promised to ensure there will be a strong contingent of the watch present to head off any problem, and allow Shay to leave Rivermouth to return to her own domain.

That leaves me assured for now, but Craya's planned raid still leaves me nervous. It's true that she commands a large and powerful army. Her Honeyfield and Cattlebridge troops alone should be sufficient to overcome any opposition. In addition to them I have called on significant forces from my own resources. Thus she will be reinforced by strong levees from Chalcliff, SE Coast and Downs, as well as smaller levees from several others. Her plan is for all these troops to muster in Cattlebridge whence they will set off. Initially, she expects to make for Midborough, where she can be sure of a good welcome, and maybe even further troops to swell her ranks. Hers will be no ordinary raiding party of fewer than fifty or so, enough to overcome any barbarian resistance. Her force will be a veritable army, the like and strength of which has not been seen before in the history of the Theocracy. Even in the civil war between Wapentake and Temples, the largest deployed armies never exceeded 512 women.

I can't imagine Shay being able to resist her march north. Yet I have a nagging feeling that this reaction by Craya is just what she wants. And since, as I said earlier, she is no fool, I'm sure she has a plan and that much bloodshed will ensue.

I know that Cray, too is similarly fearful of genuine war breaking out. She has tried to dissuade her daughter, but to no avail. Craya is determined to arraign Shay for treason. I, and Cray, suppose that Shay is indeed technically guilty. If rumours are in any way correct, she has been trading in metal goods and technology with the wild lands and giving men military training. Both these acts are illegal, and treasonable if carried out on a large scale.

Cray has also made both Craya and myself promise that whatever fate we have in store for Shay herself, that Shar will be protected and left unharmed. She was so adamant that she told Craya that she would be disinherited if she allowed any harm to come to Shar. I may be conflicted where Shay is concerned but I think I applaud Cray's stance. I'm sure she would do what she could to protect Thar if the situation were reversed.

Twin Worlds III

Dateline: 22 Autumn

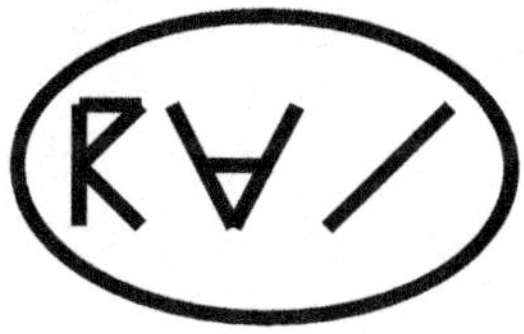

That council meeting was just too much. Shay makes my blood boil. At least Thay seems to have woken up to the danger at last. Even so, in private, she tried to talk me out of my plan to challenge Shay's nonsensical ban, which that woman has neither the right nor the power to enforce. As I said to Thay. What could possibly go wrong? My army is unmatched in History. We'll march north, resting in Midborough on the way, before we continue through Knot into the wild lands. There we'll pick up a few barbarians and march back south again. Sure, Shay may try to persuade us to turn back. But really she hasn't a chance. If she leaves us alone, her ban will be seen for what it is, mere political posturing. If she dares fight, we will smash her and bring her back in chains as the traitor she undoubtedly is.

As I expected, Mum also tried to dissuade me. She still has a soft spot for Shay and forced me on pain of disinheritance to guarantee to leave Shar unharmed. Thay was no help in that, so I reluctantly agreed, with all the potential that will have to nurture a scorpion in our bosom.[18]

Morrowphase I will lead my Honeyfield militia to Cattlebridge where we shall meet up with further levees from across the South of the Theocracy. I expect to lead at least a townfull of soldiers in my march north.

---

18 There are no snakes on Duplos, at least not on Isla or the continental lands known to humans - so Craya could not have use the term 'viper' here, but in English idiom, that's what she meant.

Cattlebridge: Dateline: 26 Autumn

Here I am, standing on a dais raised in the centre of Cattlebridge market place. Beside me are the Mayor of Cattlebridge, my two most senior officers and the High Mistress of Cattlebridge College. Standing in the square are the more than 1024 soldiers of my army and a crowd of local civilians.

I won't say my address was stirring, I acknowledge I am not a great orator. It would have been much better if Thay had been speaking; but she declined to come, preferring to manage the political scene in Rivermouth. I have to say I am disappointed in Rivermouth. Just 64 soldiers from the two town hundreds have shown up to join my muster. I blame my mother who is far too powerful an influence there, and still sitting on the fence, so to speak. I hope it gives her an uncomfortable fanny. On the other hand, Thay has given strong military support with large contingents from the south-east arriving yesterphase.

In any event, my army is keen and well-prepared. I was able to assure the assembled troops of the rightness of our cause and the lack of any credible alternative. We have reached a 'do or die' moment. Either we capitulate to Shay's demands and see our men taken from us and our land over-run with barbarians, or we take a stand now to protect our civilisation and freedom. I described Shay's treasonous acts: arming and training men and trading in embargoed goods and forbidden knowledge with the barbarian hordes. Finally I expounded on our relative strength: a disciplined army of women against a rag-tag rabble force dominated by men and barbarians. I confessed I didn't know the numbers of the enemy, whether larger or smaller than our own, but I assured them that our superiority in discipline and tactics would guarantee us victory against any troops that Shay could throw against us. Finally I vowed to split Shay personally, not with an axe as might befit a more honourable traitor, but with a saw to maximise the pain of punishment. I waved such a saw high in the air to the cheers of my assembled soldiers.

28

Outside Midborough

Dateline: 22 Autumn

I hadn't been back long and was getting an update from Brinda when an arrow thudded into a tree next to me. I was somewhat startled, but surely this could only be from my erstwhile ally against Pootini. I looked in the direction from whence it came but couldn't see anyone.

Brinda went up to the tree and tugged at the arrow to little avail. "There's a letter attached here", she announced.

"Let me help." Together we managed to extract the arrow. Brinda handed me the letter. "Hmm", she observed the arrowhead is metal, iron I think. Who is making iron arrowheads in the Northlands?"

"Interesting", I responded. "But this letter. I would recognise the messy handwriting anywhere. As untidy as ever, written much too hurriedly. Wilda would give her a well-deserved telling off. Here have a look."

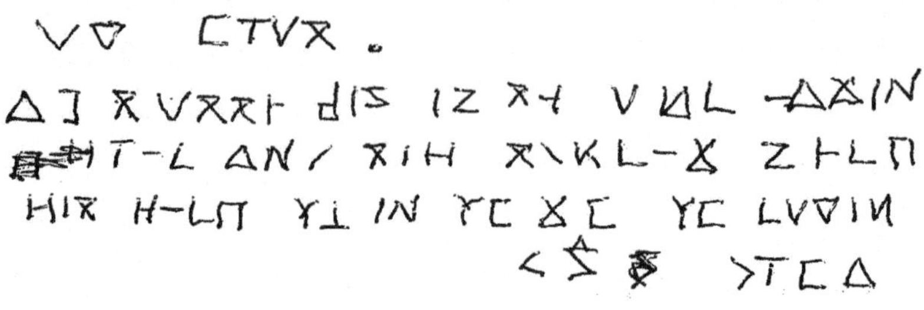

Brinda read the letter out loud.

"19 Autumn

Dear Mummy

This is my Uncle Edwin. Please welcome him and let him help you in your war.

Your loving daughter, Shar".

"Well that's a turn up for the books," she said as she handed it back to me, laughing. "Shar is growing up fast. By the way, I see she is using the single character for three instead of the usual LI, won't that get you both into trouble? She'll be taking over from you before she's even grown if you don't watch out. She'll be wanting to carry a pike herself before you know it."

"She's just been over-indulged and spent too much time in the company of the brutal and licentious. I can only blame myself. I didn't think she even knew about the war. As for her number three, which I note she has written upside down, yes technically she shouldn't know it but she saw it in some work I was doing and asked. I could get a reprimand for that, but probably not. I have told her not to use it in school and she has developed quite a sense of secrecy, for good or ill. She exhibited considerable circumspection in her dealings with Cray, somehow knowing where to draw the line. Very sophisticated for a child of any age. And she's very fond of her Great Aunt. You know they carry on quite a correspondence, yet I don't think she has once slipped up and divulged any of our military secrets. Anyway, we'd better deal with Edwin."

I looked again and saw a man in the distance. I gestured for him to come on and he waved back and approached where we stood by the tree.

He smiled and held out his hand to me. "Well met, Lady Shay. Your daughter does you credit. She was an excellent hostess and insisted on writing an introduction. It was my idea to deliver by arrow, partly to demonstrate the power of my bow. I was about half an imile away when I fired the arrow. I trust I didn't frighten you, I am a good shot and knew there would be no danger of me hitting either of you. Actually I am very grateful to her for writing, I struggle with literacy, especially if I have to write boustrophedonly. Shar says you wouldn't be able to understand my left to right method. Although I doubt that."

I smiled back at him and shook his hand. "You're correct, I think I can manage to read with all lines being left to right. I expect that Shar was showing off. Many children are not very fluent at her age. She is quite advanced and a know-it-all. Takes after me I'm afraid. You know you are very like your half-brother. Gives me quite an itch." I said this last in what I hoped was a jokey manner. This was neither the time nor place for making a pass at him. He took it more seriously than I intended; but consequently prevented me from making a fool of myself.

"I must believe you, I never knew Arval, but I do know that I take after our common father, so perhaps the resemblance is no surprise. However, I hope I'm not being forward or rude when I say that I have made a vow of celibacy unless and until I meet the vision of my Goddess. And you are not her, despite you being the most handsome woman I have ever set eyes on. I'm sure that before my Vision and Vow I would have fallen at your feet and given myself to you willingly."

"Oh dear, I didn't intend to importune you. It just came out wrong. Of course I and every woman here will respect your celibacy. We may have some internal struggles but we are all serious in our respect for men's rights. You are very kind to respond so politely and in such flattering terms."

We then got down to more serious business during which Edwin described the incredible power of his bow. Brinda was gobsmacked when he told us that his force against Pootini consisted of just thirty-two men, although he also alluded to some additional support from an ally. He offered to summon his band, currently camped on the north bank of the Lesser, west of Knot, to join us if I was willing to accept their help. I accepted this offer readily. I could see great possibilities from these longbows. Edwin then took a horn from where it was slung over his back and gave three short blasts on it. He then said his companion was at the spot from where he had unleashed his arrow with the letter. He would hear the horn and interpret it as the signal to go and fetch the rest of the band. He added that this companion also had a letter from Shar to help smooth their border crossing.

My turn to be a bit gobsmacked. Shar is eight, not eighteen. Yet here she is, basically issuing a passport for a large band of armed men to cross into the Theocracy, having realised that our border guards would be unwilling to take the responsibility for allowing such a force to enter.

I also was keen to try out the longbow myself. When I asked, Edwin shook his head. "This is a man's weapon my Lady. You really don't want to try it. You have to hold it close to your body, both for power and accuracy." He then demonstrated by firing into the air and bringing down a passing pigeon.

I was impressed, but still keen to try for myself. Edwin is big and strong. I could see that. But then I was taller and I'm sure equally strong in the arm. I could surely bend that bow. "Please let me just try."

He looked straight at my tits. They are quite impressive, though I say it myself. He pondered, seeming to calculate, before responding. "OK, If you insist, but on your own head be it."

"I do insist." I took his bow and he gave me an arrow. I noticed this one did not have an iron head but had merely been sharpened to a point.

"First, try to bend the bow without the arrow. It requires quite a force. Pull the string to touch your chin and aim with your best eye."

I did as he said. Bending the bow did indeed require a lot of strength. More than most men would have, I thought. I relaxed the bow and took the arrow. I then held the arrow in place, drew the bow as Edwin had instructed and let fly."

"Ow ow ow," I yelled. "That fucking hurt." I dropped the bow, tore my shirt open and examined my right tit. There was a bright red weal down the side where the bowstring had caught me. About two thumbs in from the nipple with blood seeping through the wound. When I had stopped making a fool of myself I noticed my shirt was cut and bloodstained where the string had struck.

"Yes, yes I know, it was 'on my head'", I said before Edwin could say I told you so. "Now I know why you said it is a man's weapon: two questions, what were you about when you were so thoughtful before letting me take the bow? And I had the impression that your allies in the north-western moors were women and also armed with these bows, how come? I'm sure we'd have heard them screaming if their experience was like mine."

"Forgive me, I was calculating the size of your tits and the likely impact point. You're quite well-endowed. A smaller woman would probably lose a nipple. I wouldn't have handed over the bow if I'd thought that would happen to you. But I reasoned that you wouldn't be satisfied until you'd tried for yourself."

"I suppose you're right. I can be stupidly pig-headed. Even if I'd known the danger I'd have tried to hold the bow differently and probably really lost that nipple. As it is I'll have a scar for a while but I expect it will heal eventually." I then burst into laughter while still clutching at my hurting tit.

"What's so funny? I wouldn't be laughing if it were my tit that had nearly been severed from my chest." Brinda was looking alarmed as she said this.

"Oh, I was just thinking that Shar would be able to get away with it, although I doubt she is yet strong enough to bend the bow. But I bet she'd be as bad as me in wanting to try. I'll have to show her my wound so as to discourage her when the time comes."

"She isn't strong enough to bend the bow. She did nag me until I let her try though." was Edwin's response.

"OK, Edwin, I'll live; but what about those allies of yours?"

"It's a long story. The Mazons are women. They originated in my community but were exiled when I was still a boy. Their leader, Zoni was determined to use a longbow. To get round the problem you have just experienced she had her own tits cut off. When she started influencing other women to follow her example she and her followers were expelled. Obviously we had to put a stop to her. Quite apart from the obvious effect on motherhood, several women died either from the operation, or from later infections. The rumour went out that it was all because they were women who only did sex with other women; but it was absolutely because of the self-mutilation."

"Ugh, how disgusting. I think we would have executed Zoni and confined any others to an isolated religious community. How come they became your allies?"

We waited until after we had done our inspecting and were able to relax after dinner before Edwin continued his story. He then told me about his vision and how he had been captured by Mazons while preparing spiritually for his campaign against Pootini.

"It was a question of 'needs must' I'm afraid. My enemy's enemy is my friend. While I bear Zoni and her Mazons no ill will at a personal level, I am as disgusted as you at her treatment of captives. Even though I understand their reasons, I can never accept what they have done, and continue to do. Nothing that you do in the Theocracy by way of slavery can compare with the cruelty and simple evil of the Mazons. One reason we tried to take no captives when fighting Pootini was that we couldn't keep them ourselves and our consciences would not let us condemn them to the Mazons' brutality. Surely a quick death from an arrow is preferable to that."

"But hadn't you agreed to hand over captives?"

"An agreement honoured in the breach. There would be no survivors to hand over."

"Right, one last thing before we retire to bed. With everything else we've had going on, I clean forgot to ask about your iron arrowheads. I didn't think you did any metal working in the Northlands. can you tell me more?"

Edwin became very thoughtful and paused a while before answering. I sat patiently, waiting for him.

"This is difficult to confess. It's down to the Mazons I'm afraid. Some communities in the Northlands do have a bit of metallurgical knowledge, but I don't know any who go to the trouble of extracting the metal from the ore. However, the Mazons are an exception. When they left our village, Zoni and her followers would have had no knowledge of metal-working, other than knowing that southerners in the Theocracy could make metal goods. They got the knowledge from captives they had taken in raids before the Pootini wars. There is also plenty of iron and copper ore in the mountains they inhabit. They had a quarry somewhere. I'm glad to say that I was never allowed to know where. They worked metal solely for weapons. Principally for their arrowheads, but they also made a few swords and knives. I suppose the knives were multi-purpose, not just weapons. During the Pootini war they allowed us some of these goods. My sword and such arrows as have iron tips all come from then. Since Pootini's defeat we have no dealings with them, and avoid contact. Peaceful coexistence is the official policy for us both, I think. By the way, one of the things I hope to negotiate with you is a supply of iron or steel to replenish our stock of metal tipped arrows."

I was interested. I wanted Edwin and his people to be our friends, and I no longer cared about the Theocracy's ban on trading in metal goods. "I'm sure we can come to a suitable arrangement. But we may not have time to start production before the coming battle. However, these Mazons. Do they do the work themselves? The unskilled labouring work is hot, bothersome and life-shortening. Here it tends to be left to men, or women from the poorer classes."

Edwin was clearly uncomfortable to admit what he knew. "No the Mazons don't do any of the dangerous work themselves. The slaves they employ are the worst-treated of all. You say life-shortening, you could say that again. The poor devils are worked to death in the quarry and forges. They are mostly men, of a sort, but a few women as well. This work is done by those slaves for whom they have no other use. Often they are people who are being punished for attempting to escape or being violent against their oppressors, or offending in some other way. Sometimes they haven't offended but are just no longer wanted for other work, or sex. Recall, I've already told you how captive women are forced to bear children so they can breast feed the babies of Mazons who no longer have their own tits. Women who can no longer serve in this way get sent to the quarry, as well as men who aren't wanted. All the men in the quarry are castrated and women mutilated to deny them the distraction of sexual pleasure. Then, as I said earlier, they are worked to death. Their legs are tied at the ankles by about a foot of rope to prevent them escaping. They are fed sufficient, if unappetising food, to keep them able to work. Men and women alike are denied clothes regardless of the weather. In winter they huddle together and get what warmth they can from the forges. If one falls ill or is injured, he or she is left to recover or die as the Goddess sees fit. As I said before, surely a quick death is preferable to such an existence. Once Pootini was defeated I couldn't wait to have no further dealings with them."

I felt sick. I know I have vowed not to interfere in the Northlands, but when this is over I must find a way of ending such misery. But, as the saying goes, the morrow is another phase. For now my first task is here and now and we all have work to do to prepare for Craya's arrival.

29
The Battle of Midborough 1

Dateline: 26 Autumn

History will record the battle of Midborough as starting with Craya's march from Cattlebridge in the ihors after mid phase on the 26th Autumn, and ending when I capture her. Technically, Craya is the aggressor. Partly because she has deliberately marched an army through opposing territory, namely Central and Midborough Rural, as a direct challenge to me and the laws of the Council of the North. Perhaps more importantly from a historical perspective because I will determine the historical record.

On the other hand, this is no surprise attack. Not only has Craya announced her intentions in the Council of the Theocracy and made a very public speech in Cattlebridge Market Square, but I have been looking for a fight, and have prepared my ground well. Also it is my forces who fired the first shots against Midborough in the mornphase of the 26th and later against Craya's march north.

It's true that my preparations were not complete when my agents warned me that Craya would march that phase. I had hoped for another phase, when the last of my troops would arrive from Knot. I decided to advance my plans. These have been thrashed out in a war council meeting between myself, Brinda, my two most senior officers and Edwin. We had considered the option of allowing Craya to enter Midborough, as we know was her initial intention. However, my analysis is that this would result in an extremely bloody assault that would completely destroy the town and result in huge civilian casualties as well as those of the military on both sides. As I told the others, a good general controls the battle before it even starts by choosing the location, the timing and the disposition of forces by both sides. And I am a good general, while Craya is not, I added. I chose my ground to the East of the town, bounded by a long bend in the Eastern river. The rivers through Midborough are unnamed and tend to be referred to as the West and East rivers, respectively. Actually 'river' is too grand a term, especially for the Eastern one, both are unnavigable and the latter really is little more than a stream. Despite this, Brinda has made much use of it further downstream in constructing her canal from Knot to Midborough. This canal terminates about three quarters of an imile from the north-eastern corner of Midborough's walls — just inside the Midborough Rural constituency - and thus in 'friendly' territory.

Both Midborough and Cattlebridge are walled towns, each with an approximately square perimeter. Cattlebridge's walls extend over three sides with the fourth side being protected by the Great River, enclosing an area of just over four square imiles. The three walls are bordered by a moat that has been created from the marsh lands where the western of Midborough's streams flows into the Great River. The land surrounding the north-western corner of the town remains marshy and treacherous and the road to Midborough veers Eastward from the North gate of the town. There are just three other roads out of Cattlebridge. Rivergate at the eponymous bridge is the main road to Honeyfield, Rivermouth and the South of the Theocracy. The roads through East and West gates are more minor. The old Rivermouth road from Eastgate is narrower and windier than the new road South of the river. The main temple is Cattlebridge College which occupies a large site on the banks of the river and features a footbridge joining the college to its lands on the South bank. The town has two further temples and a market square. This last has sides of about 185 strides (740 feet).

Midborough is slightly larger than Cattlebridge. This town is surrounded by four walls enclosing almost five square imiles. The market place is a circular ring of diameter about 290 strides, giving an area around twice that of the Cattlebridge market square. Two streams flow though the town. The West river is the larger, entering the town just south of the north-west corner, flowing out through the south wall whence it continues to join the Great River at Cattlebridge. A loop of the smaller East river flows in and out of the East wall on its way to join the Lesser river downstream of Knot. Both these rivers are important for the canals with the route from Knot to Midborough paralleling the Eastern stream, sharing the riverbed in some places. The route from Midborough to Cattlebridge makes similar use of the Western stream. The chief temple in Midborough is Midborough Abbey located in the South-East quarter of the town. There are three further minor temples in the town. Five roads emanate from the town. Each starting from the ring, two leave the north wall and one each the other three walls. The main road to Knot is the more easterly road through the north wall, Northgate, while the main road to Cattlebridge exits Southgate. The road from Eastgate leads to a junction with an older minor north-south route running more-or-less parallel with the East wall at a distance of about half an imile. This road also leads to Cattlebridge, but is narrower, slower and windier. To the north, not very far beyond the town, this road joins the main road to Knot. The area bounded by this road, two stretches of the East river and part of the town's east wall constitutes Shay's chosen battlefield. Her strategy for the 26th was to force Craya's march to take the minor road, and then somehow block her from entering the town by Eastgate.

Town Plans

The following plans of Cattlebridge and Middleborough respectively show the town walls and main water courses. Residential streets are not shown, apart form the borders of the market square/ring, Temples and public green spaces. The temples (Cattlebridge College and Midborough Abbey and their subordinate temples) all include schools, and the main temples have hospitals and secure lock-ups for prisoners awaiting trial. The main roads through the town gates are shown.

Scale: In both plans the grid squares are 1/4 of an imile (256 strides = 1024 feet).

Key

	Cattlebridge	Midborough
	Great River	
	Moat/minor rivers	West and East rivers
	Town Walls	Town Walls
	Main Roads	Main Roads
	Minor Roads	Minor Roads
●	Watch towers	
	Footbridge over G.R.	
	Public Green Spaces	Public Green Spaces
------		Boundary with Midborough Rural

Cattlebridge Town Plan

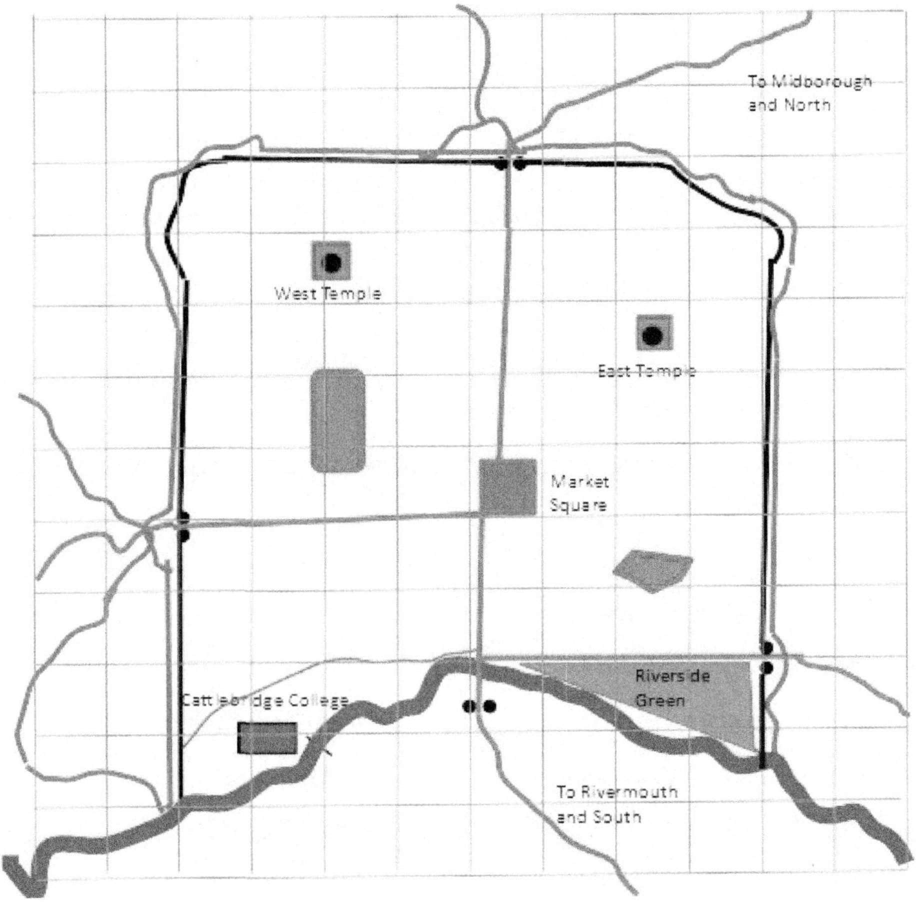

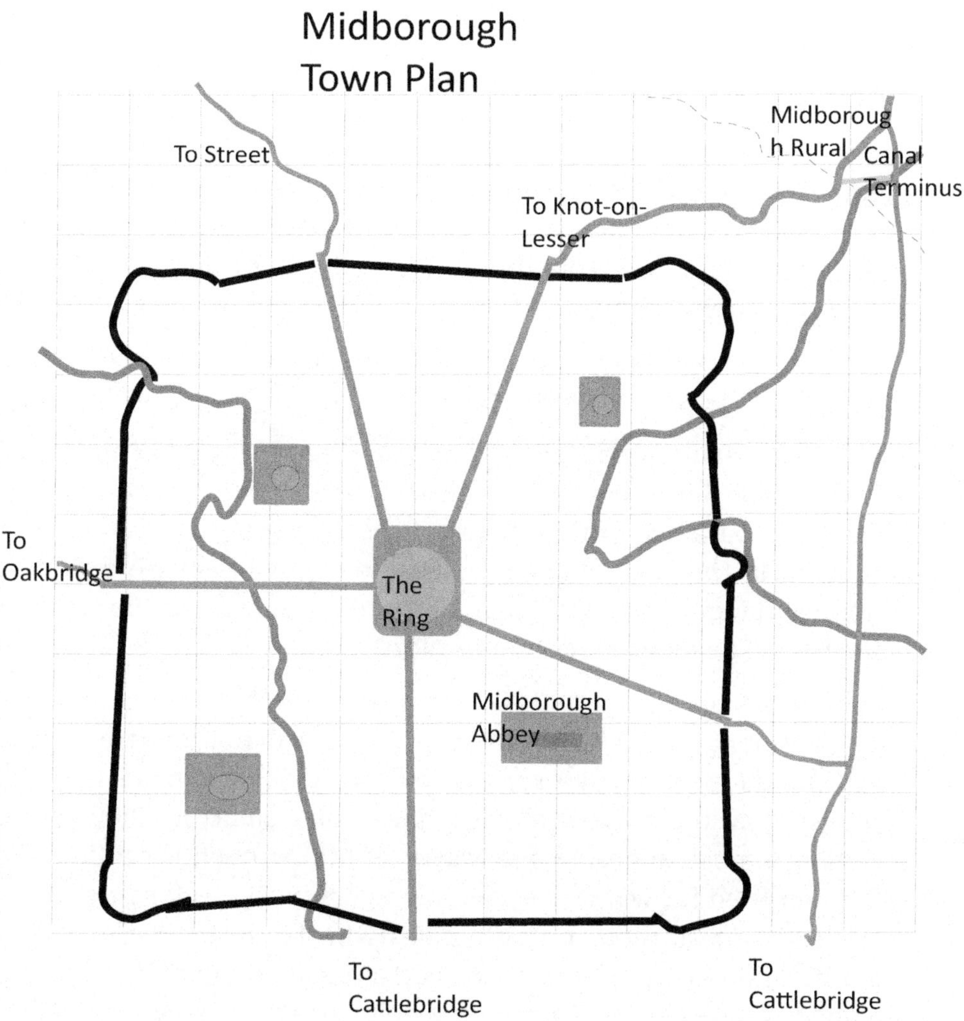
Midborough
Town Plan
To Street
To Knot-on-
Lesser
Midboroug
h Rural
Canal
Terminus
To
Oakbridge
The
Ring
Midborough
Abbey
To
Cattlebridge
To
Cattlebridge

My first move, shortly after breakfast was to send an emissary, three officers, two female and one male, into Midborough with a demand for the town to surrender. I then started to move my forces across the boundary from Midborough Rural. I didn't expect the Mayor of Midborough to accede to my demands, but felt morally obliged to try.

"I suppose we should be thankful for small mercies," was my reaction. "At least they weren't killed."

The two women had been returned. The mayor had torn up my demand. She then had all three of the emissaries stripped naked and paraded around the ring. The man was then taken to the pens in the slave market, while the two women were first publicly whipped and then marched, still naked, down the Knot road before being ejected through Northgate.

I was beside herself with anger at the breach of protocol in the treatment of a mission under a flag of truce. I immediately took Brinda and my two senior officers aside and made them promise that in the event of me being unable to do so, they will do their utmost to ensure the Mayor of Midborough is captured alive and tried for war crimes and held personally responsible for the deaths of all those on both sides who fall in the siege and capture of the town. By this time I had already brought four of my catapults along the Knot Road to within range of the North-East corner of the walls. My other two were being sent further south on the Old Cattlebridge Road, from where they could threaten the East wall and also the ground I had planned for Craya's army.

The bombardment of Midborough's North-East Corner began at the 33rd ihor, that is one ihor after midphase. The effects of the bombardment were devastating. The walls were not strong enough to withstand a direct hit from the iron balls and both balls and rocks devastated houses in the area of the north-east quarter closest to the walls. At 34 ihors a young lieutenant of the Midborough militia crept through a postern gate in the north wall and sought an audience with me. She explained that she was the daughter and sister of two Midborough town councillors who were opposed to the Mayor and had been arrested and jailed that morn after protesting against the treatment of my emissaries. Her mother represents the North-East quarter and her sister the communities without the wall. The Lieutenant told me she had a mixed party of militia, civilians and a few men who, with her, wanted to desert. I gave her the go-ahead and the lieutenant went back and led her followers out of the town to the safety of my ranks.

Also just after dawn, I had sent out a small number of soldiers to harass Craya's march with the goal of diverting them along my preferred route. All was now prepared and I awaited three arrivals; my remaining troops, my enemy and Wilda bringing my daughter.

When the first catapult fired the first shot of the campaign Craya was reaching the high point of her speech where she waved her saw and vowed to split Shay in half to decorate the two pillars either side of Rivermouth bridge.

By the main road, the distance between the market places of the two towns is about fifty imiles. The average walking speed is just over 10 imiles per ihor. Thus the journey should take about 5 ihors, and this is the amount of time that the inexperienced Craya allowed for her march. In this, she failed to consider that a large army would proceed more slowly, and require a rest break on the way. She also didn't allow for delays arising from enemy action, or for the time it would take to get her army moving in the first place.

Her plan had her leaving Cattlebridge at 34 ihors and arriving at Midborough at 39 ihors, in good time before dusk at 46 ihors at that time of year.

As it transpired it was the 36th ihor before the van of her army marched through Cattlebridge Northgate. Through the gate they could only march four abreast and the chariots and baggage carts had to go single file. Once on to the open road they were able to increase to five abreast with chariots in pairs, although baggage carts need still needed to go in single file. These last are the slowest component and an army travels at the speed of the slowest.

The marching army was configured as follows:

Two officers on horseback in the lead - a Major from the Cattlebridge 1st Battalion, and a Lieutenant from the Honeyfield 1st Battalion.

512 soldiers (female) marching behind - Battalions in marching order, Cattlebridge 1st and 2nd, Honeyfield 1st, Outer Cattlebridge, Cattlebridge 3rd, Honeyfield 2nd and 3rd, Chalcliff 1st;

Senior officers, mounted, from the above battalions, apart from those escorting Craya's carriage. Junior officers mainly marched with their troops.

16 chariots in pairs - Cattlebridge (8), Honeyfield (6), Rivermouth Central (2);

240 men - supporters from Cattlebridge (128), Honeyfield (96) and Rivermouth Central (16).

4 baggage carts, with 4 men escorting each cart from South Coast West-- One supporting woman and one other man on each cart - from New West Isla.

240 men; supporters from Outer Cattlebridge (32), Honeyfield Rural (32) , Mid-Rivers (32), Estuary (16), Downs (16), Chalcliff (64), Strait (32), Outer Rivermouth (16).

The 'headquarters' group of eight mounted officers surrounding Craya's carriage, in which Craya sat with the crippled ex-surgeon and her second in command, the Major-General commanding the Cattlebridge Militia - their horses being led by their grooms.

Those of the officers' men, who were not marching in one of the supporters blocks.

a second block of 512 soldiers, battalions in order being Cattlebridge 4th, Honeyfield Rural, Chalcliff 2nd, Strait, Combined Rivermouth, Downs & Estuary, Mid-River and a mixed battalion from other contributing Hundreds - South Coast East (24), South Coast West (16), West Isla (16), New West Isla (8).

Such mounted senior officers from the second block of battalions as were not required elsewhere.

12 chariots - 3 each from Chalcliff and Mid-River and 2 from each of Estuary, Downs and South Cape.

A further 4 baggage carts and two hospital carts, with 4 men each as well as the medical staff and other professional support.

The remaining 4 chariots - from Rivermouth Central (1), Outer Cattlebridge (1) and Strait (2) and two more officers on horseback brought up the rear.

The main purpose of the rearguard was to ensure there were no stragglers and that none of the men tried to escape.

From end to end the train was 576 strides long, well over half an imile.

And the dust raised was considerable, a rain shower about two ihors into the march did nothing to improve conditions or the morale of the PBI[19].

At first the going was reasonably easy, the main road was kept in good repair and the first seven imiles were in friendly territory. The occasional local would come out of their houses and farms and wave at the soldiers, shouting words of encouragement. Furthermore the women were fresh[20] and the late Autumn sky was clear and bright, and although the temperature was cool, it turned warm when the sun was out.

Once the road left the Cattlebridge district and entered Central, the locals were more hostile and kept clear of the invading army. No more encouraging waves, flowers thrown, or cakes brought out. It was now bolted doors and residents keeping clear. Even animals had been moved from fields bordering the road. And it rained, and it was cold, and feet began to hurt.

After three ihors marching, and only sixteen imiles beyond Cattlebridge, the column ground to halt with the women demanding a rest break. Craya was displeased but her more

19 Poor Bloody Infantry

20 Who cares about the men? - after all they're only good for one thing.

professional officers eventually calmed her down, assuring her that such a break was essential on a march of this length and that the army would perform better for it.

At first the road veers to the East, to skirt the marshes immediately to the north of Cattlebridge, where the river, known as the west river in Midborough, and the moat river in Cattlebridge, flows sluggishly and un-managed through the plain. By the time the road bends north, it is well to the East of Shay's new canal. Which it has to cross before continuing to Midborough's Southgate.

The march resumed after forty-eight imins. Two imiles further down the road the van came to the junction of the new and old Midborough roads. Brinda, on Shay's instruction had deliberately brought the canal to this point, and here was where a new bridge crossed the canal, the new road then narrowed as it crossed a causeway and, after a couple of hundred strides, the older river-bridge. Here Shay had laid her first trap. Firstly she had barricaded the road at the East end of the canal bridge and then placed further restrictive partial barricades along the edges of the bridges and causeway. Unmolested, the advancing army would be delayed by several ihors to pass or remove these obstacles. However Craya's troops were not to be allowed to pass unmolested. Shay had three boats waiting on the canal. The accompanying force was not large, but it was not expected to engage the enemy at close quarters. The ambushing soldiers were armed with javelins and hunting bows. One of Edwin's men was assigned to each boat, but had been told not to use their longbows except in emergency. Their skill was such that they were still pretty effective over the shorter range of the hunting bow. They had also taught some of Shay's own men how to use the short hunting bow accurately as a weapon. The secret being to hold it much closer to the chest than is convenient for most of the women. The women in the ambushing force were to throw the javelins and also operate the two crossbows that were mounted on each boat. Shay had not wanted to reveal her more innovative weapons at this juncture in the campaign, but reasoned that since cross-bows had been used in the siege of Fort during Pootini's war, it was inevitable that spies would have reported their existence to Rivermouth.

As the first soldiers started to dismantle the barricade, the soldiers on the boats fired a salvo of arrows and javelins. Three were killed and several wounded, the living turned and fled. One of the two leading officers rode up to see what was going on. A bolt from a crossbow took out her horse from under her. Other bolts were loosed into the leading ranks of the infantry. They didn't cause a lot of damage but did spread panic in the ranks. Assessing the situation, and observing the death-trap that had been laid for them as well as the delay to their schedule, the officers decided to divert the march on to the old road, exactly as Shay had intended.

The unhorsed officer remained by the roadside, with the wounded and a guard of eight soldiers. Half an ihor later when Craya reached the spot, she was not best-pleased but accepted that her lead officers had made the right decision in the circumstances. The new route would extend the march by about six imiles, another ihor, but that couldn't be helped.

For the most part, the canal parallels the old Cattlebridge Road (the name changes from Midborough Road at the junction) at an average distance of about half an imile. There are only a few farm bridges and a couple of lock flights along the route. Shay's boats shadowed the marching army and fired a few rounds of the crossbows every now and then to keep the enemy moving.

Craya ordered that no more rest breaks could be allowed. This was not popular with her infantry soldiers but they understood the necessity and trudged on in silence with their heads down. Most of the arrow wounds were not too serious and the wounded women had been loaded on the hospital carts and had to endure the bumps and grinds of the journey, as no transport could be spared to take them back to Cattlebridge.

It was past 45 ihors when the leading women reached the junction with the short (just over half an imile) road to Midborough Eastgate. The evening was drawing in and the road was barricaded in front of them, with more of Shay's soldiers waiting for them with various small projectile weapons, including at least two of the dreaded crossbows. While most of these weapons tended to bounce off armour, an unlucky shot might hit an eye or similar vulnerable spot, and, as the soldiers had learnt the hard way, the crossbow could pierce armour.

A few scouts did get past the barricades and avoided being shot, but discovered that the East gate of the town was locked against them. Had it fallen to Shay? They didn't know, and couldn't take the risk. The soldiers were tired and weary and in no condition for fighting in the dark. The march continued up the road, eventually halting about half an imile further, just south of the bridge over the southern arm of the East river before it enters the town. There, Craya's army made camp for a miserable night.

Key to Map of Craya's March

□ Town (Cattlebridge/Midborough)

— Great River — Canals — Roads

War of the Twins

------ Boundary between Wapentakes/Hundreds

● Resting Stop for Craya's Army

Craya's March from Cattlebridge to Midborough

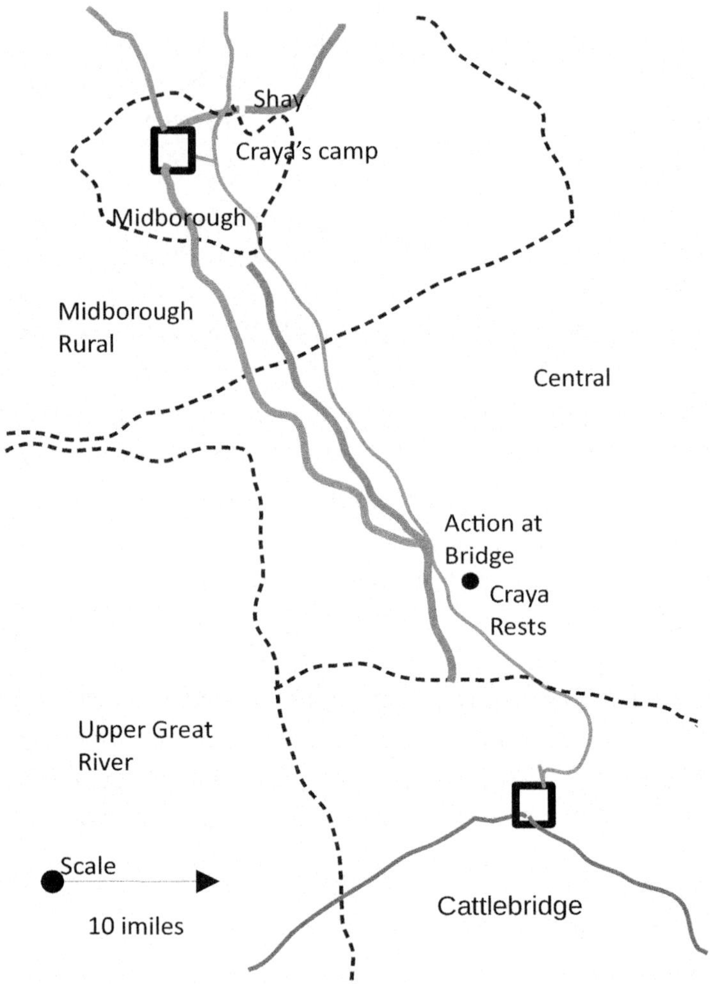

30
The Battle of Midborough 2

Dateline: 27 Autumn

Dawn on the 27th has brought a new phase, both in date and in the war. I was up early as I prepared for the phase's exertions. I was not yet quite ready to engage in pitch battle. I called my senior commanders together to outline the tactics for the phase. I introduced the Midborough Lieutenant who had defected to us the previous phase.

"Tophase I expect our army to be brought up to full strength as the last units arrive from Knot. As they will be travelling by boat, horse or vehicle, rather than on foot, I expect them to be rested and fully fit for the fighting morrow-phase. We should try to avoid a pitch battle tophase, and limit ourselves to luring the enemy across the southern arm of the river, where we will later destroy them. We already have a few troops South of the enemy camp, those that have been shadowing their march via the canal and those that have been guarding the road to Midborough Eastgate. Between them they have eight crossbows, and their job tophase will be to discourage the enemy from attempting to retreat to Midborough. Otherwise we have two catapults that have been attacking the East wall. These have been turned to face the enemy camp and will be engaged to harass their positions through an occasional bombardment. As you can see, there is a ridge of higher ground, behind which I shall hide the main force of the army, leaving four battalions of sixty-four soldiers each to occupy the ground north of the enemy camp in a defensive posture. Their job is to act as a decoy to fool the enemy as to our strength and lure them over. They are not to engage the enemy but to retreat in an orderly manner before any advance over the stream. One of these units will be the Midborough Lieutenant's force, and all units will display the standards of their constituent militias. The purpose is to fool the enemy into believing this to be our main force and that we have captured and turned Midborough. They will see two militia standards in each unit, namely: Midborough and Midborough Rural; Lesser Coast and Lesser; Oakbridge and Street; and Central and North Cape. These four units, deployed in traditional phalanx formation, without pikes, are to be accompanied by four chariots in support, for visual effect only. They aren't expected to do anything in particular. The real battle is to begin morrow-phase."

"What about the assault on the town?," asked the colonel commanding the artillery.

"You are to continue the sporadic bombardment of the north wall and Northgate, but lay off the East wall. You are not to enter the breaches but use bombardment and crossbow shots to discourage repairs or any attempts by the defenders to sally forth. I intend to hold off from entering the town until Craya's force has been defeated."

In Midborough, the Mayor also held a war council. Her military chief advised surrender because the north wall had been breached and Northgate would not hold, and she could not see her depleted militia being able to hold off a concerted attack. Yesterphase's desertion had hit hard. Her total strength was now down to about two hundred women. The East wall was left virtually undefended and the South-West guards had already been redeployed to the North-East Wall. However, she had assured the Mayor, she was a good soldier and would obey orders whether her advice were heeded or not.

Her advice was not heeded. "I have already ordered the mobilisation of all women between sixteen and fifty-four years of age, excepting only those more than two selenths pregnant or with a baby of under one selenth. Older babies and toddlers are to be handed over to a crèche in the Abbey to be staffed by the priestesses and older women from the community. This brings in a further 896 women to strengthen our defensive lines, responded the Mayor"

The militia chief considered her response carefully before finally advising. "In that case our best strategy will be to send a task force through Northgate and Streetgate to assault the enemy catapults and so end the bombardment. We only have sufficient arms for an extra 256 troops. I recommend the assault force should be led by one hundred of my militia supported by 220 conscripts, split into two equal forces of 160 through each gate. The rest of the armed troops should be held to defend the North and East Walls between the North and East gates. The remaining conscripts must arm themselves with whatever they can improvise and be held in reserve. We might also consider what men we have available to stand in support. Failing that, we might consider attacking the small enemy force outside Eastgate and linking up with Craya's larger army."

Again the mayor was dismissive of the advice. "No, we cannot afford to leave the city. We need all available troops to defend the walls and gates. Craya's force is large enough without the small reinforcement we might add and our final salvation will come when she triumphs on the field. Here, we can't trust our men. Shay has promised them freedom if they desert, and most of them will believe her. Even our own citizenry are suspect. While I'm sure that most are loyal, we have already seen some defections, and I had to arrest two ex-councillors yesterphase on account of their exhortations to surrender the town. We must remain alert to the possibility of others sharing and acting upon these treasonable opinions."

These plans came to the ears of one of my spies in the town and were carried to me, despite an order to close all routes in and out of the town. The spy concerned left via the East river, crawling through the culvert where the water passed under the wall. The soaking-wet man, for the spy was male, made his way along the river bed to my headquarters, then still at the canal terminus. Thus I learned that my strategy vis-a-vis the town was working and I could safely concentrate my force against Craya.

Wilda had made an early start from Elmhouse. She and Shar took a fast boat to Street, stopping only at Ludray farm to collect Valray. From Street they travelled by carriage and six along the main road to Midborough, before cutting off about eight imiles short of the town to travel the rest of the way on minor roads and tracks to the Knot road, and thence south on that road to the canal terminus, reaching Shay's camp at 24 ihors, just nine ihors after leaving Elmhouse. I was pleased to see them and gave Wilda a full update on the war so far and the strategy for the rest of the phase and the morrow. The last units of the army had arrived from Knot some two ihors previously and were enjoying a meal after their journey before advancing to pitch their camp alongside their colleagues behind the ridge. After spending a few imins hugging and listening to my child, I deputed Valray to look after her for the duration of the battle. Two soldiers were also set to guard them in case of any danger. "As much as I dislike her, I know that my sister would not let you come to harm deliberately; but I don't trust Craya in the slightest. She is vindictive and, even worse, she has that treacherous ex-surgeon with her pouring out her hatred. I should have killed her when I had the chance."

"Well Mummy, I'm glad you didn't kill her," said Shar. "Murder is wrong and against all we stand for. You are better than that. If she commits a crime you can send her for trial and then if the judge says she should be executed, then you can have her killed."

'Shar is strong, opinionated, principled and as stubborn as me,' I thought. 'I'm proud of her.'

What I said was, "Shar I must leave you to Valray for now. The next two phases will either see the end of this war, or I will be dead. If I am dead you are to do whatever your grandmother or Auntie Wilda tell you, and if they too are unable to look after you, you must demand to be taken to your Aunt Thay and throw yourself on her mercy. She won't love you, but she will treat you fairly."

Then I laughed and said. "But I won't die. I will triumph, and I promise you I'll pay you more attention in future and we will live happily together."

What Shar thought was: 'no you won't, Mummy. You will go to Rivermouth and have it out with Auntie Thay until you have become the chief woman in all of the Theocracy. And then you'll be busier than ever, and you'll keep promising me that next year we'll have more time together.' What she said was: "that'll be nice, Mummy. Perhaps we can go on holiday to the seaside and play in the sand and I can love and cuddle you all phase long."

I smiled, "I love you my darling now run along with your Grandma and don't go bothering the soldiers. They all have too much work to do to allow them to be distracted by a small girl."

Shar went off, but not without having the last word. She called out over her shoulder. "I'm not a small girl. I'm a big girl."

Craya's camp was not a happy place. The foot soldiers had been tired out by their ordeal the phase before, and the encampment had been set up hurriedly and not very well. A couple of rain storms in the small ihors had not helped, exposing leaky or poorly-sited tents through which little rivulets would flow, wetting the bedding and keeping the women awake. To add to this, the catapults just across the stream would remind them of their presence by firing a round every ihor or so. Timing varied to reduce predictability, thereby denying sleep. Similarly the crossbows and even, hunting bows from the force behind them would occasionally fire off their missiles. None of these was aimed in any sense as it was too dark to see other than from the camp fires of the enemy. After the first such salvos, Craya had ordered all camp fires for her troops to be extinguished, thus denying warmth or even a hot meal or drink.

In reality little physical damage was done. One tent sleeping eight received a direct hit and one baggage cart had a wheel shattered. Just three crossbow bolts found a mark. One horse killed and two men wounded. The ordinary arrows either fell to the ground or lodged in tent roofs doing no more that exacerbate the leaks. It was a good thing for Craya that the arrows were not carrying fire. However, many were carrying messages. These messages urged desertion or surrender, or promised men their freedom.

Thus it was at a late ihor that Craya's soldiers emerged from their tents and cooked breakfast. The ban on fires ended with the return of light. It was clear to their officers that they would not be fit to fight that phase. A rather half-hearted attempt was made to attack the force behind them but was repelled by crossbow and javelin, while it also seemed to provoke the catapults into action.

Looking north, Craya noticed that the army facing her consisted of just four sixty-four strong phalanxes bearing the standard of just about all the northern militias including Midborough itself. This army had only four war-chariots in support. In the distance she could see what looked like a mounted command-post on a rise in the ground and heard some noise coming from further to the North.

She concluded that the strength of the opposing army had been greatly exaggerated. Surely Shay would have some reserves but, even so, Craya would outnumber her by almost three to one. Whatever the morale of her army, she personally was brimming with confidence.

Action on 27 Autumn

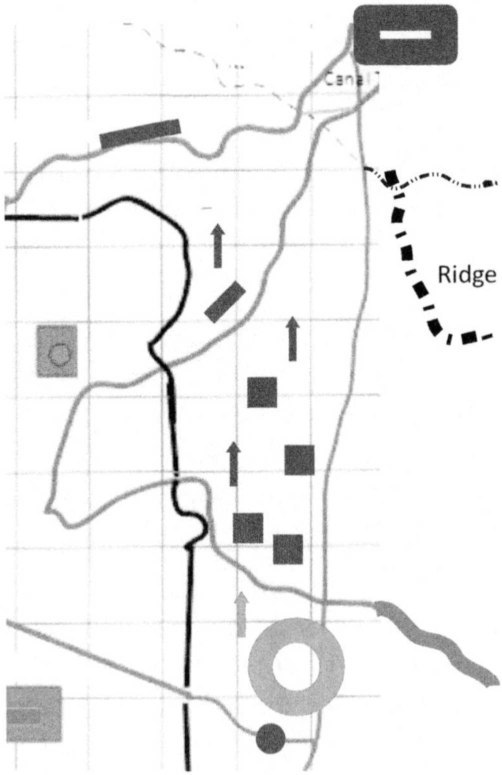

Scale: Grid Squares

1/4 imiles

Key to forces: Shay: ▬ Catapults/Crossbows:

● Small Mixed force (Eastgate Road Guards & Canal Troops)

■ Battalions (64) in decoy army: ▭ Camp & HQ

Craya:

◯ Overnight Camp

At midphase I sent out a truce party of three riders, led by a young Lieutenant from Lesser Coast. These three delivered a demand that Craya surrender, disarm and return whence she came. If she did so she would be allowed to go on her way unmolested and many lives would be saved.

Craya laughed, tore up the demand and sent the truce party back with her own demand to be allowed to pass into Midborough, then on her way to Knot and the wild lands, and then to return home with her captive slaves.

I was unsurprised. This was the outcome I expected. We responded with a renewed bombardment from the catapults and jeers from the troops drawn up along the north bank of the East stream. The catapults were firing long-range, targeted on Craya's baggage train. The rear of the encampment suffered much damage with six of the eight baggage wagons disabled. Supporting fire from the eight crossbows on the Eastgate Road killed or wounded most of the cart-horses as well as some of the male cart-drivers.

One of the iron balls from a catapult landed a direct hit on the left wing of a newly formed 128 strong phalanx. The resulting panic caused several soldiers to flee the field. Although some were quickly captured by their comrades, several got clean away and made their way back to Rivermouth or Cattlebridge. From these came premature rumours of a great defeat for Craya's army. Rumours that reached Cray and Thay in Rivermouth and caused Thay to return to her home to collect Thar with the intention of taking her back to Rivermouth where Thay herself would organise the defence against an anticipated advance by Shay's victorious army. Cray was lost in grief for her only remaining daughter, as she prayed that Shay would spare her, if only for the sake of her Goddess. "I've lost my Crayza. Please spare me my remaining daughter." She prayed to the Goddesses as she knelt in the Great Temple.

Meanwhile Craya's officers had restored order and her army marched to the stream. The catapults were now out of ammunition and were in rapid retreat northwards along the old Knot Road (as it was called when north of the Eastgate junction), each being pulled by teams of eight strong shire horses, normally employed on the canals.

As Craya's phalanxes forded the shallow stream, the decoy army retreated before them without engaging in more than the occasional crossbow shot or thrown javelin.

When dusk fell Craya's fighting force was across the stream and in control of the southern half of the chosen battlefield. The catapults were safely back near the canal terminus while half the decoy force had retreated across the northern branch of the East river and the rest were occupying the ridge.

Although the last couple of ihors had raised the morale of Craya's soldiers, they were still tired out from their disturbed night, and in no condition to pursue their advantage by fighting in the dark. The order was given to dig in for the night while their men crossed the river bearing supplies from the destroyed baggage train, and scurried about to set up the camp and cook dinner for their women.

That night the catapults and crossbows fell silent. Craya's soldiers enjoyed some well-earned rest. However the night was not entirely undisturbed. Rain fell heavily between the second and forth ihor of the 28th, while many of the soldiers were still exhibiting some nervousness on account of the previous night's experience.

Both sides counted their casualties from the phase. The decoy army had lost one killed and four wounded, all women, by javelins thrown back by Craya's advancing phalanxes, and one man killed on the Eastgate Road. On the other hand, Craya had lost over a hundred killed (mainly women but also about a dozen men) and a large number of wounded, overflowing her two hospital wagons. My force had done their best to avoid attacking these wagons, as they were clearly marked with ensigns depicting a red disc on a white background. However some collateral damage is inevitable when catapults are involved and one of these wagons had suffered two smashed wheels and some minor shrapnel damage from splintered rock.

While most of my army had an early night as they prepared themselves for the morrow's main battle, there were some who busied themselves to prepare the ground for our impending victory.

I repositioned all six catapults into the area between the Knot road and the north bank of the downstream arm of the East river. A phalanx of 64 fresh troops marched across country and along farm tracks to join the party on the Eastgate road, with the new mission of cutting off the enemy's line of retreat.

Finally, half the troops in the decoy army that had partaken in the previous phase's action retreated in the night to rest behind the main lines.

The rain was much less disturbing to my people. Our tents and other shelters were dry, warm and comfortable having been established unhurriedly and with no expense spared. Indeed some of the soldiers even made use of being woken by the rain by indulging in a quickie, with a friendly male colleague. Such had been my influence that I believe all such encounters were consensual. One soldier was overheard while sharing a man's attentions with her sister. "Why didn't we know this before? Men really do enjoy it, if only we treat them right and attend to their comfort too." Whatever exactly the man concerned then did caused her to squeal with pleasure, and her sister to shake her head in laughter.

31

The Battle of Midborough 3

Dateline: 28 Autumn

Dawn broke over the battlefield. The rain had passed over and there were few clouds in the sky. The air was fresh and on the cool side, with a slight south-westerly breeze. A good prospect for a late Autumn phase.

I rose early and enjoyed a hearty breakfast of bacon, eggs, sausages and fried bread. I had brought the bacon and sausages from my favourite supplier from the Northlands. An ipint of good ale provided a fitting accompaniment. I was looking forward to the battle, the culmination of meticulous planning. The main force fell into formation on the North-eastern edge of the ridge and waited for the word of command. Meanwhile Edwin's archers positioned themselves where they had a good line of vision on the enemy's war chariots. Theirs was to be the first hammer blow.

Craya's army was more sluggish in their preparations, and they had to get into formation under a bombardment from the catapults. Eventually at about 18 ihors Craya's phalanxes started their slow advance towards the now depleted ranks of my decoy army. The latter beat a hasty retreat, inviting Craya's chariots to chase them down. The charioteers took the bait and had soon overtaken their own infantry as they headed towards my retreating troops.

I gave the signal for the real attack to begin. The bombardment ceased as the catapults retreated towards their former positions along the Knot road.

War of the Twins

Edwin's archers appeared in front of the advancing chariots and let fly their salvos of arrows. Every one of the charioteers was taken out, as were several of the horses. Craya, now only had her astonished infantry. Isla warfare had never before seen anything like it. Then to make matters worse for Craya, My main force breasted the rise and advanced in disciplined order towards the their enemy. As we closed in on Craya's phalanxes, we lowered our pikes to the horizontal position and charged into the ranks with devastating effect. All that phalanx-ball was paying off as we pushed the enemy backwards.

Once Craya saw the advancing army, she realised she was outnumbered; but had not properly appreciated that she was also out-weaponed. She retreated to a nearby hillock where she set up her personal headquarters from which she could observe the battle from relative safety.

"We've lost, said her second-in-command, a seasoned General from the Cattlebridge militia. You must strike your colours and fly a flag of surrender to save the lives of your soldiers."

From her wheelchair at Craya's side, the crippled ex-surgeon mouthed her protest. "No, your soldiers must hold the line to allow us to escape and fight another phase."

Craya rejected her 2-i-c's advice. "We are not defeated yet. We fight on."

As the pikes smashed through the ranks, the carnage was dreadful to behold. Those few lucky enough to escape being impaled on a pike or trampled under foot turned and fled.

But there was nowhere for them to go. The Eastgate guard had come up to their rear and my chariots and cavalry chased down any survivors.

Action on 28 Autumn

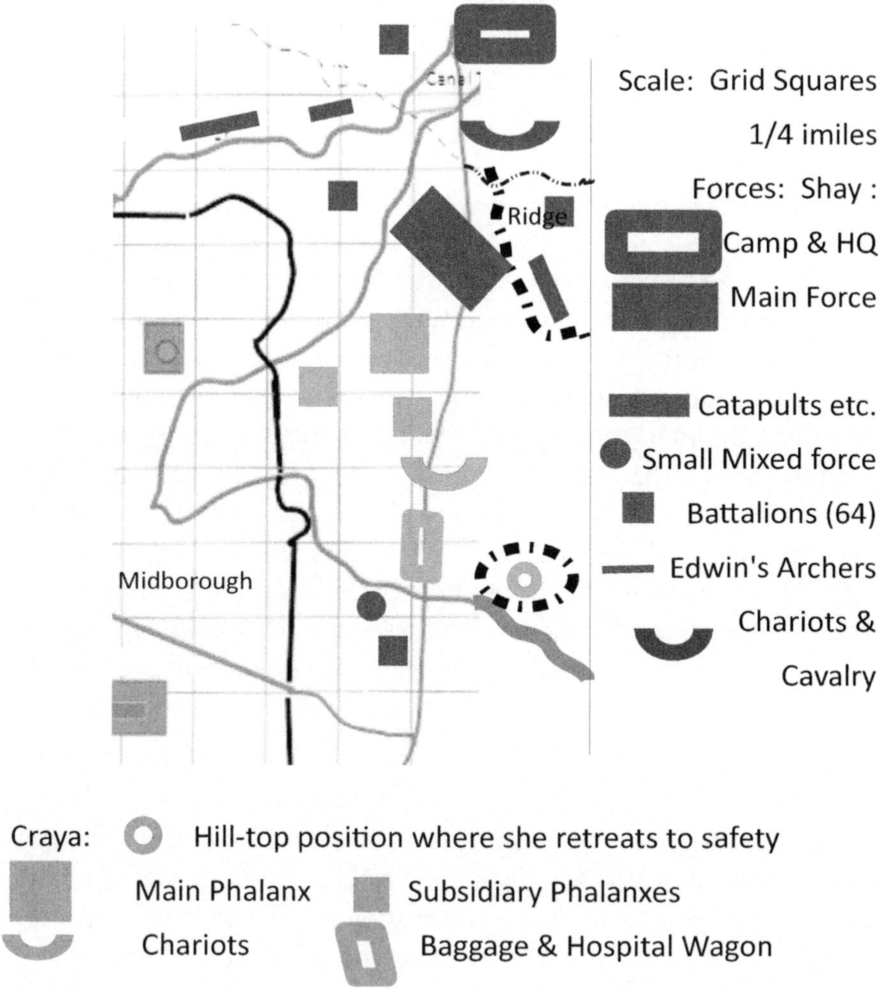

With the total collapse of her force, Craya fled the field with just a handful of her most trusted companions.

As she rode away, the 2-i-c took over command and immediately hoisted her flag of surrender. I had won a resounding victory, and all that remained was to clean up the battlefield.

When the air cleared, I could see that my own units appeared unscathed while the field was littered with the bodies of the dead and dying enemy. The rest of the phase was devoted to clearing up. The wounded were taken to our own hospital tents, where the overwhelmed medical staff did what they could, regardless of former allegiance. The remaining survivors from Craya's army were rounded up, separated by gender and held within secure compounds. Of the captives only eighty were women, with a further one hundred and twenty three among the wounded, but many of these would not survive for long, such was the massacre. On the other hand about four hundred men survived and were placed under guard. I left the female captives relatively lightly guarded while I held the men in a secure stockade patrolled by a substantial force of mainly male soldiers.

The captive men were apprehensive as to their fate. My army outnumbered them significantly, and by tradition would have been expected to gang-rape whomsoever they pleased. The men braced themselves for an ordeal that many might not survive.

It was dark by the time I had finished supervising the clean-up. Morrow-phase I will set the prisoners to the task of disposing of their dead and turn my attention to the town. In the meantime, I still had work to do.

My first call was to the stockade holding the men. I entered and called for their attention and then addressed the assembled company.

"Tophase's battle has left me with much tidying up to do. You have been soundly defeated and by long-held tradition, I am entitled to dispose of you as I see fit. I am not one for the old traditions as far as men are concerned. Furthermore, I am well aware that none of you are to blame for my cousin's illegal invasion of Central and Midborough. However, I require help with the task of disposing of the corpses of the many of your former colleagues who died during the last three phases. Morrow-phase you will be taken back to the battlefield alongside your erstwhile female colleagues, and together you will undertake the task of identifying and then cremating the dead. You will then be returned to this stockade, which will remain strongly guarded for your own protection. I don't know how long you will have to endure these primitive conditions. You will be released as soon as is practical, but I can make no promises as to when that will be.

Also by tradition my soldiers are entitled to sate their war-fuelled lusts on you. That will not happen. My soldiers are under strict orders not to molest you. Among other things, I have fought for the rights of all men to own their own bodies and to be treated fairly and with respect. Any woman here, of whichever army, who rapes any one of you will be severely punished. You have my word."

I paused to let the import of these words sink in. I was met with stares of disbelief. Such magnanimity is unheard of. Those men that would survive the anticipated mass rape, could only expect to be employed on the most menial tasks for whichever woman was rewarded with their new ownership. But what they heard was that there would be no mass rape. They would all survive to serve their new owners.

After a short interval, I continued.

"Henceforth you are no longer the property of your former owners." The men expected that, no surprises there. Anyway most of their former owners were lying slain on the blood-sodden battlefield.

"You will no longer be the property of any woman, nor of any institution. You will all be given your freedom. You will each receive a passport to guarantee your new status, you must take good care of it, lest any woman seek to re-enslave you. If you choose, you may return to your former homes, but as free men. You will also be given the opportunity to seek employment in one of my many enterprises. I stress that this is not compulsory. I mean it when I say you are to be free. In the coming phases my officers will speak to each and every one of you and then a suitable offer will be made that you can accept or reject, as you think best for you. That's all I have to say for now. Try and get a good rest before dawn breaks morrow-phase. The tasks the morrow brings us all will be hard and unpleasant. I must deal with Midborough. You must work hard to clear the battlefield. I wish you all as pleasant a sleep as is possible in the circumstances."

I then left the men to it, while I went to give a similar speech to the surviving women. Among these, there were a few officers. I gave these the additional task of drawing up registers of the dead and wounded, and then writing individually to the mothers, sisters or whoever counted as next of kin of the fallen.

When I returned to my own quarters, I first went to Shar's bedside to give her a hug and read her a story before going to my desk to write my account of the phase's events and then to start the unpleasant task of writing individually to the loved ones of the seventeen officers and soldiers of our army that had perished in the fighting.

Shortly before midnight, I heard a rumpus going on outside the tent. A childlike voice was insistent. "I must see Lady Shay. It's important and I can only speak to her. Mummy says so. I will not go away. Morrow-phase may be too late. I'll scream if I have to, I'm warning you. Ow, that hurt! I must see my Lady, NOW!"

I got up to see what the commotion was about. Two of my guards were holding on to a girl of about thirteen. The girl was struggling to get away from them.

"What is going on," I ordered.

One of the guards responded, "General, this young person thinks she can just barge in and disturb you. We've tried to stop her, but she is kicking up a fuss. I've checked her for weapons, and she appears to be unarmed, but really she should be in bed at this ihor, and in any case she is old enough to know better than to disturb someone like yourself, m'Lady."

"Well, I'm disturbed now, so I'll hear what she has to say. Come into my office and tell me who you are and why you need to see me so urgently at this late ihor." I then ushered the girl into the tent.

"Are you Lady Shay?" asked the girl, with a look of suspicion showing on her face.

"Yes, I'm Shay, but who are you and what do you want with me?

"Thank the Goddess, I've had such difficulty finding you. I'm nobody important. My Mummy is a farmer about sixteen imiles from here, in Central. A few ihors ago, not long after dark, she heard a noise outside one of the barns and there were several women dressed as soldiers. They had horses and also a carriage with a woman in a wheelchair. They were coming towards the house. I was inside and Mummy came in and told me to run away and find you outside Midborough and tell you that she had a rat infestation, and you must collect them. I escaped out the back just as these women pushed through the front door. I crept round to the stables, got a torch and my pony and rode here as fast as I could. It's difficult in the dark, but my pony and me both know the way quite well. I'll be thirteen in two periods time, can I come and join your army? I'm quite big, over seven foot already, and my tits are growing, so I should count as grown-up enough."

"Well, thank-you for telling me that news. Your Mummy is right it is important. I promise I will attend to the rat problem, first thing after dawn. I will have to send one my my most trusted officers and a number of soldiers, but you will have to lead them to your farm. You are very brave and resourceful to have ridden so far in the dark. I'm sure you can be a soldier one phase, probably an officer. But I'm afraid the law says you must be at least sixteen, however big you or your tits are. Right now we need to get you something to eat and then to bed or you'll be too tired and hungry when dawn arrives. I'll make you a bed next to my daughter Shar, who is in the small room in the corner of the tent. I hope she's asleep. But you haven't told me your name."

"Oh, I'm, Soozy, my Mummy is Sudon, because Granny was very old when Mummy came, so she was named 'Given by the Creatrix'."

I ordered a suitable supper for Soozy and then went to make up the bed. I learned later that Shar was not asleep, but had closed her eyes and pretended. She had overheard the conversation and was looking forward to having a whispered conversation with this Soozy. Shar had already decided that Soozy was going to be her friend.

It was gone two ihor in the morn before I was able to turn in myself. My condolence letters were written and sealed. Soozy's news had taken a weight off my mind. I thought to myself: 'The morrow will bring another phase'.

32
The Battle of Midborough 4

Dateline: 29 Autumn

"Another phase, another Mark," I announced to nobody in particular. I stretched and climbed out of my rather narrow camp bed. I smiled as I realised that a good proportion of my army would probably be waking up with a quickie from a male colleague — sort of consensual, but it can be hard to break the habits of a lifetime, for both the men and the women. Saying no isn't easy when you've always been expected to respond to a woman with an itch. And there is no itch more powerful than that brought on by the mixture of fear and excitement that characterises a battle. I wouldn't mind a bit myself, I mused. "Enough of that", I ordered myself aloud. "We have work to do."

Alert to my movement, an orderly coughed at the tent door and then entered with a mug of a steaming mint tea. I took it with thanks and sat down to to drink it and gradually wake properly.

"Er is there anything special I can do for you my Lady," enquired the orderly, who was a fine handsome young man, probably half my age.

"No I've a lot to do, but thank-you for thinking of me, perhaps you can just fetch me a bowl of waster so I can wash the sleep from my eyes." When the man had left to undertake this small task, I shook my head. 'Will men ever really be free?' I thought. I can't really believe that this young man wants to indulge in sex with a woman as old as his mother; but that was what he had meant by his offer of 'anything special'. He knew his place. I felt ashamed as I thought back to the times when I would have accepted his offer, and indeed demanded it if the offer had not been made, as if it were my Goddess-given right for a man to drop his pants at my whim.

When the man returned with the bowl of water, warm I noted, I gave him a smile and asked if he would be so good as to summon some of the officers to see me. I handed him a list.

I was engaged in washing myself when Valray popped her head around the tent flap. "I hope I'm not disturbing you but I thought you might want some help with Shar."

"Oh, do come in Valray. You are so thoughtful. There are two of them in there. I've heard whispering so I expect they're ready to get up and will doubtless want breakfast. The other girl is called Soozy, and tells me she is big enough for my army, at thirteen. She will need to leave straight after breakfast to escort some of my soldiers to her home, where Craya is holed up. If you could supervise them for a bit that would be most helpful."

"It's a pleasure, Shay. You know how I adore looking after my grand-daughter." Valray scurried over to the corner, lifted the flap and went in to organise the two girls.

My first interview was with the officer I had selected to secure the arrest of Craya and her party. "Take a party of soldiers, about sixteen should be sufficient, you choose who you want, and a prison cart. The girl will show you the way. I hold you responsible for ensuring she is kept safe, and her mother too, unless it is too late. I do not trust Craya one bit. Oh, I want Craya alive. I don't care if you need to rough her up a bit, but alive please. I don't care about the others. Don't kill anyone unless you have to, but the rest of Craya's cowards are disposable."

Next I summoned the Cattlebridge General and handed her a dispatch. "This is my account of the battle and my demands that Cattlebridge and Rivermouth open their gates to me and my troops. Make it clear to them that neither town has any choice in the matter. If either town fails to comply I will not hesitate to pull down their walls permanently and arraign the councillors for treason." I don't have the stomach for a prolonged war and I will punish any further resistance severely. Choose two women from your surviving army to accompany you. Go first to Cattlebridge and then either go yourself or send someone you can trust to carry my demands to Rivermouth."

The General countered. "My first duty is to the remnant of my army here, can you not send one of your own officers?"

"I choose to send you. You know the right people in Cattlebridge and they will believe what you tell them. Your survivors here will be looked after, and in due course, freed. I hold nobody to blame except Craya and the evil henchwoman who accompanies her in a wheelchair. These two will be arrested, along with the Mayor of Midborough. All others will be held blameless and released as soon as is practicable. The only cost will be to the owners of the male captives, all of whom I will set free."

The General saluted. "I shall do as you command, Ma'am." She then turned from my tent to go and choose her companions.

My last task before attending to Midborough was to appoint two officers, one female and one male, to take charge of the cremation parties.

'Time for breakfast', I thought, 'Oh, and the girls'. I got up from my desk, stretched and called in the orderly to bespeak breakfast for myself and those I needed to brief regarding the capture of the town. I then looked in on where Valray and the two girls were enjoying their substantial repast.

"Mummy, I want Soozy to come and stay at Elmhouse. Can you invite her please, in the summer when it's warm and we can play outside and swim in the river. And can she bring her pony so we can go exploring together — without a groom getting in the way. And I want to see her farm."

"You are demanding, aren't you? And you shouldn't talk with your mouth full." I rebuked my excitable daughter. "But, if she wants to and her mother let's her. Of course she can visit us in Elmhouse. But for now, we all have things to do. Soozy, I hope you slept well and didn't let this little chatterbox disturb you too much. You need to be ready to leave in half and ihor. My officer who is to go with you is organising the cage for the rats as we speak. I'm afraid I have to go and attend to that town over there, but I'll be sure to visit your mother when this is all over. Thank-you for your efforts on my behalf."

"But I don't want Soozy to go, and I've told you I'm not little and I'm not a chatterbox. I just have to say everything to you while I can, because you are always so busy." Shar was not going to let me off lightly.

"What you want is neither here nor there. We all have our duties to attend to, and yours is behave yourself and be seen and not heard. Finish your breakfast. Say goodbye nicely to Soozy and then go and wash your hands and face, and do as your Grandma tells you."

Soozy stood up. She bowed to me and said "thank-you for looking after me, and this lovely breakfast, m'Lady. I will be ready when your officer calls for me." She then turned to Valray to thank her and finally gave Shar a hug, saying "it was lovely meeting you, Shar. We will be friends and I'm sure my Mummy will let me visit you, and welcome you to our farm as well."

What a nice polite girl Soozy is. She is a credit to her mother. Shar could do well to learn from her. I know it's my fault, but Shar is becoming a bit too headstrong and full of herself, and far too used to getting her own way. I will certainly encourage the friendship.

I proceeded to the officer's mess tent where the staff were ready to serve our breakfast. I was joined by Wilda, Brinda, Edwin, my two Major-Generals, the Artillery Colonel and the Midborough Lieutenant.

"Ladies and Gentleman, please be seated and partake of breakfast. Thank-you for attending me here. The reason I asked you all is to arrange for the surrender of Midborough. I've already arranged for other essential tasks to be carried out tophase and I can rely on the various officers appointed to carry out my wishes. All that remains is Midborough."

"What about Craya," asked Wilda.

"She is being taken care of. She has been located, thanks to a very brave and resourceful young girl, and I have dispatched a party to collect her and her companions and bring them here."

So to Midborough. I'm in no mood to tolerate either a protracted siege or a bloody assault. The defenders will have observed yesterphase's action and must conclude that resistance is futile. I will require their unconditional surrender, under the threat that every woman of military age will be put to the sword if resistance is offered. Lieutenant, I'm sure that extreme will be unnecessary. If I'm wrong I will require you to identify those women who, like your mother and sister, oppose the Mayor's policies, and should be spared.

Colonel, I want no bombardment tophase but ready all six catapults in case my offer is refused. Also take command of the full complement of crossbows and have them ready also.

Edwin, I want you by my side. I hope you won't need to shoot anyone, but have your arrow trained on whoever commands their reception party. I guarantee it won't be the Mayor. Like Craya, she is a coward. All bluster and no substance. If all goes to plan, she is the only person to be arrested. Just bring one of your company with you. Get the rest to line up by the crossbows and artillery.

Wilda, I'd like you to accompany me too. Finally one of the Generals should stay to command the troops here. I think a force of about 256, with say, eight chariots and sixteen cavalry, should be sufficient for our initial parley and the other of you two should accompany me in operational command of this force. Work out between you who is to take which role. And, oh yes, pikes are to be carried and displayed very visibly. Let us all hope there is no actual fighting. Any sane defending commander should be intimidated by this show of strength, after yesterphase's demonstration of our power. Any points, or questions?"

There were none. I asked the Lieutenant to stay behind to brief me on the personalities, especially the militia commander and the various political factions. We set off an ihor before midphase.

War of the Twins

In Midborough the inhabitants were restive, not knowing what fate would befall them. The battle on the previous phase had been watched by many from the battlements atop the East wall. The breaches in the north wall were sufficient to admit a full phalanx of 64 or even 128 soldiers. The north gate was shattered and the smaller breaches in the northern end of the East wall were also concerning. The Mayor had locked herself in her office and refused to meet with those pleading for her to capitulate.

The Militia commander had a restless night wrestling with her conscience. In law she owed her allegiance to the civil authority. That is to the Mayor. But her military expertise told her that surrender of the town was the only viable option. The carnage consequent on further resistance could not be justified. The annihilation of Craya's army meant that could be no relieving force from outside. She reminded herself, yesterphase was not a simple defeat. It was a massacre. There would be nobody left to fight another phase. When she rose at dawn she was confronted by protesters in the streets. Women fearing for their lives, clutching their daughters and pleading to be spared the oncoming assault.

When she reached her command post she was met with depleted ranks. Over half the regular militia had abandoned their weapons and posts, and almost all the conscripts had dome likewise.

That did it for her. The Mayor had lost the confidence of the population and thus forfeited her right to rule and to command the loyalty of the militia. She gathered sixteen of her best remaining troops, women whose loyalty was to the town and not to the personality of the Mayor. She announced, "the Mayor no longer represents the interests of this town. I am declaring martial law. I want you to accompany me, first to her office to place her under arrest, and then to the Abbey, where dissident councillors and other opponents of her rule are being held. I intend to release these women and appoint the Senior Councillor for the North East Quarter as Mayor pro tem, to negotiate the surrender of the town to the victorious Lady Shay.

So it was that when Shay's party showed up at the broken Northgate an ihor before noon, they were met by the Commander of the town militia and the Senior Councillor for North East Quarter and Mayor pro tem, mother of the Lieutenant defector.

So my plans had been unnecessary, and the town surrendered without me having to fire a shot or issue a threat. I was relieved. As was the Lieutenant who couldn't help herself but rushed into her mother's arms. I found it easy to forgive this lapse in military discipline.

I confirmed the new Mayor pro tem, and also the martial law, to last until the emergency was over. Which would not be until I had entered both Cattlebridge and Rivermouth and 'negotiated' a settlement with Cray and Thay.

I then entered the town with my infantry force, but stood down the chariots and cavalry. We all marched to the Town Hall.

The deposed Mayor was still in her locked office with the door guarded by four of the town militia. I called to the Mayor through the door demanding she come out and surrender herself. The only response was her shout of "Never".

I asked the guards to step aside and my troops brought up a battering ram and broke down the door. The Mayor was seized by women from her own militia and carried out screaming abuse. I read a formal arraignment on charges of abuse of office and failure to obey the legitimate instructions of the Council of the North and the criminal treatment of emissaries sent to offer peace terms under a flag of truce, this last being a war crime, punishable by death. She was then taken to the Abbey to be imprisoned while awaiting trial.

Once this necessary preliminary was completed, I turned to practical matters. My field hospitals were overwhelmed by the wounded from Craya's army. Under the martial law, I ordered all medical personnel in the town to make themselves available to help treat these wounded, and for the Abbey and other hospitals to make their facilities and services available for the same purpose.

The Abbess started to object. "By the treaty between Wapentake and Temple, we are not subject to secular law and your orders are illegal."

"Ah," I said. "Obviously I have not made myself clear. Forgive me, I apologise for my short-cut language. As you so rightly remind me, the Abbey is under temple, not secular, jurisdiction. For the duration of the emergency, all senior temples in the northern Hundreds and Wapentakes are the be under the authority of Oakbridge Abbey and your orders come from there. Is that not so, Wilda?"

If Wilda was surprised by this sudden promotion, she didn't show it, but merely nodded her assent.

"First I've heard of it", retorted the Abbess, "and I cannot be subordinate to another Abbess, we are of equal rank, and only the High Priestess of Rivermouth Great Temple outranks us."

"Oh dear, you misunderstand me again, I must do better, I did not mean to imply that the Abbess of Oakbridge outranks you. But for the duration of this emergency it has been agreed that the Northern temples must speak with one voice and that Oakbridge, while not of a higher rank, is to be the first among equals, prima inter pares, so to speak. Of course you might find this difficult at a personal level, in which case I'm sure a suitable retirement package can be agreed. After all, that happened in Knot, didn't it? Anyway we can send to one of the other Abbey's for an interim replacement while the Goddesses consider who should be your permanent successor."

"I wouldn't want to put Wilda to such trouble."

"Oh I'm sure it would be no trouble, would it Wilda? I recall that only the other phase you were telling me about some up and coming priestesses who deserved promotion. One of yours in Oakbridge, I think, and then that Theologian from Fenwold, yes she would be ideal."

"The abbess of Midborough nearly exploded. I am not retiring. I'm only 52, far too young for that. My hospital will be available for your wounded, and I will accept Wilda as Prima inter Pares, but I do not expect her to interfere in the internal running of this Abbey."

"No, no" assured Wilda, "I wouldn't dream of interfering in such a way; my role is purely for guidance in the external political affairs of the temples. The whole of the North is undergoing a reformation, and we must stick together in the face of more reactionary elements in some of the southern temples."

"And," I added, "they are not my wounded, but those of your erstwhile ally. I regret that we were the cause of the wounds, and of so many needless deaths; but Craya was given every opportunity to surrender with honour, or indeed just to turn around and return to Cattlebridge. She chose to continue in the face of a superior force. It was her cowardly abandonment of her own army that was responsible for the bulk of the losses. We must now do all we can to prevent further deaths among the wounded and to restore them to as much health as our medical arts allow."

Oh, Goddess, I'm beginning to fall for my own propaganda. Like Generals of old I need a slave to remind me that I am human, except I want to end all slavery. What is to become of me?

That thought reminded me. I ordered the release of my male emissary who had been detained on the 26th. I then went on to order that all all men from the town were to assemble in the Market Ring. There I declared them all to be freed from their owners. "From henceforth, Midborough will have the privilege of being the first town in the Theocracy to be completely free of slavery. A team of scribes from my army will come to the town hall. All men are to present themselves there and register their details. Each man will be issued with a passport confirming his free status. This passport will be honoured throughout the Northern Wapentakes, and I hope eventually to be able to extend that to the whole Theocracy. In future any man entering within the walls of Midborough town may claim his freedom. Accordingly I rename the town as Midborough Freetown, and so it is to be known from this phase forth. I then left it to others to issue the proclamation, put up posters, etcetera. And to my team to receive complaints from the former owners, informing them that the loss of their slaves was their legitimate punishment for the rebellion. After all, you may even persuade many of your men to remain with you, but as free men. That is surely better than if I had enforced my right to take them all for sale to new owners, as is my right as victor.

I needed to return to my camp to attend to other matters. I arrived back at the headquarters tent around the 36th ihor. Five ihors after entering the town. I found Craya and her party waiting for me.

I quickly dismissed all but Craya. I had them escorted to Midborough Abbey Gaol where they could languish until a trial could be arranged. I turned to Craya. I noticed a small puddle under her skirt. The coward had wet herself.

"Craya, you disgust me. I still don't understand why the Goddess allowed your sister to drown and kept you alive to poison the land. If it wasn't for your mother I'd execute you out of hand, but I suppose I must give you a fair trial before displaying you from the posts on Rivermouth bridge."

Craya whimpered, "Please don't hurt me Shay, Mummy will never forgive you if you do. I don't want to die, I didn't mean it when I said I'd split you. Please have mercy. I am your very own cousin." Tears flooded down her face, and urine down her legs.

"Yes you did mean it. You wouldn't have hesitated. You always were cruel. Cruel and cowardly. As a child you hid behind my sister as you taunted me and Crayza. You were never so brave when by yourself. There is no hiding now. Thay isn't here, and despite our mutual antipathy, I don't think she would be any less disgusted with you than I am. Do you know how many deaths you caused by your cowardice yesterphase. If I don't kill you now, surely the relatives of a thousand women in your army will. Oh do stop snivelling, you nauseate me."

"Y..y..you always preferred Crayza. She could do no wrong. But she died because she stole my man. She was worthless. You turned her into a whore. It's so unfair."

I could take no more. I called over two men. "String her up", I ordered, "and then fetch me a good sharp axe. I won't use a rusty old saw on you, Craya, I'm not as cruel as you."

The men grabbed her legs, upended her and tied her ankles to a beam. The beam was then hoisted eight and a half feet off the ground resting on the forks of two poles that had been set up for the purpose.

Craya screamed.

Yes, I know I was being cruel. But honestly, she deserved it and I could hear a thousand ghosts applauding me.

I felt a severe tugging on my arm. I had forgotten Shar. She had sneaked in to watch. She knew Craya was her Auntie and she wanted to see her. She looked up at me with horror written all over her face. She mouthed at me. Silently, but I could read her lips. "Mummy you can't. You mustn't. It's against everything we stand for. Even if she would have done it to you. You have vowed to end such cruel punishments. And think of Auntie Cray. I love her, and, and you just mustn't."

Inside I was filled with pride. If Craya were even an eighth as brave as my Shar we would not be at this pass. I bent down to my child and whispered in her ear. I won't go through with it, I promise. I give you my word. But honestly she deserves to suffer on account of all those soldiers she left to die, when one word from her would have raised the flag to end the battle. She knew she was beaten the moment my main force appeared over the ridge. Her second in command told her to her face that she should surrender. How many hundreds died because of her cowardice? And then she ran away. She has to suffer. She doesn't know I won't split her, and the terror she will feel before I eventually cut her down is her punishment."

Shar nodded, "you promise?"

"I promise".

I fingered the edge of the axe, deliberately letting it cut my finger.

I approached the captive. "You should be grateful you are tied to that beam," I told her. "If I were a traditionalist your feet would be nailed to it." There came a whimper from somewhere just below my knee. I bent right down and lifted the soaking skirt that now hung down over her head. I showed her my bloody finger. "Look the axe is very sharp, I've tested it. You won't suffer too long. A quick slice to your fanny and the bones will break and it will soon be over. You'll likely be dead before the axe blade even reaches between your tits, seconds at the most and you can then tell your woes to the Goddess."

I stepped away. "Goddess she, stinks. I didn't appreciate how full of piss she is, and that's not all, I think.

Someone please fetch a bucket of cold water the colder, the better, and chuck it over her. I really should have done this outside, but I suppose we can always move the tent. The grass should grow well next year with all the extra fertilizer." I heard a commotion outside.

33

Return from the Dead

Dateline 28 Autumn

I heard a strange whirring noise overhead. It was sort-of like one of the strange birds, only louder, much louder, maybe it's a whole flock of them.

I'm on my own here. Well, there's an old man who is supposed to be looking after me. But I'm in charge because he's only a man and so really he has to do what I tell him, except he doesn't always. I mean if I want dinner, or my bed made, or to be pushed on the swing, it's all "yes miss, whatever you want miss" and he sets to it, but if I want him to give me extra sweets, or leave me alone to ride where I want. He goes. "I'm sorry miss but I can't let you do that, your Mother would disapprove." When is a slave not a slave? Huh! Anyway I don't approve of slavery. Or I don't think I do. My sister is really adamant on the point, but Mummy seems less sure. She says we must treat our men well and with respect and consider their feelings, but she doesn't know how society can function if women don't own their men. She says that usually men aren't very clever, and without women to tell them what to do, they'd end up in all sorts of trouble and everyone would be much less comfortable. She also says my Father was very clever.

So it can't be all men that are stupid. And there are some girls I know at school who are really stupid. It's all very confusing.

Anyway, I was telling you I'm home alone. Mummy has gone to Rivermouth because of some crisis. Mummy is very important in Rivermouth but Auntie Cray says she's been neglecting her duties and needs to get a grip on life, whatever that means. Well I expect it's got something to do with my Aunt, Shay. I've never met her but Shay is my Mummy's twin sister and Cray says they look exactly the same, except for their hairstyles. Shay is also my sister's Mummy. I have never met my sister but we send secret letters to each other. And when we grow up we will meet. Anyway, I overheard Mummy talking to herself. I heard her say "Fucking Shay, why did she say that in the council. And now Craya is going off on a mad expedition. I just hope it doesn't go all tits up."

Well I don't know. Grown-ups are so weird. I said 'Fucking' once and Mummy threw a fit. She said It's a very bad word that I shouldn't know, and I was spanked and sent to bed without supper. I was also told off for using the phrase tits-up, but I wasn't spanked for that. Tits is a normal word which everyone uses but tits-up is very lower class, apparently. I learnt both these expressions at school from older girls and I don't think they count as lower-class. As I said before, everything about grown-ups is so confusing.

Oh, now I've let myself get diverted. I was just trying to explain that I was on my own because the man didn't count.

I went outside and saw what looked like an enormous bird in the sky. When I say enormous I don't mean like an eagle but I mean enormous like a house. This bird actually wasn't a bird but I didn't know that then and I'm trying to tell my story like it happened.

This bird landed on the field just in front of our house and a door opened in its side and five people walked out. Three were women, one was a man and the other was a midget. She, or maybe he, was shorter than me and fat. I didn't notice tits so probably he was a man. One of the women was very beautiful and she walked up me and said. "Hello, you must be Thay's daughter. Is she at home?"

I explained that Mummy had gone to Rivermouth to see Auntie Cray, but I expected she would be home soon because she doesn't like to leave me alone.

"You're alone in this great house," said the stranger, "Surely you need someone to look after you. You can't be more than eight years old, or less for that matter." she added.

I was a bit hurt. I'm tall for my age and think I look older. Anyway I wasn't going to lie, I said. "I'm Thar, and I'm exactly eight, but I look older, so how did you guess? And there's a manservant in the house, but he doesn't really count. I'm the only female here, so I'm in charge until Mummy gets back."

"Of course you are tall and very mature for your age, I'm afraid I have extra knowledge. Your Father is a friend on mine and I know a lot about your history. Your Mummy is one of my cousins. My name was Crayza, although I call myself Créezy now. Your Great Aunt Cray is my mother."

"But you can't be. Auntie Cray's daughter is Auntie Craya, and you're definitely not her. You're beautiful. I think you're the most beautiful woman I've ever seen. Auntie Cray doesn't have another daughter, or I'm sure she would have said so. She used to have one, but she drowned like my Father."

"Right this is going to be difficult for you, but you must listen and believe me. I am not dead. I didn't drown, but finished up on the continent over the strait. You can see it from here. The same happened to your father some years later."

I was puzzled. I thought the continent was uninhabited. Perhaps it is and this Créezy was all alone until my Father arrived. I wonder if they have children.

"But nobody lives there, were you all alone until my Father came, and do you have children? I would like another sister."

Créezy thought carefully before speaking. "I'm afraid that what you've been told about Goddesses and everything like that is wrong. There are people on the continent and they are much more advanced than on Isla. Your Father and I both had a lot to learn. We are very good friends, but sort of like a sister and bother. But you do have a baby brother. His mother is one of the people with me tophase. You must meet her in a bit. Perhaps you could invite us in."

Where are my manners? Mummy would not be pleased with me. "Sorry, you must all come in and I will tell our man to bring some tea and cakes."

When we were all sitting comfortably in the library my new Auntie continued her story. Her friends are all from the continent, except the midget who is really strange. They speak a different language and couldn't say much in our language which they called Islish. Even Créezy spoke in an old fashioned way, but quite like Auntie Cray sometimes. The smaller woman was quite young, for a grown-up, she is called Rastu but has another name, Aimée, for her family and special friends to use. She told me to use it because I was now part of her family. Men on the continent are all free, just like Shar wants here. My Father is now called Arté and lives with Aimée and another woman as an equal partner. My new brother is called Artur and was born at the end of last year. He will soon be one. They are waiting for Mummy because they want to take her to visit across the strait. We went upstairs and looked across out of the window and used a special sort of extension for the eyes which made everything look nearer and bigger. Using this magic thing, they showed me a farm which my father owns which is where they want us to go.

The really strangest thing is the midget. Her name is Jezzie, and she is a she, but they don't like strangers to know. She doesn't even belong on this world. She comes from Geos. Well I know about Geos, it's the big moon that goes round our world once every period. Well I don't understand all that yet but I will one phase.

Jezzie's people are so clever that they've learnt how to travel all the way from Geos, and they invented the flying carriage that they came in, and is still sitting on our front lawn. That is how they were able to cross the strait. Which, until Jezzie came, was impossible. Anyway, we are going to go and visit my Father's farm and then we'll be brought home again. But we've got to wait for Mummy first and then Auntie Créezy is going fetch Shar and Auntie Shay, and also wants to see her own Mummy.

Auntie Créezy took me upstairs and got me to try on the most beautiful dress. It is silver and sparkly and goes right down to the floor, and has matching silver shoes and a tiara with real jewels. She says I Must wear it when I meet Auntie Shay, and she has another dress the same for Shar for when we meet our Father. It's so exciting.

Not long afterwards we heard Mummy arrive. "What is that thing on the lawn?" I heard her shout.

Auntie got up from her chair and went to greet her at in the hall. I followed.

"And who the hell are you?"

Auntie gave a laugh and said. "Don't you recognise me? I know I'm nearly twenty years older, but I recognise you; I'm your cousin Crayza although I now go by the name Créezy. I've been getting to know my lovely niece. She has been a most attentive hostess."

"You can't be Crayza. She's dead. She drowned in the Sea of Storms a long time ago."

"No, I didn't drown. Nearly, but I survived unlike my stupid sister's young man, who was with me. I clung on to the wreckage of my boat and was washed ashore on the continent. Everything you have learnt from the Temples is wrong. The civilisation there, at least in the Western Federation where I landed, is far more advanced than ours and I have prospered there. Come and join me in your library and meet my companions. I'm very worried about what seems to be going on in Midborough and I want to to put a stop to it, but first I need to know a bit more."

Mummy looked terribly confused and rather staggered into the library and collapsed on a chair.

"You can't doing anything. If you are who you say you are, your stupid sister has just lost a battle with my stupid sister. First reports suggest that the result was a catastrophe, even though Craya was leading the biggest and best army that the Theocracy has ever had. I must take Thar back to Rivermouth with me. I'm going to have to stay there for some time to try to console your mother and then help her to organise the response. You may not know but Cray is now President of the Council of the Theocracy and will have to be responsible for how we respond to my sister's rebellion."

"Well whoever trusted my sister to lead anything, let alone an army, needs their head examining. She was an incompetent cowardly child and all that will have changed is that she is no longer a child. However you are not going to Rivermouth. I shall be fetching Shay and my mother and we shall sort this out in a conference after your trial."

"What are you talking about, 'my trial', you make no sense at all. Go upstairs and pack, Thar. We are going to Rivermouth."

Auntie, then agreed that I should go and pack. I left the room, but hid behind the door to listen.

Auntie then put on a severe voice and said. "I'm sorry, Thay, but I meant what I said. If you won't come quietly, I'll have to do it the hard way. Thay, daughter of Chay, I arrest you on a charge of the attempted murder of the man formerly known as Arthay. You are to answer to a special Tribunal Court to be held at Thayview Farm, in the Islaview district of the Western Federation."

Mummy started to protest, but suddenly went quiet and I heard the thump as she collapsed on the floor. I rushed back in and knelt down beside her. I couldn't stop my tears. "What have you done to Mummy? You've killed her."

"No I haven't, she's not dead, only sleeping, Feel her wrist, you can feel her heartbeat, and check for yourself that she is breathing. I'm sorry I had to send her to sleep but it is for the best. None of us wants to hurt her. She'll wake up in about four ihors and by then will be safely tucked up in a bed on the other side of the strait."

" I wiped my face with my sleeve to take away the tears and blew my nose, which was snivelling a bit, I then checked like I'd been told. It did seem like Auntie was right and that Mummy was deeply asleep. I can't think how Auntie did that, but she was holding some sort of er 'wand' is the best word I can think of and she pulled out some sort of small dart from Mummy's neck.

"Thar now that you see that your Mummy is all right, I do need you to pack a few things, and put on some warm riding clothes. We are going to have to borrow your Mummy's best horse to carry us both as fast as possible to Midborough. I've got a special saddle to put on it so we can be comfortable and also stow our luggage safely. You must help me choose the horse."

"We don't need to ride on one horse. I have my own and am a good rider." I didn't want to be carried like a baby.

Auntie Créezy bent down to look me in the eye. "Thar, I know you are a good rider, but this will be a very tough journey and it won't be fair on your horse, which is bound to be a bit on the small side. I'll take good care of you, but it is really best that you sit in front of me on my double saddle."

The man, Esau, and Auntie Aimée put my Mummy on a sort of bed they called a stretcher and carried her to their flying cart where Jezzie had started the whirring noise. Then they flew off and I saw them disappear across the strait.

Auntie gave the other woman, Zorro, a letter and told her how to find Auntie Cray's house in Rivermouth. Zorro took one of

Mummy's horses and rode off. We waved to her and then Auntie put her saddle on Mummy's best horse, a grey stallion called River Wind, that is very strong, fast and handsome.

Auntie did ride fast. She wanted to avoid towns so we rode across country mostly. After about three ihors riding, we rested for half an ihor for a quick snack. About an ihor and a half later we came to the Great River somewhere near Honeyfield. Auntie found a ferryman who was prepared to take us across. I noticed she fished into a bag and gave him two gold coins which she said would each be worth ten marks. That's a fortune, especially for a man. I expect he usually only gets a groat. When it got dark we just rode on slowly until Auntie found what she said was a good spot to camp for a rest. I've never slept in a tent before. It was great fun. Auntie had a sleeping bag for me and she lit a fire and cooked sausages and what she called baked beans. She also had a bag of oats for River and there was a small stream where he could drink. Auntie made me wash before going to bed. That wasn't so much fun! The water was freezing. I Slept like a log and it was light outside when Auntie woke me. We had a quick breakfast and then went on our way. Just before we reached the soldiers' camp, Auntie stopped and we changed into our shiny dresses. River was tethered and we walked about two hundred strides to the camp. We wore boots and carried our fancy shoes and lifted our skirts so as not to get them muddy. Auntie's dress was gold and she looked just like a Goddess. She carried a bag with lots of stuff in it, including an enormous amount of gold coins. Auntie must be very rich, even richer than Mummy and Auntie Shay; and they are about the richest women in the Theocracy.

We paused outside a big tent with a flag on it and changed our shoes and tidied ourselves up to make an entrance. A man and a woman soldier were on guard at the entrance to the tent and tried to stop us. But they were no match for Auntie!

34
Well Met

Dateline 29 Autumn

A woman and a girl entered my headquarters tent. I say a woman, but she was no ordinary person. She was dressed in the most stunning outfit I have ever seen. She stood taller than me, and that is saying something, and on her head was a head-dress of three enormous feathers, the like of which I have never beheld. No description in my power can do justice to this vision. Her attendant, was also dressed spectacularly, but in silver, to contrast with her mistresses gold; and more fittingly for an eight-year old. I knew her at once. This was Thar, but she was not with her mother. I wondered how that could have happened. Thay is notorious for tying her daughter to her apron strings. The whole tent fell silent and stared at the arrivals.

The effect on the man standing at my side was extraordinary. Edwin dropped to his knees and bowed his head almost to the floor. My "Goddess", he said. "I have sought you long, and now I am yours to command for ever."

The Goddess approached him and took his arm. "Do get up, I don't want a slave, if you wish to please me you will stand as my equal." You may be my partner, but never my servant. You know, you do look like your brother."

She then helped Edwin to his feet and looked round the tent. She talked as if I had known her for years.

"Ah, Shay, good to see you. We must have a good chat, later. Now, Thar, put my bag down and take Shar off somewhere so you can get to know each other. You don't need to be around here for the next few imins."

Thar did as she was told. Shar just said, "Bye Mummy, I'll see you later and dashed off with her sister-cousin." I was trying to work out how to regain the initiative, when the Goddess went over to the upended Craya. She took off her headdress and handed it to Edwin, "Hold on to this for me please, I don't want it ruined by that thing," pointing at Craya with her other hand.

"You look as disgusting as ever. But I suppose your ugly fanny is more attractive than your ugly face." She looked up at the ropes tying Craya's ankles, turned to me. "Why so cheapskate, Shay, couldn't you afford nails? This disgusting creature would look much better with nails through her feet."

She then picked up the axe, "much too sharp, she won't suffer enough. Perhaps you've got a saw somewhere. That would make the coward squeal. Stop whining you're making me feel sick." She reached into the folds of her dress and pulled out a horse crop. "If you must whine, you need an excuse." With that she she gave Craya a hard whack, right between the legs. "Oh, you are even more disgusting than I remember. Someone chuck a bucket of water over her. She seems to have lost control of her arse."

Whoever this was, she certainly didn't like Craya. She wiped her crop on Craya's skirt and came over to me.

"That's enough fun for now, I think. I mustn't enjoy myself too much. I'd love to wield the axe myself, but it won't do Shay. You know that as well as I do. I'll buy the cowardly bitch's commutation. What was the damage?"

"What do you mean damage?"

"How many deaths? You know the customs as well as I do."

I was still taken aback. Who the hell is she? She seemed familiar. But, no it couldn't be. I shook my head and told her the losses. "Three junior officers and fourteen other ranks on my side, and about a thousand or so on hers, mostly women, and most of her senior officers were unscathed. I can get exact figures when my people have finished their work."

The woman laughed. A laugh that I would have recognised anywhere. Even if it was impossible. She then looked serious again. "What a brilliant victory, a good thing you weren't facing someone competent like Thay. If I recall correctly, the going rate would be sixty-four marks for the other ranks and double that for the officers. I make that 1024 plus 256 marks. I've got gold coins equivalent to ten marks. So if I give you 128 of them that should settle the weregild for your side. Her army is her problem."

"OK, I accept, but you know I wouldn't have done it. However well deserved. I promised Shar. She goes on trial in Rivermouth, unless Cray gets her out of it. I will not be her prosecutor or her judge. By the way I've charged you full price for the men. Men in my army are free, and equal in status with the women of the same rank. One of those officers was a man."

"Good", said Crayza, as she must surely be. "I wouldn't have it any other way. You heard what I said to Arté's brother."

I couldn't help myself. This was all too much. I threw my arms around her and kissed her. "Are you really my own darling Crayza, come back to me? I've missed you for twenty years. Or have I got reality wrong. Was I killed and am experiencing an afterlife where my dreams come true. You seem so solidly real, not a ghost at all. But how can that be? And if you are alive where have you been hiding all these years? And why now, why didn't you come back before? So many questions. I am totally confused and out of it."

Crayza smiled at me, and answered simply. "As I said when I came in we need a chat, somewhere quiet for just the two of us and I will explain everything. By the time we're finished I expect my mother will have got here and we can start to sort things out. Trust me I have a plan."

I offered to cut Craya down, but Crayza preferred that she was left until their mother arrived. "Also she's better looking with her face covered and her fanny on show than the other way round." She added. I was dubious, I didn't want to cause Cray that much distress, but Crayza was adamant. Cray had to be be brought to understand the enormity of her daughter's crimes.

We left the tent, and found the girls chattering away with their mouths full of cake and Valray looking on indulgently. Crayza scooped them up and sent them back to find Edwin and get him to supervise them counting out 128 coins from her bag of gold, somewhere other than in the tent being polluted by Craya's presence.

Crayza was pleased to be introduced to Valray and told her that she should also come to the family reunion when Cray arrived. Valray then scurried off after her grandchildren.

We had an interesting and very illuminating talk. Who would ever have believed it. An advanced civilisation on the continent. Arval alive, happy and prospering. Society functioning, albeit imperfectly, without male slavery. And to cap it all, aliens from Geos with the technology to reunite Isla with the continent. And strangest of all, Crayza was going to arrest me and put me on trial for my actions all those years ago. And what's more, I am content to go quietly. She doesn't have to kidnap me as she claims to have done with Thay.

The only problem with Crayza's plan is that we will be away for a period or so, leaving behind a complete mess and a power vacuum.

I suggested getting Wilda to join us and add her thinking power. I wished I also had Audreeda with me, as I really valued her wisdom. But she was probably enjoying a quiet life somewhere in the Northlands.

Crayza was impressed by Wilda, who didn't bat an eyelid on learning the truth about the continent. Well, she is Arté's sister! I've got to get used to calling him Arté. But I don't have to remember to call Crayza by her changed name. It is usual on the continent to have two names, reserving the 'private' name for close family and friends. Crayza says that I and her mother may continue to call her Crayza. When I jokingly said what about Craya. She put on a serious face and said Craya could call her Ma'am or M'Lady, but preferably just keep out of her sight.

It's ironic, I'm going to have to be reconciled with Thay, but Crayza is still to be allowed to maintain her aversion to Craya.

That was a digression. The important bit from the ensuing discussion is that Wilda is to take charge in Rivermouth during our absence. Crayza will make sure that Cray and I both sign the necessary documents and Wilda will act as President pro tem of the Council. The chief priestess of the Great Temple will be livid.

But all the northern temples will support her, and my army will have her back. Even though she won't like it, Brinda will have to occupy my seat on the Superior Wapentake, until my return. We can afford the delay to the canal linkages, which she is just itching to get on with, despite winter starting after just one more phase.

35
Mother and Child Reunion

Dateline 28-30 Autumn

It was about an ihor after sunset. I had just eaten a light dinner and was thinking about having an early night. At my age, I don't see the point of staying up into the late ihors, and I'd had a stressful phase worrying about my daughter and the rumours of a catastrophic battle outside Midborough the phase before. I was expecting my niece, Thay, to return with Thar early in the morrowphase and I needed to be at my best for the ordeal ahead.

There was a loud knock on the door. Surely that can't be Thay already? Although I wouldn't have put it past her to have ridden in the dark, or to disturb me at this late ihor. By the sound of it, no. The accent I heard seemed strange, and I couldn't place it. But it also sounded insistent and urgent. I got to my feet and opened my dining room door.

"I'm sorry to disturb you m'Lady," said my footman, handing me a letter. "But this person is insistent that she needs to see you. She doesn't seem to speak very well, perhaps she's one of those wild women. She has a horse outside that looks very like one of Lady Thay's"

"That's because it is one of Lady Thay's", said the woman in an accent that was quite strange. "The letter will explain, but you might like to sit down comfortably before you read it. And perhaps someone can take care of the horse."

I motioned the stranger into my sitting room where we both sat down. I then sent the footman to find one of my grooms to look after the horse.

I read the letter. Twice. The advice to sit down was good. I was totally taken aback and lost for words. This is what the letter said.

Dear Mother

This is to introduce my friend Zorro. Contrary to what you believe, I am alive and well. I survived the wreck of my boat, although Orcray did not. I fetched up on a beach on the continent, where I was rescued by one of the local inhabitants. Yes, our myths have got it wrong! I have been living comfortably ever since and have actually done very well for myself. I'll give you more details when we meet again.

Right now, I have collected Thar and we are on our way to Midborough to sort out the mess my sister has created. Please will you accompany Zorro to Midborough as soon as possible. I shall be with Shay negotiating the way forward. I'm sure that my sister will be ***deserving*** *of a death sentence. But, with luck, I have brought enough gold to buy her commutation. Unlike me, Thar is looking forward to meeting her sister.*

I trust I will see you soon

Your dutiful daughter

Crayza

PS My congratulations on your appointment as President of the Council. Oh, and I hope I find you in good health.

PPS Zorro struggles a bit with our language, but she has a 'magic box' with her that helps. Don't be worried about it, it is not witchcraft, I promise.

Goddess, if only this is true and not a cruel hoax. I wouldn't believe it of Shay who is surely too honourable to stoop to such depths, but it is remotely possible that she could use such a tactic to lure me into a trap.

I needed to question this Zorro. "You are Zorro?" She nodded. "Is this really true, or just a cruel hoax? How can my Crayza be alive? Surely nobody survives the sea, or perhaps I'm now dead too, I suppose I'm old enough to just die, without knowing anything about it."

Zorro replied in somewhat broken language, but this is the gist of what she said. "You are not dead, and this is not a hoax. Most people do drown in the sea, but a very few manage to hold on to something that floats and are washed up on one of our beaches. Every other such castaway I know of is a man. Crayza is the only woman I have ever heard of reaching the shore. She and I have become very close friends, like sisters who actually get on with each other. We thought it was impossible to ever return to Isla, but recent developments have enabled us to get here. I can explain some of the background on our journey to Midborough, but details should await your reunion with Crayza. By the way, I have pictures of her as she is now, nearly twenty years after the incident."

She showed me a picture of a very handsome woman in her late thirties. She certainly had a look of Crayza to her. She then showed a close up of her naked body, displaying a birthmark that I recognised instantly.

That convinced me sufficiently to risk the journey to Midborough. I instructed my man to prepare a bedroom for my guest and offer her refreshment, and then to order my carriage and four for an early departure on the morrow. I then excused myself on grounds of age etc. and took myself off to bed.

The journey was uneventful. We arrived at an inn an ihor's drive from Midborough as the sun was setting. I decided we should await dawn-light and bespoke two rooms for Zorro and myself, and sent my two grooms to bunk in the servant's quarters.

We had an early breakfast and set off for Midborough shortly after dawn. On arrival at Midborough Southgate, we were directed through the town to Eastgate and up the old road to Shay's camp. Apparently Northgate was closed for repairs following the battle and we would have encountered severe delays had we tried to go that way. We arrived at the HQ tent shortly before the 18th ihor of 30 Autumn.

Crayza and I were up early. She'd hoped that her friend, would have got her mother here the previous evening, but I was not surprised at the delay. Cray is not as young as she was. She celebrated her 70th birthphase earlier this year, and she prefers to travel in comfort, by easy stages. It's actually pretty amazing that she is as active as she is.

I was a bit worried about leaving Craya hanging upside down for such a long time, but Crayza was insistent that she deserved a bit of discomfort. I didn't want her dying on us, so I had one of my doctors look her over, just in case. "She'll live" was the verdict. However I got one of the men to strip her wet clothes and dry her off. He then covered her with a dry blanket to stave off the cold. Crayza was unimpressed by this sort of mollycoddling..

"Goddess, she is ugly. Now that she won't be allowed slaves any more she'll probably die of sex starvation. I can't imagine any man shagging her willingly. You," Crayza called to the man drying her now naked body. "You wouldn't want to fuck that, would you. At least not unless you were paid a great deal of money and even then you'd need to put a bag over her head."

The poor man kept silent. If beauty is in the eye of the beholder, then presumably so is ugliness. To Crayza, her sister was ugly. To anyone else she was perfectly ordinary-looking. Not a great beauty, I suppose, but actually nothing wrong with her in the looks department. I suspect that some men find her perfectly acceptable in bed.

Crayza took the silence as affirmatory; "thought so", she said. We then left the man to his duties to turn in for a few ihors sleep. Actually, as I'd put a camp bed up for Crayza next to mine, we talked long into the night. We had nearly twenty years to catch up on.

An ihor before dawn, we were woken by Edwin entering with two mugs of tea. He had dismissed my man and insisted on serving us himself. Crayza beamed. I shook my head in disbelief, it's clearly a case of love at first sight for both of them. I don't know what the world is coming to, but actually I am pleased for them both.

Crayza told me that she would wait until she got him home on the continent before they had sex. She also warned me that although she loved sharing with me, any invitation would have to come from him. She will never again use men as sex objects, and his wishes and feelings must always be respected.

We weren't the only ones up early. We'd just finished breakfast when Soozy and her mother showed up, bringing a totally undeserved present for Shar. Sudon thanked me profusely for being so kind to Soozy, and for the service I'd done us all by ridding the town of the Mayor and her corrupt gang.

We had a pleasant but necessarily short conversation. Crayza showed interest when Sudon mentioned that her farm was isolated, in the middle of nowhere. She then had a private conversation with Sudon, the upshot of which was that she announced that a problem was solved and she now knew just where we were going to fly from.

At a respectable ihor, Cray's carriage came bowling along the Old Knot Road. Its occupants got out and looked around to find our HQ. Crayza and I went to meet them.

When she saw her daughter, Cray almost ran to throw herself into her arms. She was in tears at the joy of seeing her darling girl again. "I could hardly believe it when that Zorro told me you were alive. I still can't take it in now I see you for myself. You have grown into such a beautiful woman. I must hear all about your life across the strait. Will you now come home, and am I a grandmother. You must be thirty-seven years old now, because Craya is forty-four."

She then noticed me standing behind Crayza. "Oh Shay, forgive my lack of manners, I'm just so distracted, seeing my Crayza again. Good morrow to you. I gather you have defeated Craya's army. I hope the losses are not as bad as the rumour mill suggests."

We shook hands; but before I could say anything, Crayza butted in.

"I doubt the rumours do justice to the enormity of my sister's calumny. You must prepare yourself for a shock. Shay would be in her rights to split her in two here and now. There really are no mitigating circumstances. However, Shay is generous, and has allowed me to pay the weregild for the soldiers she lost, and thereby commute the sentence. However, she will still need to go before a court martial in Rivermouth. She will be taken there to await our return from the peace talks which will be held in the Western Federation. Please be clear, I do this for you, not her. She's er 'hanging about' in the HQ tent. It won't be easy for you to see her but it is important that you understand the seriousness of her crimes. Oh and I'm afraid she's naked at the moment. She can't control herself, and soiled herself in her funk, her clothes were completely ruined and have had to be burnt."

We all then filed into the tent led by Crayza. I brought up the rear. Crayza whipped the blanket off her sister, saying. "Wake up, coward, Mother's here to see your disgrace."

Cray staggered back, holding her nose and trying to hold back her tears. "How could you do this to your own sister? The stench is appalling."

"The stench is entirely her own doing. Go on, tell our mother how bravely you fought. Lost your tongue have you? I'll tell her.

You were too frightened to lose face by surrendering when you saw the superiority of Shay's army. You made your troops fight on hopelessly, while you ran to safety to save your own skin. Then when you saw them dead you fled the field, caring for none but yourself. You are the most disgusting coward in history. Shay lost seventeen good men and women because of you. It cost me 1024 + 256 marks. While your army lost over a thousand. Get that, a thousand brave women and men whose life has been cut short because of your incompetence, your cowardice."

Crayza then picked up her crop and brought it down on her sister's fanny, " 1024 + 256 marks ", thwack, " one thousand brave soldiers ", thwack. "I don't want to see your ugly face again."

She then turned her back and left. "Come on we must talk in the conference room - you men, you can cut her down now, hose her off and give her some prison clothes and take her to the tumbril."

We all convened in my conference tent. By all, I mean Me, Crayza, Cray, Zorro, Edwin, Wilda and Valray with the girls. Cray was naturally very upset. Crayza took her aside. "Look Mummy, I'm sorry, but you had to face the ugly truth about Craya's actions. She'll get a fair trial, which will have nothing to do with me or Shay. Wilda will escort her to the cells in The Great Temple. Nothing will happen until you get back and I'm sure you'll be able to use your influence on her behalf. So buck up. What's done is done. We have important work to do and your part is crucial."

Crayza introduced everyone and then set out her plan. Apart from Wilda, who had a job to do in Rivermouth, the rest of us will all be going to Arté's farm, first for a trial and then a peace conference. Thay was already there, apparently, under arrest for the attempted murder of Arthay, Crayza then arrested me as an accessory before the fact. There would be three judges, Cray would be one of them, the others would be Zorro's mother and some local dignitary as neutral chairman.

We said our goodbyes to Wilda and Brinda after breakfast on the following phase, then set off across country to Sudon's farm. Crayza got out some kind of magic box, pulled out a long metal rod that had been folded inside it and started to talk to it in a strange language. I looked at Zorro, she just said, "Norse, the language they speak on Geos.

"Right," said Crayza after a couple of imins. "Jezzie will meet us here in a couple of ihors or so. While we're waiting we shall have some second breakfast which Sudon has kindly laid on for us. These two are starving." She nodded at Shar and Thar, who grinned, standing either side of Soozy.

When the time for departure came, Sudon directed us to the field that had been chosen for our transport. A big bird flew down and landed nearby. A small alien emerged and was introduced as Jezzie Peteschild, from Geos. We were shown inside and then the 'bird' took off and flew high over the country and across the strait.

36
A Brave New World

I woke with a headache. What has happened to me? The last thing I remember is coming home from Rivermouth and finding a bloody great thing on my lawn, and when I went into the house being greeted by an excited Thar telling me we had some really special visitors. I was then confronted by my dead cousin, Crayza with two other strange women, a strange man and an even weirder midget. I talked with Crayza for a bit, and then she pulled out some kind of wand and everything went blank.

I must have been dreaming because Crayza drowned nearly twenty years ago.

I don't recognise this place at all, but there's the man who'd been with Crayza, standing by the door and talking to his hand. I can't understand what he is saying. Perhaps I'm dead. Honestly, that seems to be the most rational explanation.

Now two women have come in. One of them had been with Crayza, but I've never seen the other one before. And now behind them. IT'S ARTHAY. I must be dead. But..

"Oh my darling Arthay, am I really dead? Are we reunited in the house of the Goddess? Is there really a Goddess. I'm so sorry about what I did, about what happened to you."

Arthay looked at me. I could see tears forming in his eyes. Then he spoke. "I am or was Arthay, your former slave and lover. But you are not dead, nor am I. All the things we learnt from the priestesses are wrong. We are on the continent, just a few imiles across the strait from your home. You can see it from the top of this tower. I will show you later. Here I am a free man, there are no slaves. I am no longer Arthay but Arté, the people here aren't very good at the 'th' sound. And I am no longer yours, nor will I be. These two women here are Astra and Rastu and they are my life partners. I am exclusively theirs for as long as they wish. After I was marooned here, I was helped by the father of the young man who has just left us. He had been a fisherman from the Great River who had been shipwrecked. Thanks to him I received an education here. Rastu was my study partner and best friend. Astra then became my employer. She is a distinguished astronomer. Much later, we three developed our present relationship and Rastu has recently presented me with a son.

There is one more major shock you must face. We are not alone. Geos is another world just like ours, but its people are much more advanced. So much so, that they have learnt how to cross from their world to ours. The short person who brought Crayza back to Isla, and then you to the continent is one of the Geosians. I know this is a lot for you to absorb in one go, but we will have time for you to learn and understand more.

We had hoped to approach you much more gently and have been preparing for Crayza's return to Isla for some time. Then just recently we observed changes in the Theocracy that caused us to act so precipitously. I hope Crayza, by the way over here she is called Créezy, arrived in time. We fear a great battle is to be fought and she hopes to stop it."

This is much too much for me to take in. "Crayza won't stop the battle," I said, shaking my aching head. I explained what I'd been doing in Rivermouth and how I'd come home to fetch Thar as I would be in for a protracted few phases sorting things out and supporting Cray.

"Oh Goddess, where is Thar, she shouldn't be left on her own. There's only an elderly slave in the house. She's your daughter too, all I had left of you." I began to cry, quite unlike me.

It was Rastu who answered. "Thar is with Créezy. She will keep her safe. Our friend, and Astra's daughter, Zorro, has gone to Rivermouth to find Cray. We expect them back here in a couple of phases or so. A period at the most."

I am distraught. I burst out. "I should be happy that Crayza has carried off my only child to a battlefield. Shay will capture her for sure and then what?"

Rastu was firm telling me that Shay would not capture her and that Thar was happy to go once she'd been assured that I was not dead, but only sleeping, and would be looked after.

I couldn't take this without protest, even though I couldn't do anything about it. "And Crayza by herself will succeed where her sister failed with an army. An army of the finest troops the Theocracy has seen in at least two generations."

Rastu was adamant. Crayza would succeed, but would be unhappy if she had to see her sister. Well, I got that bit. Craya and Crayza's relationship was a reflection of mine with Shay, only even more toxic. Clearly Rastu was an only daughter, she said she'd longed for a sister and couldn't understand how we could act as we do. She even had a go at her own partner, Astra, who it appears is also not on good terms with her sister.

Rastu gave it me straight. Shay and I would not be allowed to pass our feud on to our daughters. Quite bluntly, I was told that if necessary she would deny Shay and myself access to our own daughters.

I was impressed, but could hardly believe my own ears. I was being berated by a young woman who looked like she wouldn't say boo to a goose. I think I have met my match, and Shay's too; at least that's a consolation. Well if I have lost Arthay to this girl and she becomes Thar's stepmother, the child will not be abandoned if anything happens to me.

After that I was not allowed to leave the tower but lacked for neither visitors nor occupation. As Arthay had promised I was able to see my house, through a fantastical instrument he called a telescope. It looked close enough that I could touch it. We had long conversations and I learnt much of the histories of Arthay, Rastu and Astra. Rastu has even visited Geos, where her son was born, and has only recently recovered from an ordeal where she had been kidnapped, carried across Geos and then space; and had then lived among exotic creatures, on a part of Duplos that nobody had even known existed. Eventually Arthay was able to rescue her.

The fact is I really like them. I've begun to learn a few words of their language and I'm trying to wrap my head around their societal norms. I don't have a problem with the Goddesses being just mythical, but no male slavery. After all, men really are inferior, aren't they? Arthay is just exceptional. A woman trapped in a man's body perhaps, at least mentally. Well Rastu has confessed that, even in their society, men are second-class citizens; but she and Astra think that's wrong and are working tirelessly to change perceptions. Well, they'll get on with Shay then. It seems ironic that I have moderate sexual habits but am the one who finds it difficult to cope with the concept of male equality. Whereas Shay, who is anything but moderate, is not only OK with it but actively pursues it, even to the extent of provoking civil war.

I'll just have to relax more. After all, my old world is now definitely dead and I can't do anything about that. I can't change reality. I must learn to adapt. I suppose I'm even going to have to engage with Shay in a co-operative manner.

We landed next to a tower overlooking the cliff. Crayza, Edwin and the girls went into the tower while Zorro took us all in a different sort of cart along a good bit of road to the farmhouse. There we were met by Arté himself. Thay was there also. I ignored her. We were introduced to lots of people, the most important being Astra and Rastu, who are Arté's partners. Astra is also Zorro's mother.

After a while Crayza made her entrance. She was dressed in her Goddess dress which she had worn when she arrived at my camp. She now had both girls as companions dressed in identical long silver dresses, and Edwin behind her as a sort of champion. I couldn't help but notice that Rastu's eyes were on Arté's crotch. Then I saw why! The effect of Crayza's outfit on all the males present was incredibly funny to us females. We were even able to establish which of the Geosians were male. These last were extremely embarrassed. Fortunately all the partners of the men present were amused rather than outraged at this demonstration of male vulnerability.

Crayza was amazing, and clearly everything had been well prepared by her. I was really touched when Thar came up to greet me. She and Shar are very alike. You can see they are sisters, although obviously they are not identical like me and Thay. Perhaps that's part of our problem. We do each have a need to differentiate ourselves from each other.

Actually, the trial was quite cathartic. It has helped me to draw a line under the past eight years, and I suspect that it was the same for Thay. Our punishment is that we have got to learn to live together and work co-operatively. However I don't think either of our daughters will let us do otherwise. Shar has confessed to me that she has been carrying on a clandestine correspondence with Thar for nearly a year. She initiated it when I sent her to board at school. She used Cray as a go-between, and Thar responded enthusiastically. Despite myself, I can't but be impressed by her initiative and independence. I've seen much to be proud of in my daughter over the past year. I think she'll do well and be a worthy heiress.

Talking of heiresses, when Cray tried to berate Crayza for her treatment of her sister, Crayza gave as good as she got. She made it quite clear that Craya is unfit to inherit and told her mother to find another heiress, leaving Craya with a pension to be administered by someone both competent and trustworthy. She recommended Thay. Interestingly, Crayza herself doesn't want to inherit. She told me she'd buy a suitable apartment in Rivermouth for occasional visits, but that her home will remain on the continent. She has her main home in one of the chief cities, Louth, but also has a holiday house in a seaside village called South Beach, which is where Astra comes from, and has her main residence. It turns out that Crayza is extremely rich (as are Arté and the others) because of a company they founded to exploit some of Arté's inventions, that now also has a monopoly on trade with Geos.

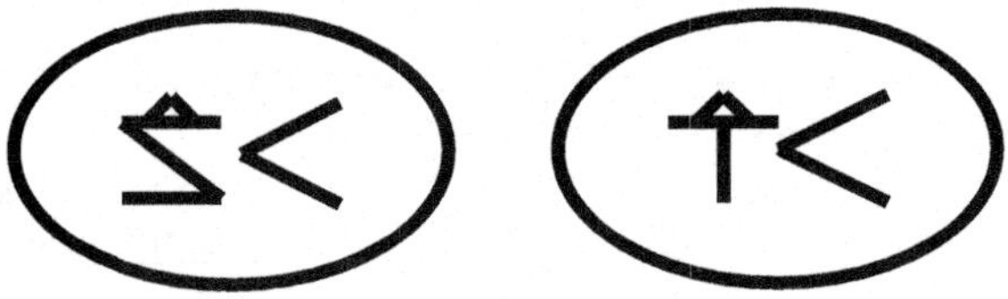

We're writing this together. We've been having a lovely time together. Isn't Auntie Créezy wonderful? It's so good to be part of a bigger family. We've now got our Father and two step-mothers, who are both very kind to us.

We are going to stay here for a couple of periods or so, while our Mummies have to go back with Aunties Cray and Créezy to sort out all the mess after the war. We're both really pleased that our Mummies are going to have to be on the same side in future. Auntie Cray thinks it will all be right in the end.

There's going to be lots of exciting things happening. Shay is going to let Auntie Brinda finish the canals to link to the Great River, but she thinks they may become redundant as we start to benefit from continental and Geosian technology. Thay is going to work with Arté on a special link across the strait from near her house to the farm we're now at. It's called a cable car. We've seen the work that's already been done at this end and now Thay has given permission for the work on the Isla end. That means it will be possible to cross over the strait without having to persuade the Geosians to fly us in one of their aircraft.

Less fun is that we're going to have to do even more schoolwork. As well as having to learn new things from both the continent and Geos, we are both going to have to learn their languages, Contish and Norse. Auntie Aimée (that's what we're going to call Rastu) is going to arrange for extra teachers at both our schools to help us. Then when we're ten we're going to go to school here on the continent, to the Federation Grammar School in Marouth, where Auntie Aimée used to be the Maths and Natural Philosophy teacher. It will be fun going to the same school.

Oh yes, we have another sister, Thay has admitted that her Goddess daughter, Clara, shares our father. She was keeping it secret for reasons that neither of us can understand. Actually Thar knows Clara quite well, but Shar has never even heard of her. She's a bit older than us but getting to know her as a sister will be fun.

All this extra family is wonderful. We're both really looking forward to the future. In the meantime we love playing with our new brother, Artur. Of course he doesn't do much. He can't speak yet, but he has begun to walk, even though he is not quite a year old. He's very cute and we love him.

And that's it, all's well in the end. Our Mummies are going to stop being at war with each other. We're going to be in a much bigger family. All the nasty politics is going to be fixed and we face an extraordinary future. And we will enter a brave new world together as sisters who are best friends.

Appendix 1

Dates and Personalities

A note on dates:

Isla did not have a date system for years at the time of this book, indeed nor did the continent. However, once Geos had made contact, some of the characters from the end of this book adopted the Geosian system. A few years later an international conference adopted a Duplos-wide dating based on Contact Year (CY) = 0; years after that were given positive numbers and designated AC, while years before CY were designated by negative numbers, or just BC. Thus 1 BC = Year -1. (CY, Year 0 is the Geosian year 2614). In this appendix, I use the future Duplosian system. On Isla they refer to dates within a year by numbered phase in each season: thus Shar was born in the 17th phase of Spring in the year 7 BC. A phase is the period of the planet's rotation about its axis, which in Earth terms is 72 hours - 64 ihors in the local system. A selenth is the period of rotation of the moon, Selenos, which is slightly less than 30 phases, a quarter of the year. A period is the period of rotation of Duplos and Geos about their common barycentre, and is 4 phases (12 Earth days).

The events in this book occur in the decade from 8 BC to 1 AC.

The extended family of Shar and Thar

Chay (b. 74 BC d. 8 BC) Mother to Thay and Shay, died just before the opening of this book.

Thay (b. 45 BC) The elder of Chay's twin daughters. Former owner of Arté (then Arthay). Intense rival of her sister, Shay.

Mother of Thar. Lay representative for Chalcliff and Strait on the Superior Wapentake, recognised as leader by most of the Southern Hundreds.

Shay (b. 45 BC) The younger of Chay's twin daughters, and main protagonist in this book. Mother of Shar. Lay representative for Oakbridge and District on the Superior Wapentake, President of the Council of the North.

Shar (b. 7 BC 17 Spring) Daughter of Shay and Arté.

Thar (b. 7 BC 22 Spring) Daughter of Thay and Arté.

Cray (b. 68 BC) Chay's first cousin, Goddess to Shay, Mother to Craya and Crayza/Créezy. President of the Council of the Theocracy and Lay representative for Rivermouth Central on the Superior Wapentake.

Craya (b. 43 BC) Cray's elder daughter. Close to Thay. Lay representative for Rivermouth South and Honeyfield on the Superior Wapentake.

Crayza (b. 36 BC, marooned 19 BC) **Créezy** after 19 BC, Cray's younger daughter.

Edgar (b. 67 BC d. 1 BC) Escaped from Valray. War leader in the 5 Villages in the Northlands. Father of Wilda, Arté and Edwin, by Wilja, Valray and Wena respectively.

Wilja (b. 60 BC) Former slave to Oakbridge Abbey, captured on a raid by Valray in 41 BC. Mother of Wilda.

Wena (b. 59 BC d. 1 AC) Sister of Wilja, Mother of Edwin.

Wilda (b. 41 BC) Daughter of Wilja and Edgar, Sister of Arté and Edwin. Abbess of Oakbridge with a seat on the Arch Convocation.

Valray (b. 66 BC) A farmer near Street. Captured Wilja and Edgar. Mother of Arté (then Arval) by Edgar. Doting Grandmother to Shar (and doubtless, later, to Thar, Mikos Artur, Clara and any others Rastu might have).

Arté (b. 40 BC marooned 8 BC) The hero of the first book in the series - Twin Worlds First Contact. Born Arval, son of Valray and Edgar. As Arthay, slave/partner of Thay, then partner of Astra and Aimée Rastu from 0 CY. Unbeknownst to himself, father of Clara by Cora, and then of Shar and Thar. Lastly (so far) of Mikos Artur, by Rastu. Brother to Wilda and Edwin.

Edwin (b. 38 BC) Son of Wena and Edgar, brother to Wilda and Arté. Eventually, partner to Créezy.

Aimée Rastu (b. 26 BC) Heroine of the second book in the series - Twin Worlds Fair Exchange. Study partner and later partner of Arté. Mother of Mikos Artur. Daughter of Sturdon (not in this book).

Astra (b. 52 BC) Astronomer. Employer, then business partner, then partner to Arté. Mother of Zorro.

Zorro (b. 35 BC) Daughter of Astra. Friend of Créezy. Partner of Esau II.

Esau II (b. 34 BC) Son of Esau I - (not in this book), Partner to Zorro. Actually distantly related to Chay's family through his paternal grandmother who was a distant cousin of Chay and Cray.

Clara (b. 10 BC) Goddess daughter of Thay, Daughter of Cora and Arté, conceived as a result of Thay doing her friend a favour.

Others not in the extended family

Brinda (b. 34 BC) Water engineer from Barton-within-Lesser. Close friend and confidante of Shay. Honorary Auntie to Shar.

Cora (b. 45 BC) Farmer and Vineyard owner. Old Schoolfriend of Thay. Honorary Auntie to Thar. Mother of Clara.

Robina (b. 36 BC) Tribal leader in the Northlands.

Joanna (b. 35 BC) Cousin of Robina, lives just north of the Lesser Estuary. Trade contact of Shay.

Audreeda (b. 72 BC) From North bank of the Lesser Estuary. Contact and friend of Shay. Lived for a while in Barton-within-Lesser under the name of Maudree.

Elguy (b. 66 BC) Sister to Audreeda. Member of an obscure monotheistic sect.

Hild (b. 81 BC) Founder and Abbess of Elguy's monotheistic sect.

Zoni (b. 53 BC) Leader of a Northland Warrior band, expelled from Edgar's village for corrupting young women. Allied to Edwin in war against Pootini.

Pootini (b. 72 BC d. 2 BC - maybe) Evil Dictator.

From Geos

Jezzie Peteschild (b. 32 BC) Engineer and pilot. Close friend of Rastu.

After they got back to Isla, Thay took Thar and Shar to visit her friend Cora. To help them to explain the new found family relationships to their surprise-sister, Clara, the two girls came up with a diagram of Arté's immediate family. I've reproduced it on the next page, but I'm leaving it to the reader to translate from the Islish script. More complicated diagrams to illustrate the wider family relationships are too complex to show here. In any case Shar's writing became very untidy as she delved deeper into the multitudinous interconnections.

Arté's Family

(Parents, Partners, Partners' children)

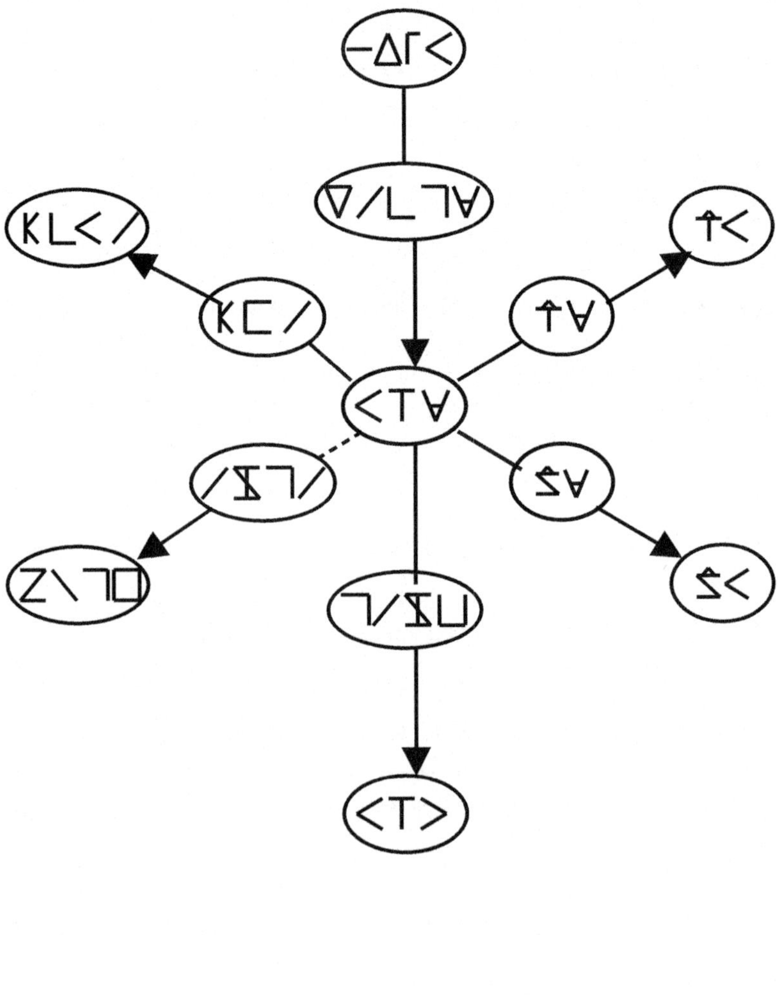

Appendix 2

Isla: Hundreds, Wapentakes and Politics

In as much as the Isla Theocracy has any central Government it is ruled by a bicameral parliament. The two houses being the Superior Wapentake and the Arch Convocation. However, don't be fooled into believing this to be in any way 'democratic'. The 'representatives' of the constituencies in the Superior Wapentake are the powerful chieftains or their appointees, while the members of the Arch Convocation are the religious heads of the most important temples and abbeys. The arrangement at the time of the Twin Worlds books was an agreed compromise following a long and bloody confrontation between the temples and secular leaders some two hundred years previously. Each house of parliament consists of twenty-five members. Their main functions are to manage disputes between the various powerful factions within and between the secular and religious establishments in the Theocracy. Twice a year the two houses meet together as the Council of the Theocracy to confirm legislation passed in the separate houses and deal with disputes between them. Presidency of the council usually alternates between the two houses on a quinquennial basis

Most secular 'Government' is carried out at local level within each of twenty-five constituencies through a local wapentake or hundred court. These are slightly more democratic in nature but even so are generally courts of the various powerful local interests rather than freely elected bodies, and naturally, men have no part to play in the processes.

War of the Twins

The map on the following page shows the twenty-five constituencies and also marks the location of the towns on the island. The tables following summarise various details.

This map is best seen in colour. It is included in the free downloads of the appendices, or the maps, from my website www.richardarthur.uk.

To count as an official town a community of over 1024 has to be so designated by the Council of the Theocracy, following a request by the representatives, temple or lay, from the region concerned. The towns shown here are those that had been designated before the year that would eventually become known as 8 BC (Before Contact) when this books opens. During the years covered here the villages of Street (Upper Street) and Steele (Lesser Coast) would both grow to exceed the required population count and would have been presented as candidate towns at a Council Meeting that was cancelled because of the crisis of the War of the Twins. In the event their designation had to wait until somewhat later, in the first meeting of a reformed council after the end of this book. Alongside the growth of Street and Steele, both Barton and Knot experienced population growth as a result of immigration from the north. In the latter case considerably so, more than doubling to around 3,200.

Twin Worlds III

Political Map of Isla

Locations of towns are marked with a black or white square. The locations of the villages of Elmhouse, Street and Mensh (birthplace of Esau in Book 1) are marked with a round dot.

Northern Hundreds and Wapentakes

Constituency	Temples	Town	Town Pop.
Borders	none	none	
Lesser	lotKBC	Knot-o-L	1536
Lesser Coast	Fenwold T&A	Barton-w-L.	1280
West Bank	Westmarch A	none	
Oakbridge & D.	Oakbridge A	Oakbridge	1408
Upper Street	Asum A.	none	
Central	none	none	
North Cape	Northwick A	North Wick	1040
	TolotE		
U. Great River	none	Southfield	2048
Midborough R.	Centre T.	none	
Midborough	Midbo. A	Midborough	4624

Northern Wapentakes are: Borders, Lesser, Lesser Coast, Oakbridge & District, Upper Street, Central, Midborough Rural, and North Cape.

Northern Hundreds are: West Bank, Upper Great River, and Midborough.

Twin Worlds III

Southern Hundreds and Wapentakes

Constituency	Temples	Town	Town Pop.
Cattlebridge	C.bridge C.	Cattlebridge	3456
Mid River	GRA	none	
O. Rivermouth	R.mouth A	none	
Rivermouth	RGT	Rivermouth	6144
R.S. & H.field	Honeyfield A.	Honeyfield	2176
Second Estuary	Low. Sec. T.	Secundum	1600
	U. Sec. T.	Channeltown	1024
W. Country R.	none	none	
White Woman	ToliW	none	
Estuary	Southbank A	none	
Downs	Southfield A.	Corona	1024
South Cape	Southwick T.	South Wick	1160
S. Coast West	West Temple	none	
S. Coast East	Isla Temple	Lanabeach	1172
	Lana Temple		
Chalcliff & Strait	Strait Abbey	Chalcliff-o-S.	3072
	St. Mouth T.		

Southern Wapentakes are: Mid River, White Woman and South Cape.

Southern Hundreds are: Cattlebridge, Outer Rivermouth, Rivermouth Central, Rivermouth South & Honeyfield, Second Estuary, West Country Rural, Estuary, Downs, South Coast West, South Coast East and Chalcliff & Strait.

Abbreviations used for Arch Convocation members are: A = Abbey, C = College; T = Temple. IotKBC = Isla of the Knotted Bends College; TolotE = Temple of Isla of the Estuary; GRA = Great River Abbey; RGT = Rivermouth Great Temple; Low. Sec. T = Lower Secundum Temple; U. Sec. T. = Upper Secundum Temple; ToliW = Temple of Isla in White; St Mouth T = Strait Mouth Temple.

Town population figures are as recorded in the Rivermouth Great Temple records as at the year following Chay's death, i.e. the year following the start of this book, which will later be known as the decimalised year 2607 in the Geosian calendar or 7 BC (Before Contact) in the calendar that will eventually be adopted on Duplos.

Towns on Isla outside the Theocracy:

Isla Marches: Fort pop. 1280.

West Isla: West Port pop 1536; Ocean View pop. 1280.

New West Isla: Fishport pop. 1280; Baytown pop. 1152.

Appendix 3

Brinda's Sliderule

In this appendix I give a more detailed description of Brinda's invention as outlined in Chapter 5. Text in italics is my commentary and written for those with Earth's understanding of Arithmetic and our decimal number representation, while normal text is used for the direct descriptions from Brinda and Shay. Recall from chapter 5 that Brinda had 'invented' a hexadecimal place value system. I shall show her numerals below but in what follows I shall use the hexadecimal characters 0,..,9,A,...,F in common use on Earth, where that seems appropriate, but mostly I will translate into our decimal notation.

Brinda started by showing Shay her number symbols.

"For the numbers one to eight, I use the symbols we are all familiar with, thus: I, L, Δ, T, Z, F, Π, X. To these I've added symbols for the numbers nine to fifteen,viz: Λ, □, Γ, Ǝ, Ш, E, W. Then I have my big innovation. Instead of writing V for sixteen, I write I: where the : stands for nothing and the symbols together stand for I sixteen plus no units. Similarly L: would be thirtytwo instead of using A, and so on. This method lets me describe any number at all. If necessary I can go higher than the tenth double or even quadruple the tenth double (*Islish for 1024 and 4096 respectively and as high as even the elite will go).*"

"Right you are," responded Shay, I get all that, but what about your machine?"

"I'll get to that soon, I promise, but first I've got one more representational trick, just using one more symbol, /. I use / to denote numbers less than one like a half and a quarter and any sum of repeated halvings. For example the number I denote as ILΔ/TZF would be *256 + 2x16 + 3 + 4/16 +5/256 +6/(16x256)".*[21]

"Wow, that's fucking magic, so /X would denote a half and /T a quarter and the last figure above — the six/sixteen times the eighth double is a number so tiny that we can't express it directly either in our language or figures!"

"Absolutely, I see you get it. Now I can describe my machine. My first attempt was very crude. Basically it's just two half foot rulers with the numbers I to X marked on them like so."

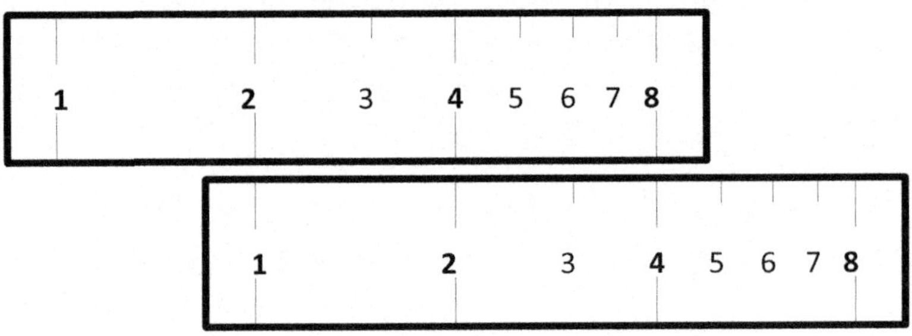

Using our figures - obviously Brinda's rulers were marked in her Islish notation.

"Sliding the two against each other you can see how they can be used for doubling if you are careful where you mark the intermediate numbers. The trick is that the distance on the ruler between a number and its double is always the same, in this case for my four thumb *(six inch)* ruler that distance is always one and one quarter thumbs."

"Neat but a bit crude, tell me more."

21 Brinda's use of / is analogous to our use of a decimal point. But in her case it is a hexadecimal point.

"As you say, a bit crude, but this was just to establish the principle. My practical model is a foot long and marks up to sixteen. It's also made with a sliding centre rather than relying on two identical rulers sliding against each other.

As you see I've marked out an even scale from nothing to sixteen in the centre, making sixteen equal major divisions at half thumb intervals *(a thumb is an eighth of a foot and thus is 1.5 inches so these divisions are at three quarters of an inch intervals)*. Further you see I have subdivided each of these major divisions into sixteen equal subdivisions so my foot rule is divided into 256 (the eight double) equal parts. I use these to help me position the intermediate numbers on my doubling scale."

"And how in the name of the Goddess do you do that?"

"Well, thereby lies the crunch. The calculations are quite fiendish even with my special notation. Obviously the first thing I do is position the doublings which will always be four units apart. Thus the numbers one, two, four eight and sixteen are placed at the major divisions, 0, 4, 8, 12 and 16 respectively. Also note that when I've placed an intermediate number that will imply the placement of its doublings. Thus if 3 occupies some position, which obviously must be between 2 and 4, then 6 will be that plus 4 and twelve will be plus 4 more.

OK, with me so far?" Shay nodded. "Good, now comes a long iterative process. Consider 3, It must be placed between 2 and 4 and closer to four — the intervals get ever smaller as the numbers increase. So it must lie between positions 6 and 8 somewhere. *(Describing all this without algebraic notation gets tedious for an Earthly reader so I'll move away from Brinda's necessarily round about description and continue as if she had the benefit of our mathematical language).*

So as a first guess if 3 is at position x, then $6 < x < 8$. Now imagine that we have as long a ruler as we might care to have and mark all the numbers on it. In practise I found 128 to be sufficient. The 32, 64 and 128 will occupy positions 20, 24 and 28 respectively. But 27 would have to occupy position 3x so we have $3x < 20$ and thus $x < 6$ and 2/3 reducing our gap considerably. I then did lots of similar things with the other numbers; iterating, refining and re-estimating until I got down to very small intervals for the placement of all the whole numbers between 1 and 16. For example 3 and 5 finally get placed at approximately 6 + 87/256 and 9 + 37/128 respectively."[22]

"That's impressive."

"Well it was a lot of tedious work, burning through many candles in the dark ihors. Anyway after all that, my final touch was a sliding square of glass with a vertical line etched in the middle that allows me to line up the slide accurately and take appropriate readings. Using this I have made multiplication tables for all the numbers up to fifteen, and those are sufficient to let me do any multiplication of numbers of any size with complete accuracy using paper and pencil, although that can still be tedious. But in those cases, where I only need to calculate approximately, my ruler enables me to work very quickly. Oh, and finally, I recently made a circular version with two concentric discs with the inner one rotating and the scales on the circumference in the same doubling format that works in a similar manner to the ruler."

---

22 In Brinda's notation that would be F/ZΠ and Λ/T☐ respectively (6.57 and 9.4A in Earth hexadecimal)

Twin Worlds III

Illustration of Brinda's sliderule but with fewer subdivisions and using Earth's hexadecimal numbers and omitting the glass cursor. The central section slides along grooves, the outer sections are connected at the back to form a rigid structure.

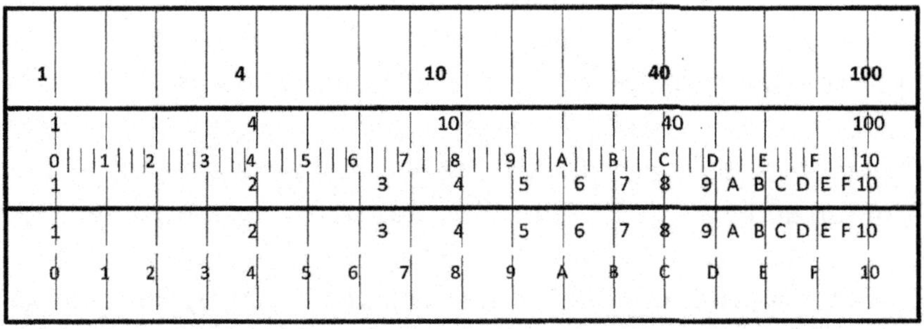

Appendix 4

Military Notes

In the Theocracy it is usual for all official military units to consist only of women. Men serve in a supporting role and only fight in rare situations. The usual arrangement is for the main force to fight in close formation, a phalanx, normally in a wedge shape protected with shields. The women wear helmets and light armour and fight with swords or spears. They are supported by charioteers, usually wealthier independent women. The war chariots sport some quite nasty weapons, spikes, knives and so on. Most are pulled by a single horse, but occasionally two horses in parallel are used. Usually the chariot is driven by a groom, leaving both of the fighter's hands free for fighting. While bows and arrows are used for hunting, these are short bows, between two and three feet, and are neither very accurate, not powerful and are rarely used in war. The usual opponents are from the wild lands beyond the Theocracy and tend to be ill-disciplined and no match for a well-organised force fighting in Phalanx.

Any independent force of 128 or more such infantry will be referred to as an army. Such a sized force is unusual. In the even more unusual event of very large armies (for example at the Battle of Midborough) subordinate units of 128 or more are referred to as Brigades or Divisions — depending on size and function.

There is no standing army in the Theocracy but each of the 25 Wapentakes or Hundreds maintains a militia, most of whose members are part-time. Within the militia units are usually organised into Battalions and Companies. Organisation is as follows.

A Battalion has a nominal strength of 64, but can vary from 48 to 80. It is commanded by a Colonel and usually has a Major as second in command, often this is the more/most senior of the company commanders. Companies are nominally of size 32, but can vary from 16 to 47. Company commanders are usually Captains, though larger or more important companies might have a Major in command while companies of 20 or fewer might be led by a Lieutenant. Most companies will have one or two Lieutenants in a subordinate role. At the bottom of the hierarchy, a unit of eight is usually led by a Sergeant or Corporal. Senior officers (Major and above) are usually supernumerary to the official strength, while junior officers are counted within the strength, and fight inside the phalanx, while the more senior officers often supervise from horseback.

Above the Battalion, an army is commanded by a General, while subordinate Brigades or Divisions may be commanded by a Major General.

Most fighting units try to maintain a ratio of one male supporter to every two soldiers, two women being expected to share the services of one man — including sexual services which are considered to be an essential part of the male role. Officers usually maintain their own exclusive male servant(s). Charioteers, who will be women of independent means, are normally considered to be officers, (Lieutenants in the main) with leaders of chariot squadrons having higher rank.

One of Shay's innovations was to include male soldiers, and even officers. She more-or-less did away with the 'male support' role and enforced a consent rule for sex. Her other innovations were in weaponry: catapults, crossbows and pikes, as well as making use of Edwin's company of archers with their longbows. She also introduced cavalry.

The armies at the Battle of Midborough were constituted as in the tables below.

Craya's Army: General: Craya: Major-General from Cattlebridge						
Militia	Battalions	Officers	Other Ranks	Chariots	Men	Non-Com
C-bridge	5	36	298	9	169	7
H-field	4	16	250	8	136	2
RM C	0.5	2	32	1	17	0
Out. RM	0.5	2	32	0	16	0
Estuary	0.5	2	30	2	18	0
S Cape	0	0	0	2	2	0
Mid R	1	3	60	3	35	1
Downs	0.5	2	30	2	18	0
SCE	0.375	2	24	0	12	0
C & S	3	9	186	5	101	4
SCW	0.25	1	16	0	8	0
W Isla	0.25	1	16	0	8	0
New WI	0.125	0	8	0	4	0
Total	**16**	**76**	**982**	**32**	**544**	**14**

The abbreviations for the Hundreds/Wapentakes should be obvious, from Appendix 2. The total number of supporting men excludes the personal servants of senior officers but includes the grooms of charioteers (all men). The non-combatants are women serving in such roles as the medical staff or chaplains.

In contrast Shay's army is mixed sex, although females dominate among both the officers and other ranks. Many of the non-combatants are male servants of the soldiers, performing traditional support roles. Shay also has a cavalry. Details on the next page.

The female/male split is:

Officers: F 96 M 20, Other Ranks F 1113 M 578, Chariots F 25 M 1, Cavalry F 36 M 3, Non-combatants F 25 M 242.

The most senior males are Edwin and two of the battalion seconds in command in Shay's Own militia who all have the rank of Major.

Chapter 34 included the figures for Shay's losses. The details of Craya's losses are in the table below. Here wounded means survived, died is died of wounds. Total deaths were 1026.

Craya's Casualties						
	Officers	Other Ranks	Chariots	Grooms	Men	Non-Com
Deserted	0	45	0	0	7	0
Unscathed	8	63	0	0	303	9
Killed	60	762	32	32	99	2
Wounded	7	85	0	0	92	3
Died	1	27	0	0	11	0

Shay's Army: General: Shay: Two Major-Generals						
Militia	Battalions	Officers	Other Ranks	Chariots	Cavalry	Non-Com
Shay's Own	6	31	364	8	16	43
Edwin	0.5	2	30	0	0	0
L Coast	3	10	190	4	4	14
O-bridge	3	11	192	4	6	15
U Street	2	7	122	2	2	23
Lesser	4	13	248	3	3	99
Borders	2	9	128	0	2	12
UGR	0.5	3	32	2	0	17
N Cape	0.5	4	33	0	0	8
Central	2	11	128	2	4	22
MBR	1.5	9	96	1	2	14
MB	1	1	64	0	0	0
Marches	1	5	64	0	0	0
Total	**27**	**116**	**1691**	**26**	**39**	**267**

Acknowledgements

My thanks to Philip Bannister for the cover design, to Philip Bannister, John Ramsbotham, Joyce Ramsbotham and Helen Walton for reading the manuscript and offering constructive criticism and to my wife Mary for putting up with me throughout the writing of this book.

R. A.
Worcestershire, UK
Earth

Author's Note

Thank-you for reading my book. I hope you enjoyed it. If so, please leave a review on Amazon. It doesn't have to be long but is really important for independent author's such as myself. This is because it is through the review system that Amazon positions books in its search listing. Please also visit my web site where I shall give news of sequels and occasional blogs by some of the characters. I also welcome any feedback or other comments via email to author@richardarthur.uk.

Also by Richard Arthur

Twin Worlds - First Contact

Twin Worlds II - Fair Exchange

About The Author

Richard Arthur was born in India just before he and his soldier parents were ejected following independence in 1947. His earliest years were spent as a camp follower of the British Army, until his father retired to spend more time with his family. After Prep School in Buckinghamshire and Grammar School in South London, Richard spent six years studying mathematics at university, emerging with a PhD. Richard then spent three years as a lecturer before joining GCHQ. Since retiring from the day job he has maintained some academic links and consulted in Information Security. He still enjoys mathematical problems, but spends most of his time helping his local pub to survive and growing fruit trees in rural Worcestershire. The Twin Worlds books are his first foray into writing science fiction. Richard is married and has a daughter and grand-daughter.

www.richardarthur.uk

Email: author@richardarthur.uk

Printed in Great Britain
by Amazon

49070292R00185